Summer Nineteen Forty-Five

A Novel

Summer Nineteen Forty-Five

A Novel

John Lucas

GE

GREENWICH EXCHANGE
LONDON

Greenwich Exchange, London

Summer Nineteen Forty-Five
©John Lucas 2017

First published in Great Britain in 2017
All rights reserved

Printed and bound by **imprint**digital.net
Typesetting and layout by Jude Keen Ltd., London
Tel: 020 8355 4541

Cover design by Narrator (www.narrator.me.uk)
info@narrator.me.uk
Tel: 033 022 300 39

Greenwich Exchange Website: www.greenex.co.uk

Cataloguing in Publication Data is available
from the British Library.

ISBN: 978-1-910996-12-6

For friends of days at Reading:
Tom and Diana, John and Joy, Don, Mollie, and Pam.

"What can this mean?" exclaimed Dr. Johnson. "It seems very nonsensical – I am in Arcadia." "The King could have told you," replied Sir Joshua. "He saw it yesterday and said at once: 'Oh, there is a tombstone in the background. Ay, ay, death is even in Arcadia.'"

Erwin Panofsky, *Meaning in the Visual Arts*

Although one dies
    With nothing to bequeath
    Enough of love survives
To make us grieve

Samuel Menashe

1

Thirty years later, when he is in the middling part of his life, *nel mezzo del cammin,* Peter Howard, needing to remember the events of summer, nineteen forty-five, will think, yes, that's when it all began, that afternoon in early May in the village of Stonely in the English Midlands, where his younger, ten-year-old self sits at the kerbside watching the German prisoner-of-war as he repairs a bomb crater in the road outside the house where Peter and his mother are living.

He can even remember Hans' words.

"You like to watch this? You like this monster?"

As he grips the steering-wheel and eases the clanking, huffing steamroller backward and forward over lumps of rock, crushing and levelling them, Hans looks down from his high seat and grins enquiringly at his enthralled spectator. Hans is filling in an irregular cavity in the road, one some six feet long and the width of a slit trench. It has been made by a bomb dropped two years previously.

"You like what I do?" he calls through the grinding noise.

Peter doesn't reply directly. Instead, shouting to make himself heard above the engine's throaty wheeze, the grumbling of the high wheels and heavy roller, he shouts his own question. "Is it for next Tuesday?"

"Ja. For the Royalty." And Hans, grinning, takes one hand off the steering wheel in order to salute. "How are you knowing this?"

"We were told at school."

"You cannot have been to school. On a Friday? This is not possible."

Hans is joking. "We got let out early," Peter tells him. "We have to make flags for Tuesday."

There is a pause as Hans leans over from his seat to inspect his work. "A bit more and we are complete."

"Then what?"

"Then tar. Then it must a bit cool. Then more rolling."

"Is that why you've got this?" Peter points to the brazier near where he sits, a metal drum with holes punched in it through which he can see the glowing fire, heat making the air above it shimmer, adding to the afternoon's warmth, the bungalow across the road seeming to quiver and buckle in the haze.

"Ja."

Two buckets hang from the back of the roller. They hold pitch and, as Peter knows from having watched Hans repairing other road cavities, the buckets have to be heated over the brazier, then the contents poured slowly onto the hardcore and allowed to cool, the keen, medicinal, hot, acrid smell beginning to die away before Hans can roll the machine across the glistening patch.

Hans the trusty. He is one of forty or so German POWs stationed in a small barracks at the far end of the village, some of whom are let out to undertake farm work, others to work on their own. You aren't supposed to go near them, or talk to them, ever, but a few of the more daring boys and girls have been known to creep up to where the men in their distinct uniform, trousers and jackets of cheap brown cloth work in the fields, shout out *"Fritz, Fritz, you're useless nits,"* and then scarper. The prisoners can't follow, of course. From time to time a stone is thrown, and one of the girls screamed when a POW shook his fist at her, but for the most part the men keep their faces turned away from their tormentors, faces which are, so the boys in particular report, pig-like, some, even, with snouts. Tusks? No, tusks is going too far. But horrible.

All except Hans. Tall, blond, always smiling, Hans is by now a familiar sight about the village. Hans who seems to be given more freedom than the other prisoners and who is trusted not to try to escape, though as Ronnie's mum says, where is he going to escape to? And once, in reply to her son's objection that the same could be said of all the others, she said decisively, "Wouldn't trust any of 'em far as I could throw them, would you, duck," looking to Peter for support as he sat sharing tea at their table. "Lock 'em up and throw away the key, or shoot the lot, that's what I say. Except for Hans. He's all right. Considerin' he's a Jerry."

Her remark, uttered with a smile that took off its ferocity, didn't really make sense, he thought, but watching her as she coughed her way through yet another Woodbine he felt unable to do more than nod. Besides, he likes Hans. The German, as they all know, had been captured three years earlier, when he parachuted to earth from a bomber that had crashed in fields a mile away. Two of the crew got out alive, but one, who broke his back from falling into a tree, died before an ambulance could be fetched to take him to hospital. So only

Hans remained to explain that his Heinkel had been brought down not by Ack-Ack fire but by engine failure. He told the tale to anyone who would listen, and before long, plenty did.

Because somehow, though nobody seems quite to know how, Hans has become accepted in Stonely as an all-purpose odd-job man, ready to be at the villagers'disposal. Though most of the work he does is for the council – ditch-clearance, road-mending, even some walling – he also finds time to fork over the odd garden plot, put a shed door back on its hinges, weed a cinder path. Sally Parsons, a friend of Peter's mother who lives further down the road, has from time to time asked him to attend to the large garden behind her house, and Annie Frisby, an old woman living at the end of the village, has even allowed him indoors to mend her carpet-sweeper and then tack up more shelves in what she calls her sweet shop, though the nearest thing to sweets in the smeared screw-top jars kept in the front room of her terraced house are crumbling sticks of medicinal liquorice and sticky clumps of what Annie calls dolly mixtures and which those who buy them reckon are concocted from paste and coloured with cochineal moistened by Annie's own spit.

On the few occasions Annie Frisby makes a sale, she'll hook out the coagulated contents from one of the jars with mittened hands, their finger nails grimed from her habit of rooting about in musty sacks of potatoes and turnips, another source of income, as are the slices of bread sold for a half-penny once they have been cut from what Annie claims is a fresh loaf, while for those whose hunger overrides caution you can, for a farthing a dob, buy a crust green with mould. Once and once only, Peter bought one of these crusts on his way to school, and pushed it into his jacket pocket. When he reached for it at break time he found it had crumbled to powder.

The prisoners aren't allowed to take money for the work they do, but everyone knows that some, Hans in particular, receive presents, payments in kind. To pay him for the work he does for her, Annie is rumoured to give the German some of her home-made cake, though Ronnie says it can't have been home-made because Hans still has his teeth.

Every morning, it seems, as the boys walk up to school, they see Hans in his brown, sagging uniform, waiting in the village square, ready for work. Every evening he goes back to camp – a long, slatted, wooden building ringed by a tall wire fence – though once or twice, Peter, on his way to choir practice, has seen the German going into the Crown and Anchor, which is directly opposite the church; and when on these occasions he calls out a greeting, Hans gives him a cheery wave.

Perhaps Hans will be allowed to go to the pub this evening. For now the war is won he's no longer an enemy soldier, surely? Peter thinks this as he watches the man bring his machine to a halt, jump easily down from the driver's seat, and go to unhook the buckets.

"Where is your friend Ronnie?" Hans asks as he lifts the buckets free.

"Ronnie? He had to go shopping with his mother."

"Ah, Mister Slater is a good boy."

The German is grinning but Peter wonders if Hans intends some criticism. "I do a lot of shopping," he says, then, to change the subject, asks, "Will you be going back to Germany now the war's over?"

Hans pauses, sets the buckets down beside his boots, then straightens, flexing his arm muscles. "This I am hoping." He pauses, "Here is good." He grins again, his blue eyes gaining extra brightness from the brazier's glow. "But here is not my home."

"Is it true that before the war you played proper football? Got paid?"

But before Hans can reply, a voice Peter knows all too well calls from across the road.

"You two. Either of you seen Lorna May?"

Man and boy turn, startled. A few moments earlier Peter had watched Mrs Herbert marching down the road, her black coat buttoned close despite the warmth of the early May afternoon, shopping bags gripped in both hands. She had glanced across at the German on his steamroller, and Peter could imagine the sniff that accompanied her cursory nod in his direction before she turned in at the bungalow where she and her husband live. Now here she is again, standing on the far kerb, divested of her coat, grey-cardiganed arms folded across her plain pinafore. The look on her face suggests anger, directed as much at them as at the missing girl.

Hans looks at Peter, shakes his head, shrugs, and picks up both buckets.

"No, Mrs Herbert," Peter says.

She stares from one to the other as though she doesn't believe them, as though at least one of them must be responsible for Lorna May's absence from the bungalow. "Well, if you *do* see her you can tell her from me that she's supposed to be here, getting the tea ready."

Mrs Herbert always sounds in a bad temper, although it seems to Peter that the look now on her sharp-featured face includes a measure of vexed anxiety or, more likely, plain vexation. Shopping over, she wants her tea. Noticing that, arms now by her sides, her hands are opening and closing in a kind of frantic irritation, he thinks that Lorna May will be in for a further dose of punishment when she does, finally, appear. Fancy having Mrs Herbert for a mother.

Peter watches as she marches back up the garden path to the bungalow, the solid brick walls of which once more begin to waver through air trembling above the brazier's glow. Or is that shaking brought on by the force with which Mrs Herbert slams the front door behind her.

And at that moment he hears his own name being called.

2

"What did Mrs Herbert want?"

"Lorna May," Peter says, settling himself at the table. "She has to make the tea and she's late in."

His mother hands him a piece of bread, sheened with a yellowy substance. "They treat that girl like a skivvy. Poor thing."

She's said it before, but now he asks, "What's that?"

"What's what?"

He takes the jam pot from her. "Skivvy. What's a skivvy?"

He meets her eyes, the slight frown of concentration that slowly relaxes into a smile. Then she says, "A drudge. Someone who has to do all the housework. She was probably needed to prepare tea for her Lord and Ladyship."

"You don't like the Herberts do you?"

The frown deepens. Has he gone too far.

"Well." She reaches for her cup of tea. "I wouldn't treat a daughter of mine they way they treat her." .

There is a pause. "But, mum," Peter says, pretending to be fair, "she isn't their daughter."

"Then they ought to be even more considerate." And, as though to bring the discussion to a close, she says briskly, "There's jelly to follow the bread-and-butter. But only if you eat two slices. Look at you. You're thin as a rake." But she's laughing.

"Perhaps I'm a skivvy."

"*You?* You're waited on hand and foot." And, as he opens his mouth to protest, she adds, " I'll grant you do some shopping and run errands for me. But who does all the washing? *And* cleans the house? *And* makes the beds? *And* keeps the garden tidy."

And, who, he thinks, looking at her neat, hand-knitted bottle-green jumper, the face above it with its curved lips, the large brown eyes, is different from other mothers. "Perhaps when dad's back home he'll help."

"Oh, he will," she says, laughing, "I'll see to that." Another pause. "But that, I'm afraid, may be some way off. The Japanese aren't done for, not by a long chalk."

To calm the sudden anxiety that clenches his stomach he takes another bite of bread, swallows most of his glass of milk, before he's able to say, "But dad won't have to go there, will he?"

She looks at him, a long, unwavering look, and he can see that the question troubles her. "Let's hope not," she says at last. "There's enough for the British army to do in Berlin."

Does she mean it, or is she trying to reassure him? Gone from her expression, steady, concerned, is any trace of the wild joy with which, two days earlier, when they heard the end of war announced on the wireless, she'd danced him round their back room, swung him off his feet, dizzying him as she shouted, "We've won, we've won, oh, Peter, we've *won*."

Ronnie, who was there at the time, looked on amazed, and when Peter went to bed that evening, blackout curtains thrown wide to allow a full sight of the deepening sky, he imagined aeroplanes coming toward him, not, as during the past years, carrying the threat of bombs, but heavy with returning soldiers among whom would be his father.

But the only sounds that came to him were not from the empty sky but the usual, muffled clanking of coal-trucks heard through his open window.

And now, he thinks, looking at his mother across the table, perhaps the war isn't over. Not fully. Not yet. Perhaps Hans and all the other Germans will have to stay in the village. And this means he won't yet see his father, and the head-and-shoulders photograph of the man in army blouse and beret with its tank badge propped on his bedside chest of drawers will still be all he has by which to know him.

She's standing. "I'll fetch the jelly." Then, pausing, she looks back at him. "Let's hope your dad'll be home by Christmas. Before you've grown so thin that he'll wonder whether I've taken in a stray."

He is momentarily shocked by her words but she shakes her head, laughing. "Joke," she says, coming back to him. Her arm goes round his shoulders, she kisses the top of his head, then leans her cheek against his. "Oh, I so want us all to be together once again," she says, her voice now low, almost a whisper.

Gathering up the used plates, she makes to leave the room. "See," she says over her shoulder, gaiety restored, "I'm the skivvy here."

Skivvy. Lorna May. Lorna May Perry. Left alone, Peter thinks about the evacuee the Herberts had taken in soon after the war started. Tall, stringy, dressed in a series of shapeless cardigans, jumpers and bedraggled skirts, Lorna May – she insists on being addressed by both names – has become a familiar sight tramping the fields on her way to and from the village shops, usually weighed down by bags that, as his mother once said, look too heavy for someone twice her age and size. Soon after her arrival, he'd once or twice gone to call for her, prompted by his mother to ask her to join him for tea. But she never did. "She's busy," Mrs Herbert always said. And the dorr would shut on him.

Sometimes on one of his fruitless visits Peter would glimpse Lorna May pushing the carpet sweeper about in the front room, or at the kitchen sink washing up, or scrubbing saucepans, or aloft a stool and cleaning windows, and whenever she saw him looking, Mrs Herbert, standing guard at the door, would say, "She's got her work to do," her tone suggesting that Peter ought to know better, though on one occasion at least, staring severely at him and speaking loudly so that the girl herself could hear, she added that the work was a punishment for Lorna May's bad behaviour.

And there was the morning when, in a moment of unexpected familiarity as Lorna May and he, with his friend Ronnie, walked up to school, the girl listed the punishments doled out for different forms of such behaviour. For refusing to eat the food put before her, extra washing-up. For not making her bed each morning, extra cleaning duties. For pissing in the bed – she made it sound as though that was no accident, so the boys were partly shocked, partly in awe of her wildness, – washing, drying, and ironing her own bedding and being allowed only bread and water for two days running. For hiding in the back-garden shed or staying out when she should have been indoors, not being allowed out all weekend except to accompany the Herberts to chapel for Sunday service.

The punishments don't stop Lorna May from offending. On more than one occasion Peter has seen her trailing around the village when she should have been back at the bungalow, and Ronnie, allowed out into the evening fields, reckons he's seen her returning by the light of the moon to whatever penalties await her.

"You'll cop it," Ronnie called out to her, one Saturday morning, early, as she sat high up in a tree the boys were walking beneath on their way to the village. "Get yer 'ide tanned, you will."

"Don't care," she called down to them, pretending indifference.

"What have you got in your satchel," Peter shouted up to her.

"Wouldn't you like to know," she shouted back. Then, "Bread and water. Going to stay here all bloody day, see if I don't."

She'd pay dearly for that, they knew.

But poor thing? Lorna May is older than either Peter or Ronnie, and although she sometimes joins them for Bandits and Outlaws in the nearby fields and woods, where she can both out-run and out-climb them, she is contemptuous of ball games. "Sod football," she once said. "Bloody waste of time."

Taken aback by the daring she showed when she first arrived, the boys for a while even fantasised about her as an otherworldly Being in disguise. After all, as Ronnie once said, "we dunno where's she's come from. Could 'ave slid down to Stonely on a moonbeam." But that fancy soon fell away. Lorna May is not merely all skin and bone, as Ronnie's gran claims, she is tough, too. A fighter. Too much for any of the village bullies, who keep well away from her.

Ronnie claims not to be scared of her, but Peter certainly is. All three go to Stonely's village school. Because of her age Lorna May is in the top year, Ronnie and Peter are a year below, and until the previous autumn they walked up to and back from school together. The route took them past a lane where a retired dentist, Mr Harrison, lives alone in a large, detached house with a high-walled garden beyond which you can see the tops of apple trees.

As the three came toward the house one afternoon last September, Lorna May said, jerking her head toward a cluster of apples that hung tantalisingly close to the top of the wall, "We could be doin' with some of them."

"Fat chance. Old Harrison wouldn't let us near 'em," Ronnie said dismissively. Like the others, he was in low spirits. The entire school, all a hundred or so of them, had been made to assemble in the school hall to hear a boring talk by the vicar about the need to pray for victory in the war, "now that Hitler is beginning to learn God's displeasure." And even after they had gabbled prayers for Hitler's downfall, they had to sing 'Onward Christian Soldiers', trying not to giggle as Laurie Chamberlain substituted the name "Aston Villa" for Christian Soldiers, and then there was a final prayer before they could be let out.

The unlooked-for delay in release from school had soured the mood. And it was perhaps for this reason that when Lorna May said to Ronnie, "I'm not goin' to *ask* 'im, you daft bugger, I'm goin' to scrump 'em," the words were accompanied by a look of contempt.

And with that she began to unbutton the shabby yellow cardigan she wore over what emerged as a ruched, salmon-pink blouse, one of Mrs Herbert's cast-offs. Having thrust the balled-up garment into Ronnie's hands, she grabbed a fistful of skirt, hoiked it up and stuffed much of it into the elasticated bottoms of her long, blue knickers. "What you lookin' at, fish face?" she said to Ronnie, grinning as she went on cramming skirt into knickers. He blushed, averted his head.

"Right. I'm goin' over that wall." She looked swiftly up and down the lane, but there was no one in it apart from the three of them. "And while I'm in there you two are goin' to keep a lookout. OK?"

"How do we do that?"

She grabbed Peter by the shoulder, swung him round and pointed to the wrought-iron gate let into the wall, beyond it a gravelled path that led to the house's front door. "You keep looksie and if the old sod so much as opens the door you holler to me. Got it?"

Before either boy could answer, she was clambering up the wall.

The cry, when it came, was not from the house, but from the garden.

"What do you think you're doing? "Then, louder, "*Stop.*" Then, louder still, "*THIEF.*"

Without hesitation, Ronnie and Peter ran.

They were across the fields and within sight of their own road before they slowed, Ronnie still clutching Lorna May's cardigan.

Doubled over, hands on knees as he fought to get his breath back, Peter said, gasping, "Do you reckon he caught her?"

For answer, Ronnie, straightening up, jerked his head in the direction from which they'd just come. "Look."

And there she was, walking determinedly down the field toward them.

As she came close, they saw the torn skirt, now released from her knickers, the bloodied knee.

She stood facing them and Ronnie held out her cardigan to her. Lorna May snatched it from him, slapped him round the face, hard, and, as Peter backed away, said, "Don't worry, you bloody custard. I wouldn't dirty myself touchin' you."

Then, turning back to Ronnie, she said, "I thought you were my friend," and Peter saw the unshed tears glittering in her eyes.

With that she turned and walked off.

Watching her as she disappeared into the road, Peter said, "What did she mean by that?"

"By what?"

"You being her friend."

"Dunno," Ronnie said. But the way he spoke, the awkwardness of his look, the way his eyes skidded away from meeting Peter's, suggested that he did know.

In silence, the two boys made their way home.

***

As he spoons up the green, translucent jelly, he thinks that, although since the previous autumn he's not spoken to Lorna May, has indeed taken good care to keep a distance from her, he and Ronnie are paying for their cowardice in leaving her to Harrison's mercies. Not that there have been official repercussions. The fact she was able to get away from the dentist and that he presumably didn't recognise her, let alone the boys, meant that, although for several weeks of sleep-disturbed nights Peter feared exposure, the head teacher didn't call Lorna May out to the front of assembly in order to identify her to the other pupils as "a bad example" – which happens whenever one of the children has been caught in some petty crime; and even though her torn skirt and bloodied knee must have led to Lorna May being punished by the Herberts, she still appeared in public every day, going on her errands, marching up to and back from school.

But since then she has ignored Ronnie and Peter, making a point of turning her head away whenever she sees them. Or, if they unavoidably meet in the road, she brushes past without a hint of recognition. He and his friend don't discuss this, but Peter knows they are both shamed by her contempt.

***

Thinking about all this now has taken away his pleasure in the jelly put before him. He pushes the bowl aside, stands, and asks, "Can I go back outside."

His mother looks puzzled, startled even. "But you've not finished your food."

"I'm saving it till later."

He can't explain his reason for abandoning the jelly.

His mother, going to sit by the wireless and tuning in for the news, open book in lap, says, "Tell your German friend to take extra special care with his work."

"Why?"

"We don't want the Duchess of Kent disappearing into a crater." And she laughs.

He, too, laughs at the thought of a car disappearing into a hole in the road. "I'll tell Hans what you said," he tells her. Then, "Do you know why she's coming here?"

"Not to see us, that's for sure. She's on her way to visit some of the nearby cities. Thank them graciously for their contribution to the War Effort. Making a Right Royal progress across country."

She reaches for her cigarettes. "And of course that can't be done if the roads are in a mess. So. Call in the troops, even foreign troops, and let's have everything tickety-boo. Even the factory closed early today, did you know? Hoskins. The workers have been given time off to make front gardens look at their best, just in case the Royal eye should be cast over them. It wouldn't have happened this time last year. But now that the Germans are done for … " A pause. "And come Tuesday there'll be another half-day to down tools. Everything stops for tea – and Royalty."

He senses the mocking edge in her voice. "We're going to have the whole day off on Tuesday," he says. "And before then I have to make a flag to wave when her car goes past. Can you help me, mum?"

"More skivvydom," she says, her mock-sigh accompanied by a nod.

Moving the book to the arm of her chair, she selects a cigarette. "By way of celebrating," she says, lighting it and exhaling smoke that danders upward to the ceiling, "I may award myself an extra cigarette this evening." She's following with her eyes the strands of grey as they spread and dwindle, smiling to herself, and he thinks how happy she suddenly looks. What is she thinking of?

"Off you go now," she says," turning to him, "and don't be late in. The war may be over but bedtime goes on."

***

He stands in the porch, listening to the familiar, rapidly contracting series of metal collisions that come over the woods and nearby fields – "coffling" the locals called the sound – as the buffers of coal-wagons slam into each other, and with the sounds comes a picture of the interlinking lines of Ashton's marshalling yard, the myriad curves of sleeper-pegged steel that snake across acres of coal-dusty ground. A teacher has told them that in ancient times the whole of England was covered by forests.No wonder there are so many mines, although gazing across to Farmer Connolly's fields and registering beyond them the haze of green marking the local wood where he and Ronnie spend so much time, he thinks, as so often he does, that you'd never imagine on the far side of what seems to be an endless mass of trees, of sycamore, lime and hazel, are pitheads whose latticed iron cagewheels stand up behind the rulered lines of small brick houses framing the bus route into Ashton.

And thinking this he remembers the time he was taken on a bus ride by the man who is his father, and how he watched from the top deck of the bus a train steaming across fields toward them and he recalls his dread certainty that very soon the train would crash into the bus though no one on the bus was worried, and at the last moment, as he tensed himself for the impact, the train disappeared, and a moment later it was on the other side of the bus steaming away from them and the man who is his father was laughing as he put an arm round him and explained that the bus had gone over a bridge and he thinks he hears the man's voice telling him that one day he will take Peter for other bus rides so they can see more of the country where they live.

And then, still standing in the porch, he knows why his mother is happy.

3

The steamroller idles at the side of the road, unattended, faint sighs and rumblings coming from its barrelled interior. Peter thinks of the cat which in winter sometimes wanders unbidden into their house and settles down in front of the coal fire, blinking once or twice at the flames before it curls to sleep; the regular, deep whisperings that are in time to the heave and fall of its ribbed sides are very like the sounds that come now from the steamroller. Treading carefully to avoid the new-laid tar that stretches for several feet behind the machine, he stands on tiptoe, trying to peer more closely into its workings when, from the edge of his vision, he sees Hans jump down from the stile on the far side of the road and come running toward him, khaki trouser bottoms flapping round his ankles, his old green work shirt, tied round his waist, singlet outlining the deep chest above which the corded muscles of his neck are browned by weather.

Without speaking, the German swings himself up onto his seat, fiddles with the controls and watches as gouts of steam belch from the machine's tall funnel; and then, as he looks over his shoulder to site the crater's covered length, he announces, as if to the world at large, "Now we are ready for the action."

He lets off the hand-brake, its tall lever with the gleaming brass catch, and slowly the huge wheels begin to reverse and the steamroller trundles, clanking, backward over the former crater.

Backward, forward, backward …

"Finish," Hans shouts some ten minutes later and the steamroller judders to a standstill.Peter gets to his feet as the German clambers from his seat, and, leaping off the footrest onto the kerb, goes to inspect his work. He jumps up and down on the glittering surface, then, satisfied, raises both arms in mock triumph, a boxing champion. "Now, how you say. She is fit for a king."

He himself is an image of fitness, his tall, lean body, muscled arms, suggesting an athleticism very different from the bodies of the older men, teachers Peter is used to seeing at school, or the shopkeepers stooped behind their counters or the workers going to and coming from the hosiery factory, Mr Herbert among them.

"Duchess of Kent," Peter says, "that's what the road has to be fit for," watching Hans as the POW marches up and down the levelled patch, a one-man, parodic military parade. From now on, Peter thinks, nobody will know about the bomb that fell one night three years ago – "dropped by Jerry when he'd had enough of trying to flatten Birmingham" one of the local farmworkers said – and which was collected the following morning by Bomb Disposal after they'd made it safe.

"It must have been a big bomb," Peter says now, looking at the stretch of tar where Hans is parading. Almost as long as a cricket pitch. "It was a big hole."

Hans stops abruptly, brings his heels together and pretends to straighten to attention. Then he swivels to face Peter. "You did not see the bomb?"

"No." Aware of Hans' speculative look, he adds, "But everyone in the road had to go up to the village hall. We walked there in the middle of the night. We couldn't even get dressed. Had to go in our pyjamas and dressing gowns."

He remembers the scene in the hall: the tea urns and paste sandwiches on trestle-tables and how he'd been far too excited to go to sleep on one of the folding beds that were waiting for them, in rows, as if they'd arrived at a makeshift hospital. "Next morning the men took it away on the back of a lorry. When we were allowed back there was only the crater to look at."

He doesn't tell Hans about how awkward he'd felt walking home in full daylight still in his pyjamas and dressing gown. His mother at least had a proper coat to wear over her nightgown.

"And now there is no crater." Hans looks down at his boots then around him. There is a pause. "And the war, it is finished. I think it will take much time to repair *all* the damage," he says slowly, as though to himself.

He shrugs, raises a hand and flaps away invisible flies. He smiles across to Peter, winks. "Perhaps your Royal Family must go around the world, waving to people, then everywhere will be made good. Like the Duchess when she come on Tuesday. No bumpy-bump. A nice smooth ride."

"I don't think mum cares about whether she has a smooth ride or not," Peter tells him. But when he sees Hans' enquiring look, or is it surprise, or disbelief, he says quickly, "Anyway, the Duchess won't be stopping here, she's on her way to a big town. That's what we were told."

Hans, who is now fixing the buckets to the back of his machine, picks up the long-handled spade used to spread tar, throws it up onto the space behind his seat, and says "I come from a big town. Hamburg. A city."

From the floor of his steamroller he retrieves a piece of cardboard, and, stepping up onto the kerb, goes to peer into the still-glowing brazier where it stands on the grassy verge. "This. It must stay to get cold. I will come to take it tomorrow." And, crouching, he props the cardboard against one of its legs.

Peter looks over the German's shoulder, sees the word he is scrawling in chalk on the cardboard, GEFAHR, and asks, "What does that mean?"

"It means danger."

"Oh." Peter thinks about it. "I don't suppose many people here will know that."

Hans looks round and up at him, grinning. "You are right." Balling his hand into a fist he rubs the word out, and hands the chalk to Peter. "Please to write."

Peter takes the stick of chalk, crouches down beside Hans and writes DANGER on the card, adding under it, HOT. DO NOT TOUCH.

Hans nods, impressed. "Good. Very good. People will understand that, yes?"

But Peter is thinking of something else. "Did you play football for your city?"

"For one of the teams, yes."

"What position?"

"Centre-half," Hans says.

As the two of them stand, he turns to face Peter. "Who knows? It may happen again. I hope perhaps so. If I am proving to be fit. And if soon I am going home."

"Do you think you will be."

"This I hope."

"And just now, were you running to keep fit?"

Hans looks startled, but at once recovers his smile. "You were watching?"

"I only saw you when you came out of the field." Peter feels as though he should apologise. Perhaps Hans does not like being watched. "But Ronnie says he's sometimes spotted you in shorts running round the village cricket ground and once I saw you from the bus. You were running along the road into town."

Hans smiles briefly, shakes his head. "Ah, so. In a small place everybody knows everybody's business. Is that not what you are saying?"

"I wasn't spying," Peter says, feeling himself blush.

But Hans, relaxing perhaps, laughs. "This I believe," he says, his blue eyes fixed on Peter. Untying the shirt sleeves of his work shirt, he pulls it on over his head, tucks the tails into his trousers. "Now I, Hans, am fit to meet a duchess."

He turns, goes back to the steamroller and levers himself up onto his seat. "OK. I will take this beast back to the depot. Like the wind we will go."

"How did you scratch your cheek?" Peter asks.

"My cheek? I have scratched my cheek?" Again the surprised look. Hans lifts his hand to his left cheek, feels with his fingers, then peers closely at them. "It is not blooding," he says.

"Bleeding," Peter says.

"It is not bleeding." Hans is still looking at his fingers. "Ach, I know." He speaks as though trying to remember. "It was when I bent under wires at the bottom of the field. I wanted to run some further distance." He pauses, looks at Peter, smiles, assured that memory has come to his aid. "This is when I scratch myself." He releases the catch on the handbrake and as the steamroller in motion begins to rumble slowly away he lifts a hand in salutation. "Bye bye, Peter," he shouts above the noise of the engine and the grinding sound of the rollers. "See you tomorrow." Adding as an afterthought, "I hope."

Later, lying in bed, grateful for the evening light that filters round curtains no longer burdened by the black-out material that had been stitched to them for the past five years, Peter thinks about Hans. Hans who has said he hopes to see him tomorrow although soon after that, may be, the German will be gone. For there are village rumours that, as Ronnie reports his mother telling him about the POWs, "Now it's all over, they'll be off our backs." With the thought comes a sudden pang, an unexpected sadness. He likes Hans. Hans the German. Hans of Hamburg. Hans who before he had waved goodbye said or did something that nags at Peter's mind, puzzles him, though he can't think why. He thinks instead, as at different moments of his adult life he will find himself doing, about Hans the footballer who took off his shirt in order to go running and who is tall and strong enough to be a centre-half. Like George Mason, perhaps, the Coventry centre-half someone once told him could head the ball half a pitch's length. Or Leslie Compton of Arsenal who, so he has read, is so strong that players simply bounce off him. One day, perhaps, he, Peter, will see these players, and others whose faces are familiar to him from his growing collection of cigarette cards.

Propping himself up on his elbows, he wonders whether there is still enough light from the window for him to look again at the cards stowed in the cupboard beside his bed, some given him by adults but more won in the playground game at which he has discovered he is surprisingly good, usually able to outflick his opponent if they play for length, or, if for "covers," then getting his card to flutter down on top of the other boy's. Raich Carter, Peter Docherty, Neil Franklin, Eddie Hapgood, Stanley Matthews, Joe Mercer, Frank Swift …

He slides back down, pulls the blanket up over his head. If he ever becomes a real footballer, he'd like to be Frank Swift, goalkeeper, last line of defence, the mudlark with his flat cap and green, high-neck jersey, flinging himself across goal in order to keep out shots reckoned to be unstoppable …

The loud knocking on the front door jerks him into wakefulness. What time is it? He peers at his bedside clock. There is still just enough light for him to make out where the hands are pointing. Eight thirty. The knocking comes again, and he hears the door open, and a man's voice, but it is indistinct and anyway he is too tired to listen…

4

On Saturday mornings Peter is allowed to sleep late. Even so, when he comes downstairs his mother has not yet returned. Saturdays is when she goes down to Farmer Connolly to pay the rent and collect milk for the weekend.

His breakfast has been laid for him on the dining-room table. A plain, rimless white bowl for his cereal, and beside it, a red-and-white patterned plate with two slices of bread. Home-made marrow jam in the squat, earthenware pot his mother bought, so she once told him, when she and his father, newly married, were setting up home together in Manchester.

He shakes Force Flakes into the bowl, and as he pours milk over them, repeats to himself the rhyme on the side of the packet.

High o'er the fence leaps Sunny Jim,
Force is the food that raises him.

Minutes later, shovelling the last of the cereal into his mouth, he hears a knock on the back door.

"Anybody in?"

Ronnie.

"In here," Peter calls, "I'm finishing my breakfast," and a moment or so later his friend's face peers round the dining room door.

"You 'eard the news?"

Peter spreads jam on a piece of bread. "What news?"

"Lorna May. She's gone missing." Ronnie comes to stand across the table from Peter, wide-eyed with excitement. "Mi mam towd us. The police come round last night, asking if we'd seen owt."

"Sergeant Locker?"

"Who else would it be?"

They take delight in the village policeman's surname. Locker. Sergeant Lock-up Ronnie calls him. "Like Happy Families," Peter's mother once said when Ronnie was having tea with them and they were laughing over the policeman's name. "Mr Lock-up the policeman. You'll have to be a roof-mender when you grow up, Ronnie."

"Slater? Not me," Ronnie said, "Mi mam reckons I'll be a tinker.

Sez I'm one already. Any road, what work does an 'Oward do?"

"Designing," Peter had said.

"Designin'! What's that when it's at 'ome?" Ronnie's laugh was a mixture of scorn and incredulity.

But he isn't laughing now. Shifting impatiently from foot to foot as he rattles out his story, he says, "She never come in for 'er tea, and mi mam said Mrs Herbert 'ad to run over to Mrs Bailey to use 'er phone."

"Why?"

"*Why?* To phone the cop-shop. To ask Sergeant Lock-up to get on 'is bike and come down. Investigate." He speaks the word as though it contains an immeasurable weight of significance.

Before Peter can ask more he hears the back door open and his mother calling out, "Peter, are you up yet?"

"In the dining room," he shouts back. "Ronnie's here."

She comes in, cradling two eggs in her right hand. "Your mother got four," she says to Ronnie, a hint of envy in her voice.

"Fair enough," Ronnie is unimpressed. "Cos there's four on us, what with Nance and mi gran." But it isn't that he wants to talk about.

"Your mother told me that Nancy's over the worst of her injury. I'm pleased to hear it."

Ronnie's big sister, who works in the village's hosiery factory, has been off sick after trapping her hand in one of the machines.

"She's OK. Goin' back to work next week."

"She'll be pleased."

"Not so pleased as mi mam. She reckons she wants Nance out from under 'er feet." But he grins as he says this. "Any road she's been out earnin' a bit, doin' some baby-sittin' for Mrs Parsons." Then, "You 'eard about Lorna May, Mrs 'Oward?"

She nods. "Sergeant Locker was here last evening."

So *that* was who had been knocking at the front door.

"Come batterin' on our door just as mi gran was just puttin' on the kettle for 'er eight o-clock cuppa. So old Locker 'ad one. When did 'e get to you?"

"Later," she says, smiling at his triumphant tilt of the head, the gesture that says *beat you!* But there is genuine concern in her voice when, looking first at Ronnie, then Peter, she says, "Poor Mr and Mrs Herbert. I called in on my way back from Farmer Connolly's. They're at their wits' end. The girl is still missing, I'm afraid." Her look invites them to share her concern, though Peter is sure that she likes the

Herberts no more than he does.

As far as he knows his mother has never before been to the bungalow. Apart from his own, long-abandoned visits to seek out Lorna May, only the postman and Mrs Connolly, with her milk pail and scoop for ladling out milk, regularly open the low, green-painted wooden gate and crunch up that narrow cinder path to the Herberts' front door.

"Perhaps she's trying to get back to London?" he says. Several of the evacuees at school have already either gone or are about to be collected and taken back to the cities they've come from. He wonders whether to add, "I wouldn't blame her."

But Ronnie laughs dismissively at the suggestion.

"She ain't got nowt to go there for. U-boat did for 'er dad and 'er mam's scrammed."

His mother's surprised glance overcomes what, for all her amusement at Ronnie's ready knowledge, Peter guesses to be her disapproval of his friend's manner of speech, an apparent matter-of-factness which he, Peter, knows isn't flippancy though it's certainly learnt from Ronnie's mother and old gran. Mrs Howard looks at Ronnie, genuinely curious.

"Ronnie? How do you know that?"

"Mrs 'erbert towd mi mam."

"When?" His mother seems taken aback and Peter wonders whether Ronnie has made the story up, especially as Ronnie looks almost embarrassed when he says, "Can't remember. Last year, I reckon." And, as though trying to change the subject, he says, "Mi gran reckons she's gone off to join a circus. Lorna May, that is." But his laugh tells them that he knows the old woman isn't serious.

"Well, wherever she is, it's to be hoped she's not come to any harm." The hint of disapproval has returned to his mother's voice. "If nothing's heard of her soon I imagine the police will have to get a search party up."

"A *search* party?" The two boys speak together. Looking from Ronnie back to his mother, Peter asks, "You mean to go around hunting for her?" Would he be allowed to join in. Would Ronnie? "What will they do when they find her. Arrest her?"

Ronnie says, "*If* they find her." Then, judiciously, "Anyway, she ain't done nothin' wrong, as far as I can see. What they goin' to arrest her for?"

"For running away?"

Ronnie is contemptuous of Peter's suggestion. "Can't blame 'er for *that*," he says. He doesn't like the Herberts, either.

"Oh, I'm sure she'll turn up," Peter's mother says, though she sounds less than certain. "It's such a large area to cover and only a few police. And no one saw the poor girl go. Who knows *what* direction she may have taken. She could be miles away by now. Or, of course, hiding somewhere nearby."

"Perhaps the prisoners could help look," Peter says, thinking of Hans.

"Could be one of 'em's done 'er in."

"Ronnie, *really*." The rebuke is lightened – just – by her smile, but as if to put an end to outlandish speculation, she stands, says briskly to Peter, "After you've washed up, there's some shopping I need you to do. Penny a job, and one for Ronnie, too, if he'd like to help."

For all her occasional tut-tutting at his way of speaking, Peter knows that she likes Ronnie. "He's a caution, your friend," she'd once said, laughing at the recollection of Ronnie's reference to one of their school mates as "a right mardy". "But you don't like me using that word," Peter protested. "It doesn't sound right when you say it," she'd told him.

***

As they begin their journey to the shops, Peter asks Ronnie, "Where do you think Lorna May could be?"

"Don't know and don't care. Long as she stays away from me, she can go where she bloody likes." The stinging slap is neither forgotten nor forgiven.

For some moments they tramp along in silence. But for all that his friend has implied he's done with her, Peter knows that the news of Lorna May's disappearance is bothering Ronnie. And sure enough, as they near the shops, he suddenly says, "I'll tell yer summat fer free." He stops still, as though deliberating whether to go on, then, head down, staring at the pavement, he says, "When we was friends, she give me an owd exercise book for safe keepin'. Said I 'ad to look after it."

"Why did she do that?"

"Dunno." Ronnie shrugs, takes a step, again stops, turns, and looks at Peter who is just behind him. "Never said. Probably nicked it and didn't want it found on 'er. Owd man 'erbert, he'd 'ave gone potty if he thought she'd nicked it. Could 'old a clue to where she's gone."

Does Ronnie mean that? "Will you look to see?" Peter asks him.

But, with a shame-faced grin, Ronnie says that he's hidden the book and can't remember where. "So she can't 'ave it back even if she wants it." He's probably thrown it away.

Swivelling to face the direction in which they are heading, he once more lapses into silence, and the two boys do not speak again until they reach the village shops.

Years later, when he comes to write about this period of his life, Peter Howard, recalling his younger self's envious resentment at the friendship between Ronnie and Lorna May, will understand why the evacuee should have felt so much closer to his friend than to him, a closeness on which she must have depended, and the betrayal of which – trivial as it seemed – must have so wounded her. But in the summer of nineteen forty-five, the ten-year-old Peter Howard can do nothing to break the silence between himself and Ronnie as he hauls his filled basket along the road out of the village.

A rising howl, as of some huge animal, jerks him out of his sullen mood. The howl fills his ears, seems to shake the pavement beneath his feet, vibrates through his body and sets his teeth on edge. The twelve o'clock factory hooter. The end of the working week.

"Can't stand that noise," Ronnie says as the howl slowly sinks into silence, a worm of sound disappearing into its hole. "Nance reckons they'll soon be back on peacetime work." The awkward silence between the two boys is, thank goodness, broken.

They cross the road, and as they pass the red-brick, single-storey factory, **HOSKINS HOSIERY** over its double front doors, skirting the knots of men and women who, work now finished, stand about on the pavement or spill into the road as they bend over cupped hands and then draw their heads back, cigarettes newly alight, or adjust caps and head scarves, most of them chatting with friends before they disperse, some to the nearest pub, others, mounted on bikes, wobbling off home to their dinner, Ronnie tells Peter, "A mate come down to see 'er yesterday afternoon, let out early. Towd 'er it was supposed to be so's they could tidy their gardens for when 'er nibs, the Duchess, comes. But he reckons the real reason was that they was running short of oil for the machines. Mi mam said that wouldn't 'ave bin let 'appen a year back."

"Perhaps it's because the war's over," Peter says.

"Could be," Ronnie says. Then, "fancy a game of cricket then, 'utton? See if yer can score mor'n two off of me?"

***

Ronnie calls for Peter after lunch and, following a brief inspection of Hans' work – "Don't reckon Lorna May's buried under that lot, do you?" Ronnie asks, making a mock grimace – they climb into Connolly's field and set up stumps.

There is still no news of the missing girl, so Peter's mother has told him, and Ronnie has heard the same from his mother.

"Reckon she's somewhere sleepin' out of doors," he says now, throwing himself a catch as they pace out the length of a cricket pitch in the tussocky grass. "Must be barmy." He gives an extravagant shiver. "Think of all them slugs slimin' over yer body if you laid down under a 'edge, like old Whistling Billy."

Peter pushes in the last of the stumps. "Whistling Billy," he says. "We haven't seen him for a long time."

"'e'll be off trampin', that's why," Ronnie says. "That old bath he sleeps in down Fox Spinney, some dirty bugger's gone and put cow shit in it." Then, looking past Peter and down to the bottom of the field, "Let's ask Keith if it were 'im, 'e's daft enough for owt."

Peter turns in the direction of Ronnie's gaze. Keith Bailey is shambling up the meadow, ungainly body outlined against the oaks and sycamores that stand up from the bramble hedge dividing the bottom of the field from the woods beyond. Keith is what Peter's mother calls "simple", though she is always quick to insist that for all his "ways", he means well and isn't to be mocked, especially as his mother, Maureen Bailey, is "kindness itself". Having the keenest memory of how, a year past, he'd been stretched out prone on the sheeted dining-room table, shorts and underpants round his ankles while Mrs Bailey, a district nurse, first squeezed and then dressed a large boil that had gathered on his right buttock, Peter has his own views on the nature of the nurse's virtues, but he keeps them to himself.

Keith, who is now almost upon them, seems only to notice the boys when he is a yard or so away. He stops, looks from one to the other, but, saying nothing, hauls at his grey trousers so as to bring into view cracked brown shoes and black socks that droop round his swollen ankles. The wool of his out-of-shape sweater, a faded maroon, is snagged and, as the two of them watch, Keith lifts an arm and begins to scratch at his armpit.

"Aye up," Ronnie says, breaking the silence. "What you bin up to, then, Keith? Chasin' nits?"

Keith looks at him suspiciously. "I've been down to the woods," he says.

"See any teddy bears?"

"I went looking for flowers." Keith pauses. "Bluebells," he says.

"'ell's bells," Ronnie says. "*Bluebells.* Why not redbells?"

"It's my mum's birthday tomorrow. She likes bluebells." The answer is shaded by truculence. The youth may be slow but once he is roused to anger he has been known to lash out at a tormentor.

"But you didn't find any?" Peter says, gesturing at Keith's empty hands. "Hard luck."

Suddenly a smug expression, almost a smile, twists Keith's heavy lips. "That's where you're wrong," he says, "I found plenty, but I'm not going to pick them till tomorrow. I want them fresh, see." The smile vanishes. Scowling now, he says, "So don't you go down there looking for them, trying to nick them. Do that and I'll come after you. I'll bash you. Both of you."

"Where'd you find them bluebells?" Ronnie asks. "I'm only askin' cos if Peter and me know we won't go there. Don't want to tread on yer flowers, Keith."

"Not telling you," Keith says. "Only don't go near the hut, that's all."

"Oh, right," Ronnie says. "We won't then."

Keith begins to move and they step aside to let him pass.

As he reaches the stile, Ronnie calls after him, "Don't suppose you saw Lorna May in the woods?"

Keith turns, stares at them, perhaps weighing up the possibilities of some insult he can't decipher, then slowly shakes his head. "She's gone, run off," he says, preparing to mount the stile, "Everyone knows that." He pauses, then adds, as an afterthought, "good riddance, too."

He swings a leg awkwardly over the stile's top bar then drops into the road and lumbers away.

Watching the youth as he disappears from view, his words "Good riddance" seeming to hang in the air, Peter remembers the time when Lorna May had followed some way behind an unsuspecting Keith as he made his way up their road, imitating his walk, the clumsy, uncoordinated movement of his limbs, and how, alerted by the laughter of others, he'd turned and run awkwardly after her, though she was far too quick for him, so that he soon stopped, came back toward where Peter and Ronnie stood, his face, they saw as he neared them, contorted with rage. For a moment they wondered whether he was going to lash out at either or both of them, but, mouth working speechlessly, he turned in at his own gate, and for what seemed an age they stood side by side, motionless, without themselves having anything to say.

Is Ronnie remembering that moment? No, it seems not. "Right," he says, "so we know where Keith's found the flowers for 'is mum, then." He grins. "Still, better let 'em be. You to bat. Who you goin' to be this time? Bradman?"

"Hutton," Peter said, "of course."

"Get ready to duck. I'm Larwood."

As he watches Ronnie marking out his run-up, Peter calls, "Hans is in training for football."

Ronnie turns to look at him. "Ow'd you make that out?"

"I saw him yesterday afternoon. When I came out after my tea he was just finishing. He'd gone for a run while the tar cooled off."

"So he'd gone for a run. What's that supposed to prove?" Ronnie doesn't like anyone knowing more than he does, especially about Hans, whom he seems to regard as a personal friend. He is forever repeating to Peter what he claims the German prisoner has told *him*. For once Peter can put one over on Ronnie.

"It proves that he wants to be a proper footballer again. I asked him if he was training and he said yes."

"More like 'ed gone for a quick fag," Ronnie says, trying to regain the upper hand.

"He doesn't smoke." Peter makes his block hole. "Anyway, he wouldn't take his shirt off for that, would he?"

Ronnie shrugs, momentarily silenced.

But soon enough he regains his voice. Dismissing the subject of Hans, he says, "Ok 'utton. Let's see you try to keep Larwood out." And he begins his run-up.

A moment later the old leather ball, stitching split and leaking grey fluff, comes harmlessly to rest a foot in front of Peter.

"A warm up, that was," Ronnie says. "Chuck us it back. Next one's for real."

But as he lobs the ball back to his friend, Peter is thinking not about Ronnie's threat but that he now understands why something Hans had done the previous afternoon so puzzled him.

5

A medley of sounds, of sighings, coughs and clearing of throats, the rustling of dresses and creak of pews hard-pressed under heavy bottoms, the congregation settles down for the Reverend Chard's sermon.

From his place in the choir stall, Peter can see his mother, just. Wearing her fawn mackintosh and the neat, dark-green hat, almost like a man's trilby, tilted jauntily to one side of her curly hair, she is sitting, as always, at the end of a pew near the west door. She likes to escape before the vicar gets to the porch to shake hands with worshippers making their exit. As soon as the final blessing is given and while the choir recesses up the aisle, heading for the vestry, she'll be on her feet. It isn't, she once explained to her son, that she dislikes the vicar, but she disapproves of the unspoken rule that you should take your place in the queue waiting to be greeted by him, that what she calls the high and mighty must always come first, and that the rag, tag, and bobtail are supposed to bring up the rear.

But who *are* the high and mighty, he'd asked? "Oh, you know. Those people who own the manor, the Garlands, Doctor Flynn … " She was being deliberately vague.

This morning, he notices Mrs Bailey, decked out in what his mother might call her finery: grey belted coat and black hat with a mini-veil. As for Keith, hunched awkwardly between Peter's mother and his own, his long-dead father's tweed jacket strained tight across his shoulders, he is gazing about him, open-mouthed, as though wondering why he's at church at all. Following the direction of the youth's slow stare, Peter finds himself looking at old Harrison in his dark blue serge suit, stiff-backed in his accustomed pew almost below the pulpit, the upward tilt of his head calculated to assert the unwavering attention he chooses to devote to whatever the vicar may have to say.

Don't worry, you bloody custard. The sudden, guilty memory of Lorna May's words makes him involuntarily look away. Surely the dentist can't have anything to do with the girl's disappearance? For a moment he lets himself wonder whether she's been caught in the act of scrumping and is now locked into Harrison's garden shed, waiting for the police to fetch her. But no, he tells himself, don't be daft. It isn't the right time of year for scrumping, and anyway he doesn't even know whether Harrison has a shed.

His gaze roaming now about the crowded pews, he notices that everyone seems to be dressed up. There's a festive air in the way people smile at each other, in the clothes that are more than their ordinary Sunday best, or, if their usual garb, are today being worn with added dash. The comparatively few men are in suits that look as though they've been freshly taken out of wardrobes or lifted down from hangers, and how brightly coloured the ties are beneath their starched collars, and among the women are far more hats than headscarves, while coats glitter with brooches or, in one or two instances, are topped by fur stoles.

The village is celebrating the end of war. One woman, further along the pew from where old Harrison sits ramrod straight, has a fox tippet wrapped round her neck, and as she tilts her head toward the pulpit, the fox's head itself seems to skew up and a pair of beady eyes become trained on the vicar, an expectant, toothy grin on its tight-drawn black lips. Peter bites his lip. Mustn't laugh.

"Today my sermon is taken from Jeremiah." Pause. "Thou art my refuge in the day of evil." Hands grasping the near-black wooden pulpit in front of him, bald, waxily-white crown of his head gleaming in light that filters through the plain-glass windows set into tall, greystone walls above the nave, the vicar pauses to adjust his surplice, allowing time for the import of his words, so gravely uttered in a hoarse whisper which seems nevertheless to reach all parts of the church, to impress the worshippers above whose upturned faces he looms.

He peers down at his notes before he pronounces "Chapter Seventeen, verse seventeen." Further pause. "Some of you here will recall that I took these same words for my evening sermon on that fateful Sunday, September 3rd 1939. The day our then Prime Minister, Mr Chamberlain, declared our nation to be at war with Germany." Pause. "And now, five and a half long years later, peace has come to much of our troubled world, although not as yet to that part of it where Japanese forces choose to continue their campaign against the Christian gospel of peace. There will come the day, and may it be soon, when they will be forced to surrender. But until that day comes, we may feel tempted to say with our prophet, 'Bring upon them the day of evil, and destroy them with double destruction.'"

Several members of the congregation nod at these words. One or two exchange looks, smiling.

"Let us, however, remember that as Christians it is our duty to practise forgiveness to our enemies, even those that have done us most grievous harm. And let us not forget that we ourselves in order to achieve peace may practise what some men think of as evil."

The smiles slowly dim and then fade.

By contrast with many sermons Peter has heard the vicar deliver, this one is short. The Rev. Chard emphasises the need to give thanks to God for delivering Britain and the Free World from Hitler, to remember with gratitude all who have died fighting fascism's wickedness, to commiserate with those millions who have been the enemy's innocent victims, both here and abroad, and to pray that the peace which men in arms and wise statesmanship have between them and with God's help achieved will prove to be a lasting one, although there is only one truly everlasting Peace and that is the one which comes from following the ways of Almighty God. Amen.

The vicar lumps his heavy body down the pulpit's steps, the choir stands, the organ begins its drone, the congregation gets slowly to its feet, and the opening words of the hymn "Now Thank We All Our God" falter into the morning air.

At the end of the service, the vicar, before administering the final blessing, reminds his congregation of the royal visit planned for the following Tuesday which, though fleeting, will, he hopes, occasion a good show of support from all those who can spare half-an-hour to line the route the Duchess of Kent's car will be taking. Then, voice dropping to a suitable gravity, he invites those present to join in a prayer for all troubled souls in the parish, "including those who are not of our congregation but are in our hearts and thoughts and whose woes at this time of peace remind us that we are all in the great hand of God and that He must be our refuge."

The prayer that follows lists several names which mean nothing to Peter. But three do. "We pray for Mr and Mrs Herbert and for the safe return of their 'charge', Lorna May Perry. Amen."

"Amen," the congregation replies, the word reverberating round the church. The girl's disappearance is by now common knowledge.

***

37

Walking home with his mother, who has waited at the church gate while he changes out of his surplice and cassock, Peter asks her why she thinks the vicar included the Herberts in that final prayer. "I mean, they don't come to church."

"It wouldn't be very Christian, would it, only to care about those who do? Besides, Methodists are Christians. I walked up the road with them this morning. They were off to chapel. I imagine prayers for the girl's safe return will have been said by their minister."

He thinks about it. "What were they wearing?"

She pauses, looking at him in mock enquiry as she repeats his words. "What were they wearing? What an odd question. Why?"

"Because everyone in church seemed as though they were dressed for a party."

She laughs. "Oh, I see. Yes, it's true, people *were* in their glad rags. Well, almost." But the laughter fades. "The poor Herberts have nothing to celebrate, I'm afraid. Not until Lorna May comes back."

Poor Herberts. She wouldn't have called them that before Lorna May went missing.

They turn into the road that leads downhill to their own house. "Look," she says, for a moment quickening her stride, "there they are."

And sure enough, he sees, on the far side of the road, ahead of them by some distance, the Herberts, their black-coated figures moving briskly in step, and he can tell from the set of their shoulders, the way they face unwaveringly forward as they stride along, Mrs Herbert surprisingly small beside her husband's burly height, that they are silent with each other. It's as though they have no other thought than to concentrate on reaching their destination as quickly as possible.

And without her saying so, he knows as his mother slows her speed that she is suddenly fearful of speaking to them, that she is thinking, as he now is, it will be better to leave the couple to themselves as they hurry to their bungalow. They must be hoping that during their absence Lorna May has stolen back in.

***

But no. Because before he and his mother begin their midday meal, she says she'll "just run over the road to see if there is any news."

She is back within a very few minutes. "No luck, I'm afraid," she calls out to him from the kitchen, above the clatter of saucepans and the brass-band music coming from the wireless he has switched on as soon as they got in. "Poor people, they're worried out of their minds. If anything, he looks even more harassed than she does."

Harassed Herbert. Peter thinks he'll save that for Ronnie. When they are out after school, the boys occasionally meet the man as he comes home from his work, in the black suit that denotes his position as supervisor at the hosiery factory. A sallow-faced, cheerless man, who rarely acknowledges their respectful greeting by more than a grunt, although once, when Lorna May had been with them, he stopped long enough to tell the girl she was due home in a few minutes. Lorna May had grimaced at his retreating back, but nevertheless soon left them to trudge back down the field to where her duties waited for her.

"Glad I don't 'ave 'im for a father," Ronnie had said. "Old misery guts. That's what me mam calls 'im. Turn the milk sour, 'e would."

***

The midday meal is soon done with. Cabbage, which he dislikes, is niftily disguised by an onion sauce he slathers over his roast potatoes and the sausages left in a slow oven while they were at church.

Sitting opposite him, his mother shakes her head in wry, amused wonder at his choosing to mash all the food together before forking it up. "Just like your dad," she says.

He looks at her, expectantly. Has she perhaps heard any news of what she calls demob. "When's dad coming home?"

"I only wish I knew." She gives the small sigh he knows goes with her attempt to throw off discontent. "As soon as the army can spare him, I imagine."

"In time for Christmas?"

"I certainly hope so." Pushing aside her half-eaten food, she says, "I'm praying he won't be sent to the Far East. He's been away for quite long enough." She allows herself a smile. "Besides, he doesn't know Japanese."

"Egypt, Italy, Germany," he recites. He has followed his father's progress on a wall-map pinned up in his bedroom. Pencilled stars for the important places along what he thinks of as a travel route exotic as Marco Polo's. Cairo, Alexandria, Palermo, Naples, Rome, Milan, and, finally, Berlin, from where his father sent the note that had arrived yesterday morning. *Journey's End*, he'd written. *Next stop,*

England!!!! Fingers crossed. Love to you both.

"Does Dad know Egyptian?"

"German and Italian. Which is probably more than half in Intelligence do." Then, gathering up their plates, she says, "Sit tight and I'll bring in the pudding."

"Steamed sponge?"

"Coming up."

Cairo, Alexandria, Palermo, Naples, Rome, Milan, Berlin. For years the adult Peter Howard promises himself that one day he will freely undertake the journey his father was forced to take as part of his army service. But he never does.

***

An hour later, having changed from his Sunday clothes into sandals, old shorts and white, short-sleeved shirt, he and Ronnie are again setting up stumps in Farmer Connolly's field. Ronnie, who never goes to church, has, so he tells Peter, spent the morning roaming up and down Fox Spinney, hoping to catch a glimpse of Whistling Billy. "Not a sign of 'im. Mi mam reckons it's a miracle nobody's took that old bath for scrap. Only thing I see was some broken-off 'azel, so the Gyppos must 'ave bin through, peg-makin'."

Then, as Peter is about to set the bowling stump into a patch of grass where he stands, Ronnie shouts, "Not there. We'll be runnin' through cow shit."

And looking about him, Peter sees that Farmer Connolly's dairy herd must have been in the field the previous evening, or even earlier that day, because there are cow pats everywhere, black-brown pancakes as big as dinner plates, some partly crusted over, though not enough to deter flies glinting green-gold as they swarm above the still-liquid surface areas.

"We'd better try further down," he says and as he does so, Ronnie, who is staring toward the bottom of the long meadow, says, "Aye up, looks like trouble."

Peter turns to where Ronnie is pointing and sees Keith Bailey drop from the stile at the field's bottom edge and come, half running, half-stumbling toward them. The youth is calling something out but is too far off for them to be able to make out his words.

"Could be some bugger's nicked 'is bluebells," Ronnie says, his voice touched by laughter, but when Peter stares at him, he says, "Not me. Towd yer, I were in Fox Spinney. Never went near the woods, God's truth."

"You don't believe in God," Peter says, but he believes his friend.

As Keith labours toward them he stops shouting and now they can hear what sound like sobs issuing from between his red, wet lips.

Within a yard or so of the boys, he comes to a sudden halt.

"I've seen her," he says, gasping. Looking from one to the other, he takes a deep breath and they see that he is trembling. "Right by the bluebells. Right by the hut." His eyes are staring, a mixture of disbelief and fear.

"Seen who?" Ronnie asks with surprising gentleness. "Calm down, Keith, and tell us."

Taking a step forward, he stands directly in front of the bigger boy and puts a reassuring hand on Keith's arm, which is still sleeved in his dead father's jacket.

Keith looks at the hand then at Ronnie, his face contorted with bewildered grief, as though he can't believe that Ronnie has failed to understand.

"Her, of course," he whimpers. "Her. Lorna May."

.

6

"Crimson or scarlet lake?"

"Crimson. Scarlet lake's too dark."

"They drape flags over coffins, don't they?"

"Big flags, they do. Not these. And they only do it for the nobs."

Ronnie and Peter sit facing each other across the dining room table, empty tea plates pushed to one side, between them newspaper spread under a jam jar filled with water standing next to a tin box of water-colour paints. They are putting the finishing touches to their paper flags. They speak in near-whispers, motioned to do so by Peter's mother, who, in her accustomed chair by the fireplace, is listening intently to the six o'clock news.

Hearing the name "Berlin" coming from the wireless, Peter stops what he is saying and looks expectantly across at her, but without turning to him she shakes her head and sighs. "He's telling us that Berliners are without food. And water."

Another, posher voice now. A man reporting from the German capital, someone who has returned from what he calls Concentration Camps, where he has seen …

His mother abruptly switches off the wireless.

"Don't you want to hear?" Peter asks her.

"I can't bear it," she says.

"It's about all them Jews being starved and killed," Ronnie says.

"I know about that." With his paint brush Peter points down at the paint-spattered newspaper. "It's in here."

"Well then," his mother says, "let that do for the moment."

Standing, she comes over to inspect their work. "Not bad," she says, a hand on Peter's shoulder and including Ronnie in her approving smile. "Budding artists, both of you."

"Or designers?" Peter looks up at her.

"Is this the kind of thing yer dad does, then?" Ronnie asks.

"Not really." She moves to sit down again. "Furniture rather than textiles is what Peter's dad is an expert at designing. Chairs a speciality."

Ronnie looks first mystified, then sceptical. Who needed a chair designed for them? Chairs have four legs, a back and a seat, and that is that.

He indicates the chair she's dropped into, "is that one of 'is?'"

"As a matter of fact, yes."

Ronnie, lips pursed, studies the chair's angled, padded back, the slight wings, the grey-green material.

Perhaps to draw him away from some caustic remark or thought, she says, "Now, tell me again what happened. There are parts of the story I still don't know."

It is, Peter thinks, a strange thing about grown-ups. They can talk about one thing, then another, then a third, switching between subjects as automatically as trains switch tracks when points send them off in different directions.

Whereas he, and, he's sure, Ronnie, are still so full of the afternoon's events that since coming indoors, at his mother's suggestion, to share tea and flag-making, they've talked of little else.

But then his mother hadn't been present when Keith came stumbling up the field to blurt out his discovery. Nor had she been with them when they followed the youth to his mother's house.

Because after dinner, as on most Sundays, she had taken herself down the road to visit Sally Parsons. Sally Parsons has twin girls, born a few months after her husband, a fighter pilot, was killed over France. That had been in the early days of the war and since then Peter's mother and Sally have been regular visitors to each other's houses. And so it was only when, as she returned from her visit and saw Peter and Ronnie at the stile – "guarding Sergeant Locker's bike, like 'e towd us to do" – Ronnie explained, that she heard about Keith's discovery.

She was still silent, still pale-faced, as the boys told her how they'd run home with Keith, how in Mrs Bailey's absence Sergeant Locker had phoned the police station … and then, while they were telling her all this, she turned from them and they saw she was watching Sergeant Locker as he marched up the field, Keith lumbering along behind him.

"Afternoon Mrs Howard," the policeman said, hoisting himself onto and then over the stile. He touched the peak of his helmet with a forefinger. "A right mess we've got here."

"You've found Lorna May." She was trembling as she spoke. "Her body?"

Sergeant Locker was suddenly on his guard. "Formal identification will be necessary." After glancing at her face he spoke more softly. "It's her, I'm afraid. Poor lass." Jerking a thumb at his companion, he said, "It was Keith here found her. And 'body' it is. She's dead right enough. Been there some time, if you ask me. Half-hidden in brambles. Easily missed." And again he said, this time sighing, "Poor lass."

"How ... have you any idea what happened?" The trembling had stopped, but her eyes gleamed with tears.

"We have to be careful about advancing theories." He straightened his back.

But as before, softened by her evident concern, he dropped into familiarity. "If you ask me, she fell and broke her neck. That's what it looks like."

Keith said to nobody in particular, "Sergeant thinks she fell off the roof."

"*Roof?*" Ronnie and Peter spoke together

"Roof of the hut. That's where I found her. Beside the hut." Keith looked around, his earlier expression of bewildered panic now replaced by one of dazed pride. "That's where she was. Her legs were sticking out of that old bramble bush. You know." He appealed to Peter and Ronnie for corroboration of the bush's existence.

"Careful what you say, lad. I've already taken one statement from you. We don't want too much coming out before it can be verified."

But Peter and Ronnie were looking at Keith. They knew all about the bush, just as they knew about the hut, an old, partially collapsed structure deep in the woods, once used as a woodman's store but for years in a state of abandonment and increasing decay, a place where, although the boys occasionally used it as a hiding place, the mildewed smell of rotten planking, the rustling of heaps of festering leaves, and the stinking, unnameable objects piled in corners, soon drove them out. As for the roof, it was partly fallen in, its tarpaulin cover torn and holed, most of the struts and thin lathes to which the tarpaulin had once been nailed long fallen away.

Climbing onto it was a risky business, but if you took care you could balance on the deep overhang and from there launch yourself out into air and down to the thick carpeting of grass below. Sometimes, if you fell awkwardly, you winded yourself, or, if you jumped off the roof without taking good care to check where you'd land, you got scratched by the brambles, menacing as barbed wire, that sprouted to one side of the hut; but otherwise the worst that had happened to any of them was some bruising of elbow, or knee. Nothing worse. They'd never thought of it as dangerous.

44

Until now.

"Poor, poor girl."

"As you say, ma'am." Sergeant Locker made a tight-lipped gesture of assent to Peter's mother, jutting out his chin. " We'll have to order an ambulance here, pronto. I need to phone from Mrs Bailey's, then get back to guard the body. Shouldn't really have left it, but, like they say, needs must … "

They watched as he bustled up the road, Keith doing his best to keep up.

A few minutes later, minutes during which Peter, his mother, and Ronnie stood, not meeting each others' eyes and nobody spoke, Sergeant Locker marched back, this time alone.

"Right. The ambulance will be here soon as ever's possible, I'll get back to the corpse … to the girl, and perhaps you lads wouldn't mind waiting for the ambulance. Make yourselves useful, will you, by showing the men where they've to go." It wasn't so much a suggestion as an order.

"What about Keith?" Peter knew what Ronnie meant. Keith really ought to be the one to lead the men to the hut. It seemed only fair. He'd after all been the one who found the girl. He knew exactly where she was.

Swinging a leg over the stile, the policeman said " Keith's done his bit. And now he's waiting for his mum to come home. They're due their tea." A pause, as he clambered down into the field. "I'm told it's her birthday. She's had to go out on a case but she'll be back soon enough." He made it sound as though birthdays were luxuries a policeman could expect to go without.

Watching him as he set off to tramp down toward the far tree-fringed bottom of the field, Peter's mother called after him, "I take it somebody's told the Herberts?"

Sergeant Locker turned to her, and, perhaps offended by her suggestion that he had been in any way remiss, said emphatically, "I can assure you that I've been and knocked, but there's nobody at home."After a moment to let that sink in, he added, "I slipped a note under their door, asking them to contact me. Not a lot else I can do." Having said which, he swivelled and set off down the field at a determined plod.

"Probably gone 'untin' for 'er on their own," Ronnie said.

"So they don't yet know." The words came out with unguarded feeling. "Poor people. Oh, this is *awful*."

Peter watched his mother put a hand to her mouth, an habitual gesture of concern. Her previous coolness toward the Herberts had quite vanished. Concern now thickening her voice, she murmured, as if to herself, "I'd better get back home." And to Peter, she said "Once you've shown the ambulance men where they have to go, come up for your tea." Her smile troubled, though attemptedly reassuring, she added, "Would you like to join us, Ronnie? The usual bread and scrape, but I can probably find a slice or two of cake."

There was, though, nothing usual about this Sunday afternoon.

"Ok," Ronnie said, then, remembering his manners, "Thanks, Mrs 'oward. I'll 'ave to let mi mam know."

"I can do that for you," she said, "I'll be going past your house. And your mother will want to know about Lorna May."

***

Sitting at the table, watching the painted flags drying on the hearth, Peter says, "I don't think there's much else to tell you, mum. All Keith told us, and all he told Sergeant Locker, was that he'd found Lorna May lying under that bramble bush."

"Probably thought she were asleep," Ronnie says. "Soon found out she weren't."

Reaching for a cigarette, she asks, "Why was Keith in the woods?" She means, Peter knows, why did Keith Bailey go there on a Sunday. Mrs Bailey might be 'a dear', but in common with most of the villagers she regards Sunday as the day of rest. On Sundays you are supposed to put on your best clothes and, apart from going to church or chapel, you stay indoors or go for decorous walks. You don't, as Peter and Ronnie are allowed to do, roam the woods. And thinking this, Peter recalls that Keith was still wearing his church-going jacket when he came stumbling up the field, carrying the burden of his discovery.

"'ed gone lookin' for flowers, bluebells," Ronnie says. "Me and Peter saw 'im yesterday when we was playin' cricket. Towd us he'd found some and ud be goin' back for 'em today. Wanted 'em for 'is mum's birthday. Let on as they was near the 'ut. That's 'ow he come across Lorna May's body."

As she watches smoke coil toward the ceiling, she says, reflectively, "Which rather suggests the girl couldn't have been there when Keith was down there yesterday – Saturday."

Looking at each other, startled, the boys nod speculative agreement. They hadn't thought of that.

"And yet Lorna May went missing on Friday."

They hadn't thought of that, either.

Peter says, "Perhaps he simply didn't see it. *Her*."

"Or the body weren't there," Ronnie says. Then, as she looks sharply at him, "I mean, perhaps Keith wasn't near the 'ut. 'E could 'ave found the bluebells in a different place, couldn't 'e? There are plenty on 'em around."

"But," Peter says, "he warned us not to go looking for the flowers he wanted for his mother. Told us he'd bash us if we tried."

"What, you reckon Keith was tryin' to make sure we kept away? Wanted to keep the discovery of Lorna May's body to hissen? Don't make sense.' E'd 'ave towd us there and then. What's the point of waitin' till the next day."

"Don't go leaping ahead of yourselves." She nips off the end of her half-smoked cigarette. "Tell me about what happened when the ambulance arrived."

"It wasn't a real ambulance," Peter says, and Ronnie nods agreement. "It was an army truck with a canvas hood and a red cross on each side."

"Short of proper ambulances, I reckon. But they was proper 'ospital blokes in it."

"And once we'd told them where to find the sergeant and Lorna May, they ran off down the field carrying a stretcher."

An' come back up with 'er body on it. Except we couldn't see owt 'cos they'd covered 'er with a sheet."

"And Sergeant Locker came up with them and got on his bike and rode off," Peter says.

"An' no reward. We'd stood there mindin' it all afternoon. Never 'ad time fer a game of cricket."

"I imagine he had rather more on his plate than apologising to you two for any inconvenience he may have caused," she says, her smile one of wry judgement. "I'm sure he at least thanked you."

"He said he'd come to take statements from us tomorrow. After school."

"Hmm." She kneels on the hearth-rug, inspects their flags, touches one with an index finger. "The paint's dry," she says brightly. "Here, Ronnie, this one's yours, I think. Have you got a stick at home you can attach it to?" She holds the piece of paper out to him, a signal that it's time for him to go.

And thanking her for his tea, Ronnie goes.

***

Now they are on their own, Peter asks her, "What do you think will happen?"

From the chair where she once again sits, abstracted, she looks at her son before, speaking slowly, she says, "I imagine there will have to be an inquest. To determine the cause of death." And having explained to him what the word means, she adds, "But poor Mr and Mrs Herbert. It's *dreadful* to think that they'll be the last to know what's happened to the girl they took in."

He risks saying, "But you thought they weren't very kind to her."

"I did, I admit it. And I wish now I hadn't." She stares into the empty hearth. "They weren't very loving, perhaps. Not as far as anyone could tell. But I suppose they were unused to having children about the place." She lifts her eyes, turns to him. "I'm certain, though, that they'd have wanted the best for her, looked after her according to their lights."

"What does that mean?" he asks. "According to their lights?"

She holds up her hands in rueful confession. "I'm not a hundred per cent sure, my love. The light of the religion they follow?" A pause. "One thing I *do* know. They'll be distraught when they hear about Lorna May. Distressed beyond words." Her look is one of sad reproach. He knows what she is thinking. I shouldn't have allowed you to speak so openly and so often about how you dislike them both. "We'll all have to make an effort to be kind to them."

Yes, he thinks but doesn't say, there's not much doubt that being kind to the Herberts won't come easily.

And years later, remembering that moment, it's his mother's words he recalls most vividly, her remark, "They looked after her, according to their lights." And he sees her hands raised, that gesture of confession. I'm not a hundred per cent sure.

7

As soon as he comes through the back door he hears his mother's voice calling to him "Peter. Come and join us."

"Here he is," Mrs Bailey says as he pushes open the door to the front room, her smile welcoming him in.

She and his mother are in easy chairs facing each other across the hearth rug, and Sally Parsons sits on the settee.

The photograph of his parents, taken immediately before his uniformed father went off to war, has been pushed to one end of the low coffee table, to allow space for the tray bearing the best china: tea-pot, milk-jug, plates, all of them in angular yellow-and-black patterns. Slices of fruit cake are neatly arranged in a large glass dish. Three small glasses for sherry, only taken out of the cupboard on what his mother calls High Days and Holy Days, two of them with small amounts of brown liquid in them, stand beside a dark glass bottle in which the cork has been loosened.

"We're helping to celebrate," his mother says, and he remembers that yesterday had been her near-neighbour's birthday.

"Have a piece of cake, Peter," Mrs Bailey invites him. She raises her cup of tea and smiles at him over it. "I've had some good news."

"Maureen's birthday cake," Sally Parsons says, as he goes across to the table and deliberates over the glass dish.

"Though it's not only a birthday we're helping to celebrate," his mother says.

"Keith's got a job," Mrs Bailey says. "He's been taken on at Hoskins. He's to start next week." The contentment in her smile is matched by his mother's look of pleasure in her friend's happiness.

Sally Parsons says, "It must be such a relief to you, Maureen."

What she means, Peter understands, is that given Keith's problems, his backwardness, as most call it, let alone his clumsiness, he's lucky to find any work.

To break the awkward silence, his mother asks, "And how was school?"

"We had prayers for Lorna May," he says, "and Ronnie and me had to give our statements to the police." He pauses. "At dinner break."

"I thought the sergeant said he'd be coming here?" His mother is surprised and, he thinks, offended by this information.

"It wasn't him that talked to us. He was there, but the man who asked us questions was from the town. A detective."

Maureen Bailey says to the other women. "Probably the same one that came to see Keith." She turns to Peter. "In a brown suit?" He nods. "Yes," she said, " it'll be him. Humphreys is his name. Came this morning by car – all the way from Ashton." He is aware of the satiric edge in her voice. Ashton is no more than two miles from Stonely. "Sergeant Locker was with him, but it was Mr Humphreys who asked the questions."

She picks up an empty sherry glass, twiddles it between thumb and index finger. "Keith coped well. Told them, told Humphreys, what he'd seen. After which 'I gave my account' – " she puts mock-emphasis on the phrase – "of how I'd been out and so Keith had to give permission for the Sergeant to use our telephone."

And she puts the glass back on the coffee table.

Looking at the other two women in turn, Sally Parsons says, "Surely it's highly irregular for a policeman to ask a boy of Peter's age questions without an adult being present." She seems to be treating herself as a person of authority. "Where did all this happen?"

"In Miss Wheelock's room," Peter says. "She sat behind her desk while he spoke to me. And she did the same when Ronnie was called in."

"Miss Wheelock's the headmistress," his mother explains. "Still, I'm surprised I wasn't asked to be present." And to Peter, "Did he make you sign anything?"

He is puzzled. "Sign? No. He said he only wanted to know when I'd last seen Lorna, and if I could remember what Keith said to Ronnie and me after he'd found her. We told him that we were playing cricket in Connolly's field when Keith came running up. He kept calling her Lorna, even when we'd told him she made us call her Lorna May," he added.

As he repeats words he'd earlier spoken to the detective, he remembers that he hadn't said anything to the man Humphreys about Ronnie and him seeing Keith emerging from the woods a day earlier. But that was before the discovery of the body, so it didn't count, anymore than did Hans' emergence from the field on the afternoon before *that*.

"It all sounds very informal," Sally Parsons says. "Did Keith have to sign?" she asks Maureen, then colours faintly. Keith can't write.

But Maureen Bailey says, "Neither of us had to put pen to paper. They told us they were making preliminary inquiries. I think they wanted to get matters clear in their own minds as to whether there could have been anything at all odd about the poor girl's death."

"Suspicious circumstances, you mean?" Sally Parsons rises as she asks the question, places her teacup on the tray and says, "I shall have to be getting back. Thanks so much for the tea, Kay, and Maureen, too, for the delicious cake. A rare treat nowadays, being allowed to eat something with real butter and eggs in it."

She brushes invisible crumbs from the front of her pleated, grey skirt, and Peter notices her glance at herself in the mirror hanging over the fireplace, adjust the collar of her cream blouse, and fiddle momentarily with a pearl earring.

Smiling ingratiatingly at Peter so that he notices the scarlet bow round her teeth, she asks him, "Would you mind bringing me my coat? It's in the hall. I'm afraid I rather draped it over the newel post."

Newel post? He is mystified. But his mother says, "At the bottom of the banisters."

When he returns with the camel-hair jacket and hands it to her he is aware of her perfume, its cloying sweetness. Before shrugging her jacket on, she gives him the sherry bottle, now re-corked, to hold. It feels, he thinks, very light.

And as if to confirm this, Sally Parsons, as she takes the bottle back from him, says "Hardly worth lugging this back with me, I suppose, but then again … "

His mother says, laughing, as she pushes herself upright, "Sally, dear, don't you dare to leave temptation in my way." Then, more seriously, "I hope the twins have behaved themselves in your absence. It must be a treat for your mother-in-law to see them after all this while."

Looking up from tightening the belt of her jacket, Sally Parsons says with a brief smile, "And quite a treat for me, too, to have a few hours off duty. Now that trains are beginning to run more normally, I sincerely hope she'll be able to come up more often." A small sigh. "But Cornwall is, I'm afraid, a long way off. And now that your friend's sister is back at work," she says turning to Peter, "I've lost my baby-sitter."

"Nancy?"

"Nancy," she says. She looks down as though inspecting her

brown suede shoes. "Rather a slatternly girl, but she means well. At least, Kay, you've got your husband's return to look forward to." A pause. "Sandy and I had so little time together."

"What about your parents," his mother asks. "Won't they be wanting to visit their grandchildren?"

"*My* parents?" The question is one of forceful incredulity. "I'd rather not speak of them, if you don't mind." She turns, then, framed in the open doorway swings dramatically back. "And they've made it abundantly clear that they'd rather not speak of, or to, me. No, don't move, Kay. I'll see myself out." A flutter of her hand, as she says, "Sorry, forget you heard that," and leaves the room.

A moment later they hear the front door close firmly and the clack of her heels on the flagged path.

"Lord," Peter's mother says, "I said the wrong thing there."

"I *think* I heard that they disapproved of her marriage," Maureen Bailey says. "It was very sudden." She mouths a word Peter doesn't understand.

He goes to look out of the window. Will the fine weather hold for tomorrow's royal visit?

"Hey," he says, staring across the road to the bungalow opposite. "Someone's pulled the curtains across at the Herberts."

He turns in surprise, then back again to study the bungalow's tight drawn curtains. They are black-out drapes. Unlike most people up and down the road, the Herberts haven't yet taken theirs down.

"I've not had a chance to tell you." His mother joins him at the window, resting a hand on his shoulder. "Mr and Mrs Herbert arrived back early this afternoon."

"Back? Where from? Where have they been?"

Behind them, Maureen Bailey says, "I'll leave you two alone, if you don't mind. I don't like being out of the house for long when I'm supposed to be on duty, even if I've not gone far. You never know who might be in need of my services."

They turn now to look at her, find themselves staring at her apologetic smile. "He does his best, Keith, poor lad, but he doesn't always remember to tell me about phone messages that have come while I'm out."

"Of course," his mother says.

"But I've really enjoyed this afternoon, Kay. It's done me good. Thank you." She slaps her hands together in irritation. "I should have remembered to thank Sally for the sherry."

His mother goes across and takes the other woman's hand, palm to palm, rubs the back of her guest's with her free one. "Sherry you didn't drink?" she says, smiling. "Sally had most of it. I don't really see the need for you to thank her for that."

"Perhaps not," Mrs Bailey begins, "but … "

"But nothing," his mother says. "Thank *you*, Maureen. And I'm so happy that Keith has the promise of work. It will be good for you both. He'll be looking forward to it, won't he." She is smiling into the other woman's eyes. "Bringing some money into the household. He'll feel quite the man."

A shadow passes quickly across Maureen Bailey's face and is as quickly gone when she says, suddenly laughing, "Do you know what he's most looking forward to? Cleaner's overalls. I think the promise of wearing those excites him more than anything else." There is genuine pleasure in her laugh. She is laughing with, not at, her son.

Years later, remembering that moment, Peter Howard will understand the modest heroism that enables Maureen Bailey, a middle-aged widow with only a mentally retarded son on whom she can concentrate her affection, her love, to survive the horror of what lies ahead.

***

Left to themselves, mother and son sit in the sage-green easy chairs in the room rarely used when they are on their own, scoffing the last of the cake as she tells him about the Herberts.

Most of her information has come from Maureen Bailey, the rest from Mrs Herbert herself. It seems that the previous afternoon, increasingly worried, even desperate, about Lorna May's disappearance, the couple made the sudden decision to take a train to London, hoping against hope that the girl might somehow have made her way back to her former home and that they would find her there.

"I thought her dad was dead, and her mum had gone away, disappeared." Peter is puzzled. "That's what Ronnie said."

"And it turns out he was telling the truth." She looks at him as though she finds this a surprise. "Mrs Herbert tells me she let that information slip once when she was talking to his Mum. She admitted she was trying to explain why Lorna May was proving difficult. 'A bit of a handful,' was how she put it. What Sally Parsons calls a Street Arab. Lorna May had apparently said or done something nasty to Ronnie, and his mother went over to – well, to complain, I suppose."

Yes, he can believe that, even thinks he knows when it had been. He tells his mother about what had happened one afternoon some two years earlier, when he, Ronnie and Lorna May had been tree climbing, and seemingly irritated by Ronnie's getting ahead of her, the girl had pushed Ronnie off the branch he was straddling. In falling, he'd ripped his shorts and bloodied them from a cut to his knee. Limping home, he'd said he wouldn't tell on her – at that time he and Lorna May were still friends – but in all probability his mother forced a confession about what had happened out of him. It wasn't though enough to save him from a whacking because the shorts were new – bought with coupons Mrs Slater had saved for.

When he finishes his tale, she says, "It sounds all too likely. Ronnie's mother told me something about it this morning."

He realises that while he's been at school a great deal of discussion has been going on between various adults, all of it to do with – caused by – Lorna May's death.

But, let slip? "What do you mean by saying that?" he asks.

Because, his mother explains, a shade defensively, the Herberts are as close as oysters, aren't they, they don't welcome any gossip, and certainly wouldn't do anything to encourage whisperings among the locals about any member of their family.

Peter wants to protest against this explanation that Lorna May *isn't* family. But he realises that in 'disappearing', Lorna May's mother has done something disreputable. An image of Mrs Herbert flashes into his mind. Her purse-lipped, stony face, those tight grey curls. No, she wouldn't want anything to 'besmirch' her reputation, a word he'd once heard Lorna May use when she was telling Ronnie and him about how Mr Herbert hit her for swearing. "What'd you say?" Ronnie had wanted to know. "I told him it was bloody unfair, me having to clean the kitchen floor after *she'd* spilt some gravy on it. So then he thumped me round the ear, and *she* said that I was a disgrace to their reputation, that I *besmirched* it."

Should he tell his mother of this? But she is concentrating on her own story, of how Maureen Bailey learnt about the Herberts' decision. Mrs Herbert had apparently come knocking soon after Sunday dinner, asking whether she could use the phone? "She wanted the local taxi service to take her and her husband to Ashton station.

One of them, perhaps both, had the idea of dashing down to London to see whether they could find Lorna May and bring her back."

"*London?*"

"I know. Rather like looking for a needle in a whole field of haystacks, though it shows how concerned they were."

"But why didn't Mrs Bailey tell you where the Herberts had gone? Why didn't she tell the police? I mean, she knew that Lorna May's body had been found. Keith found it."

"Because she wasn't there when Sergeant Locker arrived, remember. She'd been called out to help with what turned out to be a difficult birth. Some poor woman on the far side of the village."

A rueful smile. "And poor Keith. He'd so wanted to make his mum's birthday a happy one, and she couldn't even be there for it. She told me she didn't crawl in until gone midnight."

He remembers then the Sergeant saying that Keith was waiting at home while his mother was out on a duty call. So he'd waited in vain. Yes, poor Keith.

"When did she tell you this?"

"When she popped in this morning to let me know about Keith's good news and then *of course* she told me about the Herberts. It was the first chance she'd had."

Sadly, she shakes her head. "That pointless trip to London. Nothing but a wild goose chase, I'm afraid."

"Because Lorna May was here all the time."

"As they found out in London."

"How did they do *that*?" He is amazed.

"Ah, now," she says, "this is the most extraordinary part of the story. They found out from a newspaper." She waits for a moment, then, "There was a snippet in one of this morning's dailies, about a young girl being found dead in woods near Ashton. The local police were asking for information from members of the public. There was more, obviously, but that was enough to set the alarm bells ringing for Mr and Mrs Herbert. She showed me the piece. It even mentioned that the girl was thought to have originally come from London."

"I still don't understand how Mrs Bailey knew."

"Because Mrs Herbert phoned her from London, to tell her that they'd be on the first train back to Ashton."

"And how did the newspaper know?"

She stands, begins to gather together the tea things, arranging them on the tray. "I imagine the police told any journalist they could get hold of. It's what they do. That's why they sometimes broadcast messages, requests for information about missing persons. And Sergeant Locker knew about Lorna May, didn't he? He'd have passed on to his superiors any information he had. 'Information that could aid us in our inquiries.'"He recognises her imitation of the official tone of voice used by broadcasters when they repeat such police requests, requests that often come before the six o'clock news.

He hands her his plate, careful not to let crumbs fall onto the dark-blue carpet.

"Lucky for the Herberts that they saw it," he says.

"I don't think lucky is the word, my love."

"I didn't mean that," he corrects himself. "I meant that it was a … "

"A chance in a thousand? Yes, perhaps. Or perhaps not. They were in a B and B near Paddington. Hadn't even gone out to Hackney, where Lorna May's parents once lived. Mrs Herbert told me that he – Mrs Herbert's husband – looked at the papers in the breakfast room, and almost at once saw the article. Well, not article. As I say, it was a snippet. But he phoned the number given, was told the bad news, and they were on the next train."

"And you saw them when they got back?"

"Not at first," she says, "but when I was preparing this room for Maureen and Sally's visit I happened to glance out of the window and noticed that their curtains were drawn, and then I knew they must be home and that they knew about the poor girl's death." She picks up the tray. "Open the door, for me, there's a good lad."

And as she passes him, carrying the loaded tray, she says,"I *had* to go over and try to offer some words of comfort. They were suffering, poor things. They didn't want to say much but I could see it in their eyes. Mrs Herbert showed me the newspaper item, a mere scrap, but it put paid to their hopes of finding Lorna May alive."

He follows her out to the small kitchen, watches as she rests the tray on the draining board.

"Miss Wheelock said there has to be an inquest about Lorna May."

"As I thought." She fills the kettle, puts it on the stove and lights the gas. "You can help me with the washing-up."

Watching her as she stirs the water into suds, he says, "I don't understand why there has to be an inquest. Inquests are for when you can't explain the cause of death, aren't they? That's what you told me."

And when she stares quizzically at him, he says, "Besides, I looked the word up in our dictionary. It says there that an inquest is for deaths that are violent or sudden or mysterious. Lorna May fell off the roof of that hut. What's mysterious about that?"

She purses her lips. "Violent and sudden," she says.

"But not mysterious." He is determined to pursue his argument.

"As far as we know," his mother says. Then, "No, I shouldn't have said that. I've no doubt the poor girl's death was an accident."

But her words leave him uneasy, wondering.

8

Tuesday morning. From his bedroom-window Peter looks out on a grey sky. Blossom from the almond tree by the front gate is scattered across the rockery beneath their hedge. Shifting his gaze, he sees that the blackout curtains in the bungalow opposite are still drawn across. "It's a form of mourning. How people signal a death in the family," his mother had explained the previous evening. And when he'd wondered, aloud this time, whether Lorna May counted as family, she said, sighing, "Well, she was all they'd got. And they were all *she'd* got. At all events, if her mother can't be found."

Perhaps she *can* be found, he'd said, looking enquiringly at his mother as she sat in her chair beside the wireless, reading. "Perhaps," she'd replied, without looking up. "The police have their methods. Notices in public places, items in the newspapers like the one that alerted the Herberts to Lorna May's death. Even an announcement on the BBC. Who knows They may run her to earth."

He tried then to imagine what it would be like hearing the name of Lorna May's mother coming out of the wireless. "Would a Mrs Perry, last heard of in London, please contact the police at Ashton where her daughter, Lorna May Perry ... "

Where her daughter was what? Lying dead? Would that be said? Difficult to believe that the name of the girl he had known and who had once almost counted as a friend might soon float out over the air-waves and be heard by thousands of people living in towns and cities across England.

"Will the police know Mrs Perry's first name?"

"Her Christian name? Bound to. Her maiden name, too, I imagine. And where she lived in London." She thought for a moment, as though to say more, changed her mind, and went back to her book.

***

As he pulls on his clothes, he wonders whether the Herberts are keeping their curtains closed because Lorna May's body is lying in the bungalow and they don't want prying eyes looking in on the dead girl. Perhaps they've been allowed to bring her from the hospital where, so his mother had told him, the couple were taken by the police car that met them at Ashton station.

But she soon scotches that idea. "They had to identify the body," she says, as she sits opposite him while he spoons up his cereal. "But they certainly wouldn't be allowed to take the girl away with them. The girl has to stay where she is until the inquest is held."

"Then what?"

"Then she'll be buried."

Chewing on his toast, he asks, "When will that be?" "No idea, but I hope for all their sakes it can be soon." Staring into the cup she's settled back into its saucer, she says, "Imagine how her mother will feel when she eventually finds out about her daughter's death."

"Do you think she will?"

She stares up at him, but it is as though she is looking not at him but some distant prospect. "How can she *not?*"

And, pushing back her chair, she stands abruptly up, leaves the room.

***

Hunched over the last of his toast, he is still considering this remark of hers, its jolting certainty, when he hears a customary tattoo being beaten on the back door.

A moment later Ronnie stands in front of him.

"Ready?" He waves his paper flag, glued to a piece of twig. "Mi mam reckons there'll be a big crowd to see 'er 'ighness. She towd mi that if we want to get a good view, we need to be in position sooner rather than later."

And, to Peter's mother, who has followed him into the room, he says, his voice blending surprise and perhaps some faint criticism as he takes in her workaday jumper and skirt, "You not goin' ter be there, Mrs 'oward?"

"I'll probably watch from upstairs." But as though feeling the need to justify her words, she adds, mock-serious, "I haven't the clothes to compete with you young bucks."

Ronnie is encased in a dark grey jacket a good deal too large for him, all three buttons done up, and sporting a tartan tie.

"Very natty," she says, as Ronnie explains that both jacket and tie are his father's and that in preparation for the Duchess of Kent's appearance his mother had shortened the jacket's sleeves by tucking the cuffs under, then sewing them up "So they don't flap free when I wave at 'er 'ighness."

"She's done a fine job. I wouldn't be surprised if as soon as she claps eyes on you the Duchess doesn't stop her car, get out and knight you on the spot."

Ronnie accepts her praise with equanimity. "You look good, too," he remarks judiciously to his friend, casting a critical eye over the sleeveless Fair Isle jumper Peter has pulled on over his school shirt.

"A couple of swells." She smiles warmly at them. "What about your mum. Ronnie, will she be watching the pageant unfold?"

Ignoring any hint of satire in her words, Ronnie shakes his head. "'er and Nance 'ad to leave for Leicester early. Nance is 'avin' 'er plaster off today. An' mi gran'll watch from indoors. She can't stand bein' out in the cowd."

A few minutes later, the two of them, Peter in raincoat against the chill wind, Ronnie determined to show off his jacket and tie, go out to join the huddle of locals strung along the road.

"When's it due?" Ronnie asks a woman beside whom the boys have found a place to stand.

"When's what due, yer cheeky bogger?" the woman asks, straining to button her coat around what Peter notices is her swelling stomach.

"'Er Nibs' car."

"Duchess of Kent to you, mister."

And she turns away.

Another woman's voice, from behind Peter, asks, "Is that where that little girl lived? That one with the drawn curtains."

Turning, he sees that the woman, who isn't anyone he recognises, is pointing across the road to the Herberts' bungalow. The woman standing beside her, a widow called Mrs Vernon who comes from further up the road, says, "That's it. You won't see them today."

"In mourning, is it?"

"Shame, more like. That kiddie led a dog's life." The words are little more than a whisper.

"Well, our Meg was in class with her," another woman says, "and she reckons she was pretty wild. Lash out as soon as look at you."

"Keep your voice down," the Vernon woman says, nodding meaningfully to where Peter and Ronnie stand. "Walls have ears."

"Don't worry me none, duck. I like to speak my mind."

And now yet another woman, this one headscarved, overhearing the conversation, says, "Can't be easy, being an evacuee. Away from your mum and dad for god knows how many years."

Mrs Vernon leans toward her, whispering something that Peter guesses will be about Lorna May's parents, or rather loss of parents.

After which the women fall silent until one says, "Look lively, here's the Law."

And Peter sees Sergeant Locker marching slowly down the road to where they stand. The sergeant exchanges words with some in the scattered crowd, nods to others.

"Making sure we don't start a riot," one of the women says, and the others laugh. "Wouldn't start a riot for him," Mrs Vernon says. "Not exactly Clark Gable, is he?"

Ronnie nudges Peter. "Let's move," he says, "there's more space further on down."

They step out into the road, avoiding the stretch of tar that marks the crater Hans has so recently filled in, cross over and, when they reach Connolly's farmyard, climb up onto its metal gate.

"Grandstand view, this," Ronnie says.

And at that moment someone in the crowd shouts, "Here they are," and advancing round the bend some hundred yards down the road Peter sees coming into view a capped policeman, seemingly all in black, astride a slow-moving motorcycle. He is followed at a short distance by a large black car, which, as it advances toward them, they can see sports a Union Jack on the front of the bonnet and, below it, fixed to the engine grille, a cut-out, gold-coloured crown.

Women, children, and the few men among them, alike crane forward as the car eases past. At its wheel is a driver in black suit, face topped by a black, stiff-peaked cap, behind him, leaning well back, two figures, either or both of whom might be women, one of them raising and lowering a white-gloved hand in response to some cheers and waving of flags.

Another capped motorcycle policeman follows behind, black trousers encased in knee-length shiny boots, silver-buttoned jacket done up to the neck, staring ahead. Nobody cheers him.

Then the car, seeming to accelerate, disappears round a bend toward the top of the road.

***

Only afterward, as they follow stragglers from the dispirited crowd back up toward their own houses, do the two of them realise that neither of them had waved, let alone raised a cheer as the car passed them by.

"Waste of bloody time, that was," Ronnie says, ripping up the flag he had taken such care to paint. He stuffs the balled-up scraps into his jacket pocket and tosses the twig into the hedge.

"At least we got the morning off school."

"Could 'ave bin anyone in that car," Ronnie says contemptuously, pursuing his own line of thought. "Our mams 'd 'ave done as well."

"Better," Peter says.

"You got it," Ronnie says.

9

"Rain, rain go away," Peter says.

"Not much chance of that, I'm afraid." His mother comes to stand beside him and together they look out at the sodden garden. "If the weather doesn't improve, I imagine the organisers will have to call it off."

But by early afternoon that Saturday, as they walk up to the recreation ground, wind has seen off most of the clouds, and the fresh-mown grass glitters in a fitful sun.

Small groups of people stand around in talk, some under the chestnut trees screening the ground, others stripped to singlets and shorts, swinging their arms to keep warm, a few of them touching their toes or running on the spot.

A blackboard propped against the pavilion rails announces
VICTORY ATHLETICS EVENT
OPEN COMPETITION
PRIZES followed by Tea in Village Hall
Evening Dance 2/6 (Servicemen and Women free)

Ronnie, detaching himself from a group of classmates, jogs across to join them. He is in football gear, black shorts and a green-and-white striped shirt, though his feet are encased in brown plimsolls.

"You gonna run in them things" he asks, staring disbelievingly at Peter's mac, open to show his grey pullover and school shorts.

"I've got these," Peter says defensively, indicating his black plimsolls hung by their laces round his neck.

"I'll leave you two here," his mother tells them. "Run well, both of you, and I'll see you later."

Ronnie looks enquiringly at Peter, who says, "She's helping to get things ready at the hall."

"She don't want to see you run?" Ronnie's disapproval is plain. "My mam's comin' soon to cheer me on. Along of Nance."

Peter shrugs. "It's not important." No point in admitting that he'd had to persuade his mother not to watch him trail along in hapless pursuit of swifter contemporaries.

By the time the boys get to the hall it has been decorated with bunting augmented by a few of the paper flags to have survived the disappointment of Tuesday, which is already being spoken of with varying degrees of sarcasm as less royal appearance than vanishing act.

Peter and his mother are among those who help clear away the crockery, including the large serving plates from which all traces of the piles of sandwiches and cake have long since disappeared, and while they wash up others dismantle trestle-tables and sweep the planked floor.

"Would you have liked to stay for the dance?" he asks her, as they walk back home with Ronnie. Ronnie's grandmother will be taking care of him while his mum stays behind for the evening's entertainment. Nancy, accompanied by a friend, has already caught the bus into Ashton. They are planning to see Errol Flynn in a film whose title Nancy seems unsure of, though telling them it doesn't matter. "We're not going for *it*, we're going to see *him*. Got to hurry, there'll be a massive queue."

"Soppy as new-born kittens," Ronnie says to mother and son, recalling his sister's inexplicable behaviour. "Mi mam's comin' back to life now Fritz has been beat," he adds. "She loves dancin' and prancing'. That's what she told me, any road."

"Dancing and prancing." Peter's mother repeats the words, though her pronunciation makes them sound odd, almost comical. "It must run in the family."

The boy looks at her, puzzled, as they turn into the road where they all live.

"Fleet of foot," she says. "I gather you won all your races. Your mum told me. She's proud of you."

"An' I come second in the 'igh-jump." He raises his arms, fists clenched. "Champion, that's me," he says in innocent pride.

Peter says to his mother, "So it's the fault of you and dad that I didn't win anything." He tries to make light of it.

"Ah, well," she says, perhaps understanding his disappointment. "Tortoise and hare. Besides, it's the taking part that counts."

But in adult life, when he hears those words sounding in his memory, Peter Howard will have good reasons think that more often than not the hare wins, and that the tortoise, true to its nature, creeps slowly over the finishing line.

"Any road." Ronnie keeps his voice down because the words are meant for Peter alone, "you ran fast enough when old 'arrison come after us." And, grinning, he digs Peter in the ribs with a sharp elbow.

Peter glances at his mother, but she hasn't heard. Her smile is for the person she sees walking up the road toward them, waving as she comes. "Sally. What can she want, I wonder?"

Sally Parsons, who with mother-in-law and twin daughters – "Trouble and Strife" she called them – had put in a brief appearance at the recreation ground in the first part of the afternoon, is now on her own.

"I've nipped out for an hour," she says, an almost conspiratorial gleam in her eye as they join her where she waits by their front gate. She steps through ahead of them, "And" – spinning on her heel as they reach the porch – "I've brought a peace-offering with me."

A bottle glints in the lowering sun.

"Gin. I've had it in the house for years, under lock and key, waiting for this very moment."

"But why a peace-offering? I wasn't aware we'd fallen out."

"Kay! Mr Hitler's war is finally over, or perhaps you hadn't noticed." Sally Parsons seems in an odd mood, her words excited, but her expression wary, even anxious. "He's dead, his henchmen are in custody, and I'm offering you a chance to toast the new world order."

"We seem to have been doing rather a lot of that lately," Peter's mother says, laughing. "However, any excuse … "

Opening the front door, she follows her guest in and, as she does so, says over her shoulder, "Peter, you and Ronnie can have an hour before bed. OK?"

Then the door is closed.

***

In the days and weeks that follow they grow to expect these visits from Sally Parsons. "Parson Sally", his mother dubs her friend, "bringing comfort with her, though she seems rather more in need of it than I am." The down-turn of the mouth which accompanies her words suggests that Sally's increasingly frequent appearances aren't always welcome. Twice, even three times a week, they hear the familiar rap at the front door, always in the early part of an evening, and Sally stands in the porch with her 'peace-offering', usually sherry, though occasionally the dark brown bottle is exchanged for the clear glass that announces gin. She and Peter's mother will sit in the front room drinking and smoking for an hour, then she'll leave, saying that she has to get back to her mother-in-law "to show civility. Though to be honest," she once half-whispers at the front door, "she drives me half mad wittering on about her precious son."

"Did she mean her husband?" Peter asks his mother that evening, when she comes up to see him as he lies in bed, reading.

"That remark wasn't intended for your ears." she says. "I imagine it was the drink talking." She looks, he thinks, somehow guilty when she adds, "I certainly did nothing to encourage her."

What does she mean? Encourage the drinking or what she sometimes calls speaking out of turn? He realises that his mother seems never to supply the drink. That is always brought by her visitor.

Turning to leave him after she's kissed him goodnight, she says as though by way of explanation, "Sally was married for such a short time and she's been a widow now for over four years." She pauses. "And she's still a young woman, you know."

"So are you," he says.

Divining the undertone of uncertainty in his voice, she comes back, lays her palm on his forehead. "I'm not a widow," she says, "and there are only two men in *my* life. You and your father. OK?"

And that, too, is a remark he will many years later have cause to remember.

***

Nearly a month after Keith Bailey's discovery of Lorna May Perry's body, the school gathers to say prayers for the girl, who is to be buried that afternoon. The coroner's inquest, which, so the local newspaper reported, had "in these still unusual times" taken longer to convene than ideal – for which the coroner apologised to all concerned – was required to wait until it received both doctor's report and police evidence. Death, the report concluded, was from natural causes and there were no suspicious circumstances 'attendant' upon Lorna May's having broken her neck, almost certainly as a result of falling from the roof of what was described as a 'dilapidated' hut in woods near her home. Accordingly, the body could now be released for burial. Sincere condolences were offered by the court to the dead girl's grieving family and relatives.

Leaning over the table, the newspaper spread open so they both can study it, Peter and his mother read that the funeral will be a private one, conducted by the Methodist minister, and that following the service Lorna May's body is to be interred in the part of the local cemetery reserved for worshipping Methodists. Mention is made of the fact that the girl's father had been lost at sea and that her mother's whereabouts are unknown. A sad story, the reporter concludes, although Lorna May, one of countless children evacuated from London at the commencement of war, had been fortunate in the loving care she received from Mr and Mrs Arnold Herbert.

"Family and relatives?" Peter says, pointing to the coroner's reported words. "That doesn't make much sense, does it? She'd only got the Herberts."

"Her mother's still alive so it's to be hoped."

"But she hasn't been found."

"While there's life," his mother says. She raises her head, stares at the ceiling, and he can see the glimmer of a tear in her eye. "It's such a sad story. A girl of that age with a mother gone missing and no one much to … to c … " She'd been going to say "care", but, stopping herself, lapses into frowning silence.

***

The day after Lorna May's funeral, Sally Parsons comes again at her usual time. All that day, Saturday, there has been rain, too much of it for Peter and Ronnie to go out into the fields, and while the grown-ups sit in the front room he is on his own at the dining room table, writing to his father at his mother's urgent request.

Should he tell him about the inquest into Lorna May's death? Has his mother already told him? Peter decides to put his head round the door to ask her.

But as he stands outside, in the hall, hand extended to grasp the door-knob, he hears Sally Parsons say, defiantly, "Well, Kay, *I* think there's something fishy about them. Keeping everyone at arm's length."

"It may not be normal behaviour but it isn't a crime. And wanting a private funeral isn't a crime, either. They're private people, they don't socialise and they may be dry old sticks but they're not *bad*."

That's his mother speaking, and that she is upset by her guest's words becomes evident from what comes next.

Sally Parsons starts it. "I know it may seem to you that I'm poking my nose in where it's not wanted. But, Kay, you were the one who said you thought they treated the girl badly."

"Yes and I wish I hadn't." His mother is keeping her voice low, but even so he can hear her words. "I certainly didn't mean to suggest that they'd do anything that might have driven her to take her own life."

"They might not have *meant* to, but I'd say that between them they're bearing a guilty conscience. All that dashing down to London. What was *that* about if not to show how much they cared."

"Because they *did* care." His mother's voice is raised now. Upset is turning to irritation, even anger.

"I know more than one person who thinks it was a ruse – a what do you call it, an alibi." Sally Parsons, too, is, from the sound of it, becoming heated.

"An *alibi!* What on earth is *that* supposed to mean?"

"It means … " Sally Parsons lowers her voice but enunciates slowly and clearly, "it means that one of them realised the girl had left them – she may even have written them a note – and so they sprang into action, not wanting to face accusations of mistreatment if and when she turned up."

A pause. He imagines his mother's exasperation, even distress. "No one mentioned a note," she says.

"Because the Herberts destroyed it. Well, why not?" And when his mother says nothing, Sally Parsons, still taking elaborate care to pronounce each word clearly, says, "I've given this some thought, you know."

"I don't want to be rude, Sally, but what you call thought I call fancy. Castles in air."

"*I* don't think so. *I* think it's quite possible that one or both of them went looking for the girl and found her lying there, in the woods, with her neck broken."

"Then they'd have told the police." His mother's voice, swift, with a hint of impatience.

"Not necessarily. They might have panicked. They could have concluded that she'd killed herself and that they'd be blamed for what had happened."

"But why on earth should they think that? Why should *they* be blamed?"

"Oh, come on, Kay. *Because of the way they treated her.*"

"And so to avoid suspicion they ran off to London? This is becoming ridiculous."

Sally Parsons' words cut through his mother's attempted laugh. "You're not listening. I'm suggesting that they panicked. And in that frame of mind catching a train to London could well have seemed a way out of their difficulty. A cover. 'Look how we care. We're out of our minds with worry. That's why we're doing all we can to find our little girl. We've even gone down to London hoping she might be there, might be looking for her original home, or perhaps for her mother.' It's happening, isn't it? Evacuees *are* going home."

"And so according to you the Herberts go down to London as cover for their own misdeeds? Nonsense, Sally, I won't listen to this. First they're supposed to have found the girl in the woods, when there's nothing to suggest they did. Then they leave her there for Keith Bailey or someone else to come along and stumble over her body. And meanwhile, so you say, they make a bolt for it because they fear the finger of suspicion will be pointed at them. You'll be saying next that they as good as planned her death."

Sally Parsons' voice comes, stiffly. "Believe whatever you want, Kay, but plenty of tales far stranger than this have turned out to be true."

"Well, I don't believe *this* tale, is all I can say."

The words are spoken with a decisiveness that makes clear she wants to put an end to the conversation. And as though to confirm this, he hears a chair creak, guesses at least one of them must be standing up, and speeds back to the dining room.

As he drops onto his chair, the door opens and his mother, her look strained, cheeks red, peers in on him.

"Are you all right?" she asks, and at once he knows she's wondering whether he's heard anything of the conversation in the front room.

"I'm finishing my letter," he says.

Smiling, abstracted, she says, "I'll see Sally out, then find you an envelope."

Minutes afterward he hears their voices bid each other goodnight, the front door shuts, and his mother comes back to join him. Hand resting on his shoulder as she looks out of the window at the rain-battered garden, she says, sighing, "I *wish* we could get back to normality."

"Normality?" He looks up at her enquiringly.

Her laugh, when it finally comes, is brief, mirthless. "The good old times, the golden age. The age when everyone thought the best of everyone else. When love was king and bulldogs all had rubber teeth. The age that never was. 'Ah,' in imitation of Mrs Mop, "'It's being so cheerful as keeps me going.'"

Then, leaning to kiss him on his forehead, she says, "Well, better to look forward. The promise of the future," and she ruffles his hair.

What promise, he wonders, but does not ask.

~ PART TWO ~

10

When he sets himself to write about the summer of 1945, Peter Howard realises he must have thought that in the days and weeks following the announcement of Victory in Europe the village of Stonely would continue to breathe the atmosphere that lit up each new day of peace. Physically, not much had changed. The POWs had gone, transferred to farm work in Norfolk, so Hans told Peter when he met the tall German running round Farmer Connolly's large field the day before the prisoners left, their hutments at once taken over by a pig-farmer – "same difference" was the local joke – but 'that apart' the village seemed unaltered, in that state of suspense which someone said was like holding your breath, waiting for peace to break out.

Yet the atmosphere surely was different. You woke up, you drew back curtains from which the blackout material had been unpinned, you stood at the window and looked across the road to the fields beyond the houses and the one bungalow, you listened for bird-song all the more piercing, exultant, now that the skies were guaranteed to be empty of thumping, cruciform shapes on whose tapering wings you feared to see the swastika (the engines of British and American bombers made different, more continuous, droning sounds), you wiped condensation from window-glass the better to see those deeper, fuller colours that must be pumping through the trees, lighting in this double summer-time the harvests which men and land girls will gather in under prolonged evening skies, light that shimmers above the far woods and gleams on the flanks of the dairy cows in Farmer Connolly's meadow.

Now: open the window, inhale the new air. Stretch out a hand to feel the breeze on your bare skin, shiver excitedly at its promise.

But no. It didn't take long to fade, this excitement, it dwindled, dulled, sank back to ordinariness.

He has read somewhere that England in 1945 was "war-weary and drab, the shops still empty, foodstuffs in short supply, the clothes shabby, the possibilities of entertainment few". That isn't how he remembers it. A shop was a shop. You went to one when you needed to and you bought what it had to offer. True, he wasn't interested in food, had no curiosity about what was put on his plate as long as it was edible; as for clothes, each day he dressed himself in the clothes he was used to wearing, clothes his mother patched and darned and washed and ironed; and he and his friends, dressed more or less as he was, went on playing in the fields, listened to the wireless, read the books they borrowed from each other. *Drab? Empty? Shabby?* Meaningless words. You couldn't miss what you'd never had.

And yet as the summer went on, so, he recalls, in the faces of people he passed in the street and in the teachers who stood in front of class, the shadow of disappointment, of let-down, and that *was* new. Or rather, it was like his boyhood experiences of Christmas. Anticipation was always followed by let-down, a bump of dejection. For weeks you looked forward to what, even in the war years, people insisted on calling the Festive Season, then it was on you; and afterwards you wondered at all the fuss. A joy proposed; behind, a dream.

A memory comes of how each December in early, wartime years, his mother would take an old, battered suitcase from the cupboard under the stairs, drag it into the front room, kneel to snap open its locks, and then lift out, one by one, the green-spiked limbs of a small artificial Christmas tree, carefully slotting each in turn into the foot-high wooden trunk. Once the tree was assembled it was moved into position beneath the bay window, after which he would help her decorate it with a dozen tarnished, chipped baubles and strands of silver paper. And then, as Christmas approached, there'd be the presents to group around the tree, presents, which, once opened, seemed so dull, so pointless, so *obvious*, that you couldn't wait for the tree to be dismantled and returned to its hiding place under the stairs.

The anticipation so great, the realisation so small. Who had said that? He can't remember, but he is sure he knows that in 1945, as May turned into June, the villagers began to look about them in disconsolate bemusement, as though, he now thinks, they couldn't quite understand why they had been desperate for the war to end.

They became snappish with each other, even miserable. They "grumbled". At all events, he recalls the word coming to his mother's lips on more than one occasion and how apt it had sounded: a growl, a back-of-the-mouth rumble that mingled protest and disapproval. Only the spivs and black marketeers were living well, she once told her son with weary disgust after returning empty-handed from a shopping trip to Ashton where she'd been drawn by the rumour of summer dresses for sale. There were no dresses, although among the luckless shoppers a rumour circulated that bolts of cloth had been snapped up by the spivs who would sell them on the black market. And *naturally* none of *them*, none of the *spivs*, had fought.

For some days, before it faded, her anger at spivs and the dress she couldn't buy spread a shadow over their daily lives, clouding the bright excitement that had showered the early summer air.

***

According to Mrs Bailey, commiserating with his mother as they walk down from the village shops one Saturday afternoon early on in that strange *après la guerre* period, there is the "blessing" that Keith is happy in his work. Peter walks beside the two women, carrying his mother's shopping bag which, as well as vegetables, contains a twist of sherbet he has bought from the village newsagent who is also a tobacconist and, so a sign over his door says, confectioner, though apart from the powdery sherbet the newsagent has no sweets at all to sell.

"Will Keith be allowed to keep his job?" his mother asks.

"You mean once demobilisation begins?" Already there is talk in the newspapers and on the wireless about what work the soon-to-be demobbed servicemen will find waiting for them when they are once again on what is increasingly called "Civvy Street".

Mrs Bailey laughs. "I don't think anyone's going to want to take Keith's work from him. If I'd risked life and limb fighting for the nation I'd want better for myself than the job my lad has." Briskly, then, she adds, "But it's fine for Keith, believe me, I'm thankful that he's so content. Happy as a sandboy."

As she is saying the words, they see the tall, black-suited figure of Mr Herbert coming up the field toward them. They pause, ready to speak, but with a nod of the head and a curt, "Afternoon," he passes them without breaking stride.

Lowering her voice as they continue on their way, Mrs Bailey says, in charitable excuse of the man's stony-faced unfriendliness, "Well, he's never got much to say for himself at the best of times."

"And these certainly aren't good times for them," Peter's mother says.

***

Later, as he helps lay the table for their tea, Peter asks, "What did Mrs Bailey mean about soldiers not wanting to do Keith's work?"

"Oh," she says, "it's right enough for him. Sweeping up, fetching and carrying." She pauses, sets down the loaded tray and, as she places a glass of milk in front of where he sits at the table, says, "I can understand why his mother's pleased. Work like that won't be under threat when the men begin to return. They'll want better than to be a … " Again she pauses, searching for the word she needs.

"Skivvy?" he asks.

She straightens up. "Which reminds me," she says. "I heard in the village that the German POWs are being sent to work on farms in East Anglia. They may have gone already."

"They have. Yesterday, or the day before." And he tells her of his meeting with Hans.

He bites into a slice of bread. "So I don't suppose I'll see Hans again." Chewing, he adds, "He's still doing his training."

"Training? What for? And what might that involve?"

"Hans wants to go back to playing professional football. That's why he's training. He runs. Round the rec. and through the fields. You know that?" And when she shakes her head, he says, "I thought everyone did. Ronnie and me, we've often seen him in vest and shorts." The memory of Hans on the occasion he came loping up the road, trousers flapping round his ankles, causes him to laugh.

"What's so funny?"

Peter tells her.

But she is not amused. "Why on earth had he left his machine? Shouldn't he have been doing what he was p – what he was sent to do?"

"He had to let the tar cool off before he could drive the steamroller over it."

"So he went charging up and down the road, like Sydney Wooderson. He must have looked a rum sight."

"He didn't run up and down the road. He'd been running up and down Connolly's field. And who's Sydney Wooderson?"

"A famous runner."

"And perhaps Hans will become a famous footballer for Hamburg."

"Hamburg!"

The sharp concern in her voice startles him.

"What's wrong with Hamburg?"

For a moment she is silent. Then, "It was very heavily bombed," she says.

He waits for her to say more. "It's a city in ruins. Thousands were killed. Buildings flattened. At least that's what the newspapers said. Did Hans have family there?"

"I don't know. He said he came from Hamburg, that was all."

She purses her lips, that gesture he knows so well. "Well, he must know what happened to the city, what state it's in."

He thinks of the photographs he's seen of London streets, of houses smashed flat or left as rubble, broken to pieces by doodle-bugs, as the newspapers call them. Has something like that been done to Hamburg?

He takes the thought to bed with him.

***

The following afternoon, Sunday, Sally Parsons comes to tea. Peter is aware that since their argument about the Herberts there have been no early evening visits, no repetition of the clinking of glasses, and he has begun to wonder whether the friendship between his mother and Sally is at an end.

"Mending fences," his mother says, smiling, when she tells him about Sally's impending visit. She bends to the oven and, as she opens the door, warm, fragrant scents of baking fill his nostrils.

"What does that mean?"

"Being a good neighbour."

Then, seeing his bafflement, she adds, "Not letting your cattle or sheep out onto someone else's land."

"We haven't got any cattle. Or sheep."

"But we do have scones. And you can help me prepare the tea tray."

"Best china?"

"Of course," she says, with a quick laugh. "Nothing but the best for our Sally." But as though wanting to dispel any suggestion of sarcasm, she adds as quickly, "Besides, we'll be doing her a kindness. She's on her own for the moment."

The twins, she explains, have been taken down to Cornwall, and Sally herself plans to use their absence to prepare the house for sale. "She'll be glad to have an hour or so away from all that work. And who knows, inviting her to afternoon tea may mean we shan't be favoured with a bottle."

***

"Well," Sally Parsons says, pushing her plate aside as she reaches for the bottle of sherry. "I can't deny that living in the country has its compensations." Then, putting the bottle back down without uncorking it, she instead uses a red-painted fingernail to dab at some crumbs clinging to her plate. He watches the tip of a tongue emerge from between carmined lips, her eyes rounding with pleasure. "Real butter, real eggs. Mmm."

His mother, sitting across from her guest, smiles. "But not enough to keep you here?"

"No. no. God, no." Sally Parsons looks as though she may be going to say more but instead shakes her head and lapses into rueful silence, her eyes withdrawn. When she speaks again, she says, as though inconsequentially, "I need to be among more people. No offence, Kay, you've been a dear." It is said with a perfunctory flicker of a smile. "But I'm still young you know." There is a knowing quaver, a pretend self-pity in both voice and gesture that don't disguise something more genuine.

And now she does take up the bottle, and pours herself a glassful of tan liquid.

"Are you sure you won't join me?"

His mother, who has put out only one glass, says, half-apologetically, "Not me, Sally. A mite too early in the day for me, I'm afraid."

"And you don't have any sorrows to drown."

Sally Parsons lifts the glass to her lips, careful not to let it make contact with their fleshy redness.

His mother reaches out, touches his arm. "Peter, love, would you mind clearing the tea things away?"

He understands.

But in the kitchen, door ajar, he can perfectly well hear their voices coming from the dining room, Sally's raised as she worries about the twins not having a father and that to find one she needs to be elsewhere, his mother's murmured reassurances, Sally's impatient "Oh, I *must* get away. I don't belong here. And now there's no reason not to move."

"Now?" That's his mother's voice, puzzled.

"Now that the war is over."

Then, silence. He inspects the soap-whisk, plunges it back into the warm water, trying with the scraps of soap it encases to create lather enough for him to wash the tea plates, wondering what Sally Parsons means when she says she doesn't belong in the village. She lives here, doesn't she? Isn't that belonging? Well, no, perhaps it isn't. Lorna May Perry had lived here, and she certainly hadn't belonged.

Lorna May. Already, now she has been buried, she is becoming forgotten. There'd been days, not so long before, when he'd thought regularly about her, or rather about her death, had heard others discussing it, agreeing that it was a mystery. Not *how* she'd died, perhaps, but *where*. *Why* was she in the woods? Why on the roof of the woodman's hut? And why, given how sure-footed she was, should she have fallen off?

In the days and then weeks following her death and, then, burial, he and Ronnie had often discussed these and other questions. Suppose she *had* been trying to get back to London, Ronnie said. She *might* have decided to hide until night-time and then make her escape. She could have planned to make her way through the woods to the railway line that lay on its far side, get to Ashton station, and from there sneak onto a London-bound train. It sounded far-fetched to the point of impossibility, but Lorna May had a daring they themselves lacked, as the episode with old Harrison proved; and Ronnie had read about American tramps – hobos, they were called – who managed to clamber aboard freight trains crossing America and go hundreds of miles in pursuit of work or simply because they wanted a change of scene. "Hobo Lorna," he said.

"But why was she on the roof of that hut?" Peter asked. "I can understand that she might want to hide inside it. But why the roof?"

"Perhaps something scared her," Ronnie said. "She scrammed. Got out of 'arm's way. Or maybe she thought some bugger might want to come into the 'ut, might want to use it themselves."

"So she got up on the roof? Doesn't sound very likely."

"OK, then. You got a better explanation?"

But Peter hadn't.

"Tell you what," Ronnie said, "the way I see it, something must have scared 'er, otherwise she'd 'ave landed safe and walked away." A silence. "It's either that," he said, "or some sod did 'er in."

Ronnie's suggestion shocks Peter. It also intrigues him. "You mean she was killed? But who by?"

"Take yer pick," Ronnie said, "Old 'arrison. Keith. Whistling Billy? Some gyppo."

"She could run too fast for any of them."

"Not if they nabbed 'er when she weren't expectin' it."

But at that point their speculation would come to an end or veer into wildly inventive fantasies. "'Ow about an anaconda?" Ronnie suggested on one occasion when they were indulging themselves. "Roostin' in the trees, come down and dragged Lorna May off the roof, wrapped itself round 'er and squeezed the breath out of 'er."

"Why didn't she see it in time?"

"'Cos anacondas is in disguise, all green and brown like the trees they 'ide in."

Remembering that now, he remembers yet again seeing Hans as he ran up the road, Hans with his trousers flapping round his legs, the faded greyish shirt he'd tied round his waist. Hans who, when asked, claimed not to know that there was a scratch on his cheek and yet who – and now the memory is sharp – automatically lifted his hand, his *left* hand to the cut and then, having peered at his fingers, said that it was not "blooding".

What does it mean? Can there be a connection between that scratch and Lorna May's disappearance?

But as he is pondering this, his mother pushes wide the kitchen door. "Sally is leaving," she says. "Dry your hands and come to wish her goodbye." She is smiling brightly, professionally, he thinks, but her eyes are troubled.

He goes out to the hall, sees Sally Parsons standing on the porch beyond the open front door, and goes toward her.

Her camel-hair jacket is draped over her arm, and the expensive-looking green wool jumper she wears above a tartan, pleated skirt makes her look not merely glamorous but, with the green of the almond tree at the end of their path framing her, as though she is deliberately posed: leaving for a world elsewhere.

She touches his outstretched hand with the tips of her fingers, smiles – more of a twist of her lips – and says, formally, "Goodbye, Peter, and good luck."

Before turning away, she glances at the poster in the front bay window.

VOTE LABOUR

She opens her mouth as though to say something, decides against, contents herself with a faint smile, and they watch her as she walks the length of the path and out onto the road, where she turns for one final wave, and then is gone.

In silence he and his mother are putting away the washed and dried crockery, until his mother says, slamming a cupboard door with sudden energy, "Well, I doubt we'll be seeing *her* again."

"Is she leaving so soon?"

Back turned to him as she arranges knives in the cutlery drawer, she says, "As far as I'm concerned, she can't leave soon enough."

She turns to him then, her cheeks flushed. "Forget I said that," she tells him. But aware of his puzzled frown, she sighs. "I don't think she and I are meant to be friends."

He doesn't know what to say, it seems such an odd remark. Not *meant* to be friends? Why not? What does meaning have to do with it?

Trying to understand, he says, "Did you fall out over something?"

She laughs, a short, bitter laugh. "There's not much Sally and I wouldn't fall out over." A pause. "Something has happened to our Sally. Something has upset her, though I've no idea what. Either that or the spots are coming out. Having been unpleasant about the Herberts the other day, this afternoon she vented her – I don't know the word I want – on poor Keith Bailey."

He looks at her enquiringly but she says, "Not for your ears, my love."

"I've heard him called the village idiot."

She is shocked into anger. "Well, I hope *you* don't use that phrase. It's horrible."

So Sally Parsons *had* used the words, or ones very like them.

But he is unprepared for what comes next. "As good as accusing him of being ... well, never mind." Then, changing her tone, she asks as she looks at him long and steadily, "Has Keith ever struck you as behaving, you know, oddly. Has he ever behaved strangely to you." She is blushing. "I mean, has he ever got close to you, touched you... "

He waits for her to finish the sentence, then says, "Keith is OK." And as her look begins to clear, he adds, "Ronnie and me, we like him."

He doesn't know whether he's saying what she wants to hear, but to his relief she relaxes her shoulders as she says, "I was sure of it. I knew it was all nonsense. Like the other things she said."

"Such as."

"Not now." She puts an arm round his shoulder. "Come on, I want to listen to the six o'clock news." He puts his arm round her waist and side by side they leave the kitchen.

Switching on the wireless as she sits in her easy chair and he kneels on the hearth rug, she says, laughing, gay, "Do you know, if I owned this house, I'd paint it red."

For some weeks past she's been telling him that a General Election is coming when a new government is, so she says, to be "formed," and that she and his dad will both be voting for the Labour Party. "And if they win Mr Attlee will become Prime Minister."

"I thought Mr Churchill was Prime Minister. Like Miss Wheelock is head teacher. I mean I thought the job was for life "

She tilts her head back, exhales smoke from the woodbine she always smokes at this hour. "Not if we get our way."

She is laughing happily.

"And will you?"

"Not if Sally Parsons gets hers." She is still laughing, but less happily.

"And will she."

She is suddenly serious. "While there's life, there's hope."

***

A week later, a Sunday evening at the beginning of July, as when earlier in the summer she heard the news of Victory in Europe, she is dancing Ronnie and Peter round the room in triumph, joyous at the wireless announcement that, with all the votes now counted, and Labour elected to govern, the new Prime Minister, Mr Clement Attlee, will address the nation on the list of measures his government plans to ensure a better future for all.

But a thought coming to her, she slows the pace of her movements and, lowering her voice, says, her arms still round Peter, "Oh, how I wish your dad was here. Wouldn't it be *wonderful* if he could share this with us." Remembering to include her son's friend in her exultant mood, she adds, "And you must wish that *your* father could be here, too, Ronnie."

Ronnie, opening his mouth to speak, is stopped by the suddenness with which she presses her fingers to his lips.

"What was that?" Her eyes are wide, her face a rigid mask.

It comes again. The front door knocker.

"It can't be," she whispers. "Your dad. No, not possible."

Fingers now pressing her lips shut, her expression is wild with hope beyond hope.

Again the door is banged, this time insistent, impatient even.

Pushing Peter out of the way, she dashes from the room and, as he and Ronnie follow behind, wrenches the front door open, almost sobbing in her haste.

"Oh."

A woman stands in the porch, a woman in a black, shabby coat, at her feet a suitcase held together by a leather strap.

"Oh." This time it is nearer to a groan, a sound leaden with disappointment. Struggling to lift her voice, his mother says, "I'm so sorry, I didn't mean to be rude. It was just that ... I mean I was hoping ... I was expecting someone else."

A pause, then, an instinct of good manners coming to her aid, she says, "Can I help you?"

"Those people over the road," the woman says, turning to look over her shoulder, before she again faces his mother. "The people who live in the bungalow. Are they called Herbert?"

The question seems more like an accusation.

"Yes." The reply is guarded. "Could I ask why you want to know?"

"They're not in."

"Oh. Should they be? Are they expecting you?"

The woman looks at Ronnie, then at Peter, then at his mother.

"I'm Mrs Perry," she eventually says. "Rachel Perry."

Her eyes flick from mother to the boys and back again.

"The mother of Lorna Perry," she says. "She's – she *was* – my daughter."

11

"Nice place you've got here," Mrs Perry says.

The three of them are grouped round the table, where she is eating the last of the cake while she drinks a second cup of tea. Her coat is draped over the back of her chair and her woollen jumper, dark green, with knitted yellow flowers that may have been intended as roses, is strained across her ample chest.

She looks at his mother, then, beyond her, at the garden. "Can't imagine this kind of thing in London. Not the kind of places I've been living in, anyway. You've no idea." She shivers, turns down her mouth. "Rat holes, half the time."

Now that she is sitting, he notices that the odd, sideways flicker of her eyes make her look as though she is never quite sure where she wants to rest her gaze. The image of a dragon-fly comes to mind, its blue, quivering needle of a body seemingly poised to land on a leaf, then of a sudden zooming, darting elsewhere, so that even as he thinks it safe to study her face, at least momentarily, he finds her eyes turned to meet his, then off, veering away. He blushes and turns to his mother, who sits across from him, leaving Mrs Perry to occupy the seat at what he thinks of as the head of the table. From there, her eyes flitter back and forward between mother and son.

His mother says, aiming for conversational ease, though her words are awkward, "It must have been terrifying for you in London, especially this last year. Those flying bombs … "

The visitor laughs, more of a snort. "Terrifying. You could say that. You never knew where they'd come down next."

Her voice is curiously flat, what he assumes to be a London accent ironed out by her unemphatic way of speaking. "Terrifying." She doesn't make it *sound* terrifying. He thinks of Hans. Hans of Hamburg. Hans who may even now be wandering the streets of his wrecked city, looking for houses and faces he once knew but which aren't there any longer.

"What part of London do you … did you live in?" He asks the question out of genuine curiosity but, as she stares directly at him, knows he shouldn't have done so.

"I was in the thick of it," she says. And this time the words come out almost aggressively. Doubt my words, do you, she might almost be asking him, her dark eyes burning into his. Then, flicking them away,and after a pause, "I kept saying to myself that I'm glad my Lorna's being spared what's happening." A shake of her head so that a grip flies free of her dark curls, lands in her lap. Quickly she traps and replaces it, pushing it into her bushy hair with fingers of her ringless left hand. "I thought she'd be safe in the country." Another pause. "Funny how things work out," she says, her eyes moving restlessly between her listeners.

His mother says, "It must be awful. To have found out about your daughter's death so long after it actually happened."

"Two months," Mrs Perry said. "Two months it's been." A pause. "And if it 'adn't – *hadn't* – been for a stroke of luck I'd still be in the dark. Though I suppose 'luck' is the wrong word."

"Yes." His mother's word isn't quite a question, but he knows what she means. There is a pause."How *did* you find out?" she asks.

Mrs Perry drains the last of her tea and dabs at both corners of her brightly-lipsticked mouth. When she speaks it isn't to answer the question. "These last years have been a nightmare, I don't mind telling you. Losing Lorna to the authorities, then Harold going down with his ship, then being bombed out, *then* being forced into moving about, looking for wherever I could find to lay me – my – head, and then, finally, this. Hearing my daughter's been taken from me. *Really* taken. Not just for the duration, but for ever."

She stares out of the window, lips apart, as though, Peter thinks, she may be anticipating some further unexpected disaster stalking across the lawn to where she sits. Her flickering gaze taking in both of them, she says, "I found out because someone I know saw the Police Notice and told me."

"Police Notice?"

"Yes, dear, Police Notice."

Mrs Perry looks at his mother, and again her voice carries an almost aggressive note. "How *else* was I to know?"

She waits for one of them to speak, and when neither does, "As far as I was aware, Lorna was safe with those people who were *supposed* to be looking after her. The Herberts."

Stung by the stress Mrs Perry puts on the one word, his mother does speak then. "I don't think the Herberts are to blame. They gave her a good home and … and I'm sure they did all they could to make her life here a happy one."

But she shifts uncomfortably at her own words. Happy? Not really, he thinks, and his mother knows it.

She tries again. "When your daughter went missing some of us thought she might be trying to make her way to London. The Herberts certainly did."

"Now why would she do that?"

His mother, more certain now of her ground, says, "To see you, of course."

"But she didn't know where I was."

And then, as though realising this is hardly an adequate reply, Mrs Perry adds, "I was so often on the move I couldn't give the Herberts an address where I could be certain they'd find me, could I now."

His mother is looking more puzzled. "But you knew where *she* – where your daughter, was."

So why didn't you get in touch with *her*, she presumably means, and for the first time it occurs to him that Mrs Herbert must have told his mother that Lorna May had heard nothing from her own mother.

"Indeed I did." It is spoken with something like indignation. "I sent cards at Christmas and for her birthday."

Her tone becoming placatory, even beseeching, she adds, "The thing is she was in a safe place here." A thin smile. "Or so I thought. I was going to send for her just as soon as I'd found accommodation where the two of us could be together."

She pauses. "Which isn't easy, believe me. You should *see* London," she says. "Millions of us fighting for somewhere to lay our heads. And there's hardly anywhere left standing. The Nazis have flattened the city. Destroyed the place."

Can it be that bad?

"But now," she says, looking from one to the other, and not bothering to answer his mother's question, "it doesn't matter, does it. I hear out of the blue that my daughter's dead, so I come on this journey, and the very people who should have been looking after her aren't even here to see me."

"Did they know you were coming?"

Flick, flick the eyes go, but again she doesn't answer. Perhaps she thinks the question doesn't deserve one.

His mother sighs, and sympathy deepens her words when she says "I'm so sorry you had to hear about your daughter's death in the way you did. It must have been … it must have been shattering."

Mrs Perry bows her head as though in acknowledgement of an apology.

"But the Herberts did their best to care for Lorna May."

"They got paid for it, you know!"

Open-mouthed, his mother gasps, as though she'd been physically assaulted by Mrs Perry's words.

When she can control herself, she says, "Ten shillings a week is hardly a fortune, is it."

This is followed by an awkward silence. "No, well," Mrs Perry eventually says, with something like ill grace and at the same time offering to make amends, "I suppose if anything was wrong the billeting officer would have moved my Lorna."

For a brief second Peter wonders whether the expression that crosses his mother's face, the momentary look of contrition, may lead her to confess that she fears or perhaps suspects that Lorna May's disappearance could after all have been brought about by the Herberts' treatment of her, that she'd run away because she had finally had enough of being the household drudge, the skivvy. Other evacuees were going home, were leaving the village. Why shouldn't she try?

But no. Instead, and speaking slowly, she says, "We were all, all of us, *appalled* by your daughter's death. It was completely unexpected." Another pause. A shake of the head. "But of course accidents *are* unexpected."

Having given time for the words to register, she adds, "Around here, you see, the children feel free to wander the fields and the woods, and the awful accident that happened to your daughter – it could have happened to anyone's child. I know that doesn't make it any less dreadful, and poor Mrs Herbert, *and* Mr Herbert, no doubt feel guilty… " Her voice rather trails away.

She starts again. "I'm sure if they'd known you were coming they'd have wanted to be here to see you."

There is no reply to this. So Mrs Perry hadn't contacted them.

More confidently now, his mother goes on, "They're often away at the weekend. Now that the war's over and travel is easier I think they go on religious retreats."

Mrs Perry flushes, her truculence now abated. "If they'd had a telephone I'd have let them know I was on my way. No point in sending a letter. A letter would have arrived after I'd got here. Anyway, letters and me don't agree."

She smiles briefly at her own unintended jingle, wanting perhaps to lighten the atmosphere, but before he can consider the meaning of the words, she hurries on, "So I got on a train as soon as I could. And here I am."

She looks round the room. "It isn't where I want to be, I assure you."

Hauteur mingles uneasily with apology. "Sorry, that came out wrong. I mean I didn't want to plonk myself on you on a Sunday evening. I was *hoping* to speak to the Herberts. But no, as I've explained, I didn't give them advance notice, and then, when I discovered they weren't in and I couldn't make anyone next door hear me knocking, I thought I'd come across and see whether whoever lived here knew where they were … "

This is said in a sudden rush as though to get her apology out of the way.

"I'm sorry to impose," she says.

The words are oddly formal, and, her smile now a blend of the abashed and the ingratiating, she asks, "I wonder – I shall have to ask whether I can impose a little more. I mean, I shan't be able to get back to London tonight …?"

She stops, looks enquiringly at his mother, who says, quickly, almost too quickly, "Of course we can offer you a bed. There's a spare room. Not five star, I'm afraid, but you're very welcome to it."

She stands, goes to the door, as though relieved to have something to do, says, "Peter, while I'm sorting out some fresh linen, perhaps you'll offer Mrs Perry another cup of tea."

The other woman, too, stands. "No need to stick to the formalities, in that case," she says. "Seeing as how I'm spending the night under your roof. My name's Rachel, well, I've already said that." Holding out her hand, "and yours is … "

"Kay. Kay Howard."

They shake hands and Rachel Perry says, "I won't have another cuppa, not for now." She drops back into her chair. Turning to Peter, she says, "But I want to hear about my little girl. Seeing as how you lived opposite each other, I expect you were friends. Played together?"

Framed in the doorway, his mother says, as she looks warningly at him, "Did Lorna May write to you about her life in the village?"

"If she did, I never got her letters. Well, you see, dear, it wasn't many months after she'd gone that the flat was bombed out. Half the street went that night. That's why I had trouble explaining to the police who I was. Who I am."

His mother comes back into the room. "Who you are? I don't understand."

Rachel Perry lets out a brief laugh. "Nor did they. The police, I mean. They'd put up this notice all around the area where I'd been living, asking for anyone with information about me or her – Lorna – to contact them."

"When was this?"

"Soon after my poor daughter's body was found."

"Didn't anyone tell you? Didn't Mr and Mrs Herbert … "

His mother stops him. "No," she says. "I see the problem You'd been bombed out, hadn't you, at the beginning of the war. The Herberts didn't have a forwarding address for you." She shakes her head. "An awful mess. Still, you'd have thought someone would have tried to track you down." Then she stops short.

Not noticing his mother's faint blush, the cause of which Peter thinks he knows, Rachel Perry says, with a grimace, "I could have been buried under bricks and mortar for all anyone knew to the contrary."

But no, Peter thinks. Ronnie's mother had heard from Mrs Herbert that, following her husband's death, Lorna May's mother went off with another man and couldn't be traced. *That* much at least was known about her.

But what of the cards she claims to have sent her daughter? They must have come from *somewhere*. Hadn't she given an address.

As though reading his thoughts, she says, "I was never in one place long enough to settle. Awful it was, you've no idea."

Meaning, presumably, that living here you lot have been out of harm's way.

Another thought comes to him, one that springs from the occasional murmurs he has heard from Ronnie's mother as well as his own. Wherever Rachel Perry found to live after being bombed out, and no matter who she was living with, she could surely have come to see Lorna May? Other evacuated children in the village had, after all, been visited by *their* mothers. Some children, who hated village life or couldn't settle with the people who took them in, had gone back to the cities they'd come from. Often, they'd claimed to be going home for a weekend, one from which they never returned. The school chair that had been occupied on Friday was empty the following

Monday. Lorna May couldn't go to see her mother because she had no home to go to. Mrs Herbert knew her mother had vanished, though how she knew was itself a mystery. Perhaps Mrs Perry had told a neighbour she was off and to forward the news to the Herberts. He harks back to his earlier thought. Even if she *was* living somewhere else in London it wouldn't have prevented her from visiting her daughter.

It occurs to him, then, that having once packed Lorna May off to safety with the rest of her school – "the authorities" as she calls them – her mother as good as abandoned her, and yet now, five years later, here she is, determined to see the people who'd taken Lorna May in, not even bothering to tell them she is on her way, and yet implying they ought to be waiting in to greet her on her arrival.

And again, as though she can read his thoughts and knows how to outmanoeuvre him, the woman repeats, "You've no idea the problems I had convincing the coppers who I was. Am. Rachel Perry. Lorna's mother. They didn't want to believe me."

"Why ever not?"

His mother's question hovers on the edge of incredulity.

"I'd no means of identification, that's why not. Can you imagine?" She pauses, her look flickering from mother to son. No, you can't, the look says. "Birth certificates, hers and mine, marriage certificate, all gone. Went when the bomb fell."

"But you must have had a ration card?"

"Oh, I got given one of them afterwards. But let me tell you, Kay, the coppers don't much trust them. Easy enough to buy one on the black market, if you know where to look; at any rate it's easy enough in London. Thousands do it. I know people who have half-a-dozen ration cards, all under different names. Live off the fat of the land. Still, it's probably different in a small place like this."

"I don't follow."

"Not like a big city, is it? It's easy enough to disappear in London or to come up with different names." And now it's her turn to colour faintly. "Anyway," she says, raising a hand and waving it as though to brush away further questions, "I finally got someone to vouch for me and here I am."

"And here you are," his mother says, smiling with artificial brightness.

"Oh, don't worry, Kay." The answering smile is grim. I know what you're thinking. "I'll not be stopping for more than tonight," she says.

"I want to visit my poor girl's grave. Then I'll make myself good and scarce." An extravagant sigh. "The police gave me the cemetery address," she says, after a pause.

She reaches for her coat, digs into a pocket and produces a piece of paper which she spreads out on the table. "Here … " She follows the hand-written words with a heavily nicotine-stained finger. "Old Lane."

She looks up, says, "You'll have to tell me how to get there. Unless the Herberts are back by morning, in which case I can have a bit of a chat with them, and perhaps one of them will have the goodness to come with me."

The gracelessness of her sarcasm is smothered under another sigh. "I ought to collect her clothes and any knick-knacks they've kept. I'd like something to remember her by. A keepsake."

"Old Lane isn't far from here," his mother says. "Down the road about ten minutes then off to the right. Not more than fifteen minutes in all."

Rachel Perry folds up the paper, returns it to her coat pocket. "Well, that's good," she says. "I'll pop over to see the Herberts, if they're in, then pay a visit to the grave, and then I'll be off back to London."

"They may be here later this evening," his mother says. "If not, then they're certain to be back first thing tomorrow. Mr Herbert has to be at work."

"What's Mr Herbert do?"

"He's at the hosiery factory."

He can sense what his mother is thinking. Fancy, she doesn't even know that. She knows *nothing* about the people who for five years have acted as parents to her daughter.

Rachel Perry says, though she doesn't seem especially pleased by the news of the Herbert's return. "Well, at least I can see Mrs Herbert."

Perhaps, after all, she isn't especially anxious to meet her.

As though to dispel this impression, she says, "I can ask her to show me Lorna's gravestone."

But the wistful tone in which she speaks is at odds with the way in which her flickering eyes take in mother and son. See, the look seems to say, I care.

"There isn't a gravestone," Peter tells her.

She focuses her gaze on him. "Isn't a gravestone? How do you mean?"

Discomforted by the intensity of her stare he blurts out "The ground has to settle. Then the gravestone can be put in place. I think it takes a few months. That's what we were told."

"A stone has been ordered," his mother adds, backing up his words. "By the Herberts."

"But how am I supposed to find where my little girl is lying?" Indignation tops any other emotion. "And who's 'we', may I ask?"

"It's what Miss Wheelock, our headmistress, told us at school before we went to lay flowers. There's a wooden cross," Peter tells her. *Lorna May Perry*, the board had painted on it in white lettering, and underneath, *1934-1945*. But he doesn't tell her that.

"And now," his mother says, decisively, "I *must* go and hunt out some fresh linen for your bed."

As she leaves the room, Rachel Perry stands up. "I think I'll take a stroll," she says. "Get some air into my lungs before bedtime."

She seems to have forgotten that she's asked Peter to talk to her about her daughter. Just as well. He won't have to admit that for the past months they've not spoken, that on the occasions they met, Lorna May looked straight through him.

But then he thinks, well, I don't have to mention that, and as he watches Mrs Perry pull on the black wool overcoat with its ragged hem, he says dutifully, "I could talk to you about Lorna May, if you'd like."

Rachel Perry looks at him. "Lorna, dear. Not Lorna May. Lorna is – Lorna *was* – her name."

He follows her down the hall, then holds the front door open for her.

"What's that?" she asks, standing in the porch.

She is listening to a sound he knows only too well.

"Coal trucks," he says, "there's a big yard at Ashton. Perhaps you don't have them in London?"

He says it as politely as he can, but she laughs away his question.

"Oh, we have them all right," she says. "I'm surprised you have them *here*, though. In the country."

And, stepping out into the evening air, she marches purposefully down the drive to their front gate.

Left to himself, he thinks as he takes her cup and saucer out to the kitchen that he'd never have imagined that the blonde, skinny Lorna May could be the daughter of this plump, dark-eyed, dark-haired woman. And why should she insist that Lorna is or was her daughter's name when Lorna May herself had always insisted with far greater fervour that she be addressed by both names? Strange.

12

When Peter returns from school next afternoon, Mrs Perry, who hadn't appeared by the time Ronnie called for him after breakfast, is nowhere to be seen.

But going from kitchen to dining room, he notices her suitcase, with the strap round it, in the hall. She's packed, then, presumably about to leave.

His mother sits in her usual chair, smoking, a book open on her lap. In July warmth, hair curling about her shoulders, she is wearing a loose, lilac-coloured dress and white, strapped sandals.

Raising her face in expectation of his kiss as he comes toward her, she says, "I hoped – thought – that might be her coming through the back door." A twitch of the shoulders. "She's been gone for hours."

"Are you all right, Mum?"

He knows at a glance that she isn't.

A smile flickers and goes. "Nothing that having the house to ourselves wouldn't sort out. I don't think I like having uninvited guests on the premises." But as though realising the words sound unnecessarily sharp, she says, "No, I mustn't be mean. The poor woman had nowhere else to stay, I do know that, and she'll soon be gone again… " She looks at the clock on the mantelpiece. "But she'll have to hurry if she's to catch the last train to London."

"Does she know what time it goes?"

"She does. Mrs Herbert has the new timetable."

He sits at the table, takes up a piece of bread from the plate she's laid out for him. "She's seen the Herberts, then."

"She's seen Mrs Herbert. I took her over as soon as she'd had breakfast. Mister had left for work long before we got there."

He waits for her to say more, and when she doesn't asks, "What happened?"

She raises an eyebrow. "The meeting? It was a bit sticky at first. They'd never met until this morning, and I think they were suspicious of each other. Prickly. Understandably, perhaps, given the circumstances. I imagine Mrs Herbert thought Rachel Perry should have kept in touch with her daughter, and as for her – for Mrs Perry – we know that *she'd* decided the Herberts were somehow to blame for Lorna May's accident – Lorna, as she calls her. Mrs Herbert's references to Lorna May didn't go down well. I said we all called her that and she said that she was her mother and that as far as she was concerned her daughter's name was Lorna. So, yes," she hunches her shoulder up, shivers dramatically. "You could have cut the atmosphere with a knife. I thought we were never going to be invited into the bungalow, that we'd have to stand there on the porch for all the world to see."

He spreads marrow jam on his bread, chews. "Not much of the world goes up and down our road," he says.

She allows herself to laugh. "Don't forget the Duchess of Kent."

"She didn't notice us."

"True." This time the laughter comes more easily.

After a moment's silence, she says, "However, I'm pleased to say that by the time I left them to it the ice had been broken. Mrs Herbert was going to take our guest to see her daughter's grave and then they were hoping to drop in on Mrs Bailey and perhaps Sergeant Locker, though I did warn her that both of them are usually out and about."

He is puzzled. "Why does she want to see them?"

"While she was having her breakfast she asked me who had found Lorna, so I told her Keith had, and then I had to explain that after Mrs Bailey had phoned the police station Sergeant Locker came down to inspect the body."

"And the ambulance? Did you tell her about that?"

"I did. I had plenty of time, the amount of tea she poured down herself. I thought she'd drink me out of house and home."

"Is that why there's no milk on the table?"

She laughs and now she is fully relaxed. "No, clever clogs, it's because in this hot weather it keeps better in the larder. You can go and pour yourself a cup, if you like."

He shakes his head. "In this hot weather I'd rather drink water."

"Adam's ale," she says. "That's what your dad calls it."

He wonders whether she is about to tell him that there's been a letter, but instead, with another glance at the clock, she says, "I don't know what's keeping her. Even if she's managed to see everyone on her list she ought to be here by now."

And, as though on cue, they hear a rapping on the front door.

"I'll go," she says, standing, "you finish your tea."

A moment later Rachel Perry comes into the room. Wearing the jumper she'd arrived in, coat over her arm, a draggled black skirt and black court shoes on the feet of her stockingless legs, she looks hot, strands of hair stuck to her forehead, beads of sweat either side of her mouth, her lipstick smudged.

Flopping down into the easy chair across from his mother's, she says to Peter, "God, the country. Give me the city every time. Paving stones rather than grass for me. My ankles have been turned this way and that until I can hardly stand."

His mother comes in with the glass of water intended for Peter, and Rachel Perry at once reaches for it and downs it in one long gulp.

"Ooh, that's better," she says, handing back the glass and then fanning herself as she sinks lower into the chair. "Traipsing over fields isn't for the likes of Rachel Perry."

She eases off one black shoe with the toe of the other, then lies back, sighing. But next moment she straightens herself up, reaches down and removes the other shoe, then begins to massage her toes while her flickering gaze goes between mother and son.

"I'm not going to make it, am I?" she says, noticing his mother glancing at the clock. Then, sighing, "I'm ever so sorry, Kay, but I'm afraid I'll have to impose on your hospitality for one more night." She looks at his mother, what may have been intended as an apologetic smile turning to a grimace. "Thing is, there's unfinished business here for me."

Holding the empty glass in her hand, his mother, trying to disguise what Peter knows is her feeling of irritation, says nothing but looks with quizzical intent at the other woman. "Unfinished?" she says after some moments of silence. "I don't understand."

"You will when I tell you." Mrs Perry sighs dramatically.

A pause, while she finishes massaging her toes. "Ooh, that's better. I'm comfier now."

She tucks her feet up underneath her. "It's been quite a day, I can tell you. Needs some telling." Cheeks puffed, she exhales air. Then, ingratiatingly, "I suppose I couldn't have a cuppa, could I?"

Unwillingly, his mother says, "I usually have one later, but ... "

"I'm sorry to put you out." Is there a hint of sarcasm in her wheedling tone? No, he decides, probably not, but he can see his mother is, as she might say, riled by the request.

A few moments later, though, moments during which Mrs Perry closes her eyes as though not wanting to speak, allowing him the licence to study her round, blunt chin, stubby nose and thick eyebrows, features in which he can see little sign of her daughter, his mother returns with a cup of tea and the refilled water glass, which she hands to Peter.

The other woman opens her eyes, senses that Peter has been studying her, and says, her eyes on him so that he at once blushes, "Thanks ever so, Kay. This will soon set me to rights."

Still looking at him, she sips at her tea, then returns the cup to its saucer and with elaborate care sets it down beside her, before shifting her flickering gaze to his mother. "Well," she says, "let me tell you all about what I've been up to since you left me with Mrs Herbert. Dora. And how long ago *that* seems."

Dora. Peter realises that until this moment he's never known Mrs Herbert's Christian name.

Rachel Perry frowns down at her lap, as though gathering her thoughts, then says, with sudden force, "Lorna's grave. Have you been to see it?"

"I'm afraid I haven't, not yet."

Rachel Perry seeming not to notice the apologetic tone of his mother's remark, says, as by way of reproof, "I see."

"It was a private funeral," his mother says, defensively. "The Herberts weren't keen to have anyone apart from themselves involved."

"But some of us from school took flowers," Peter says, reminding her of what he said the previous evening. When her eyes flicker in his direction he stops short.

His mother says, "They gathered flowers from the fields hereabouts. And woods, too. From where the poor girl fell to her death."

"Oh, when was that? *When* did they take the flowers?"

Startled by the way she asks the question, the way she swivels her head to stare at him, as though she's accusing him of some failure, Peter looks at his mother. "I don't exactly remember," he says. "But soon after Lorna May – Lorna – was buried. Perhaps a week later?"

His mother nods her agreement. "Yes, I'd say a week at most."

"And everything was all right?"

Puzzled, he says, "Yes." Then adds, "I think so," though he doesn't know what she can mean.

Mrs Perry's dark eyes are glinting. "It's been got at," she says. "Someone's been there and … what's the word?"

"For what?" his mother asks apprehensively.

"For when someone interferes with a grave.".

"*What!*" His mother looks aghast. "*Interfere.* You mean your daughter's grave has been vandalised? How?"

"Not the grave itself, but the cross. They tried to scratch out her name."

"But that's *awful.* I can't believe anyone would do such a thing."

"I can assure you, Kay, it's what I saw. If you don't believe me, ask Dora Herbert."

"Rachel," his mother says, "I'm truly sorry. Of course I don't doubt your words. But ... " She shakes her head. "I can't ... It doesn't ... It's so ... so inexplicable. Why on *earth* would anyone want to do a thing like that?"

As though she has gained her point, Rachel Perry says, her voice lowered now, more measured,"the very question I put to your Sergeant Locker."

And now his mother sits silent, looking at her guest, waiting for her to continue.

Which she does. "Dora took me up there. To his house. We had to march all the way from the cemetery. I wouldn't want to have to do that every day of my life, I don't mind telling you."

Peter tries to picture the distance between Old Lane and the policeman's house with its blue lamp, a little way beyond the church.No more than a twenty-minute walk if you cut across the fields, and even if you keep to the road you can surely cover the distance in half an hour at most. Not a long march, to use Rachel Perry's words.Perhaps in London people are used to going about by bus or tram. Or there's the tube, of course, the underground train system his mother has told him about.

"I made your sergeant promise he'd look into the matter. He's asked me to call back tomorrow when he's had a chance to inspect the damage and make some enquiries. He took notes while Dora told him all about it. I was too upset to speak."

A pause, then she says, "Lorna's name has been scratched right through." She shudders. "Horrible."

Peter tries to recall the details of the wooden cross he and the others of his class had visited. The name **Lorna May Perry** painted in white on the crosspiece, and underneath, the dates *1934-1945*. Below, finally, painted on a small stone, ***Rest in Peace.*** That was all.

And now someone has tried to destroy her name. Why? Who would want to do such a thing?

"It must have been quite recent, so Dora thinks. She's certain it wasn't there last time she went to pay her respects. On what should have been Lorna's birthday."

"When was that?"

"Two weeks ago," Rachel Perry says quickly. "I'm not likely to forget *that* date, am I." She sounds once again aggrieved, as if choosing to detect in his mother's question some implied rebuke.

Her voice now gentle, reassuring, his mother says, "You're very welcome to stay here again tonight, Rachel. You'll need to, of course, if you're to see Sergeant Locker again tomorrow."

"That's kind of you, Kay." A smile. "I'm grateful." Good relations have been restored.

"And did you manage to see Mrs Bailey?" His mother opens the packet of Woodbines she keeps on her chair arm, and, after a brief inspection, offers one to her guest.

They both light up, after which Mrs Perry, feet still tucked under her, and following with upturned eyes the thin plume of smoke as it drifts toward the ceiling, says, "Yes, yes, I did. *We* did. Plodded all the way down from the Sergeant's place to hers and Dora introduced me. I was desperate for a cuppa by then but she kept us on the doorstep."

"I'm surprised by that. Maureen Bailey is usually the soul of hospitality."

"Dora reckons she was shielding her son, that Keith."

"Shielding him?" his mother says. "I don't understand."

"Don't you, dear?"

"No, I'm afraid I don't."

The hidden antagonism between the two women is back. Rachel Perry widens her eyes, as she says, "I'm only reporting Dora's words. She told me about him when we got back to her house – her bungalow." With thumb and index finger, she lifts a shred of tobacco from her tongue, inspects it before flicking it away, and says, "I may say that trying to get anything out of Mrs Bailey was like trying to get blood out of a stone. All I wanted to know was how her son discovered my daughter's body. Anything he could have told me might have helped."

"Helped?" His mother can't disguise her mistrust of the other woman's implication.

"Help me cope. Don't you think a mother's every right to know the details of her daughter's death, especially when it's as unexplained as Lorna's is."

Flicker, flicker go the eyes and she speaks with a kind of caged anger, a raw grievance.

And again his mother tries to calm her, to warm the air between them.

"Of course you do, Rachel. I do understand."

Judging after a moment's silence that it's safe to speak again, she adds, "But I imagine Sergeant Locker did his best to reassure you there wasn't anything mysterious in your daughter's death. The coroner was satisfied that it was an accident."

"Well, I'm *not*."

His mother seems to shrink from the force with which Rachel Perry utters the words. But she says nothing, waits.

"I've been to see where she was supposed to have had her 'accident'."

She looks at them both, then, when she realises that neither is about to speak, she says, "And let me tell you why I went."

She taps ash into the palm of her left hand, looks round for an ashtray. Peter takes the one by his mother's feet, offers it to their guest, and Rachel Perry drops the ash into it, then places the ashtray in her lap, scarcely bothering to nod her thanks. It is as though she has taken charge, that they are now her guests.

"I tell you, Kay, an outsider sees things the locals miss. I'm not trying to be rude in saying this. It's always the case." She tilts her chin and releases more smoke, while his mother looks attentively at her.

"Besides there's something I don't trust about the Bailey set-up. I didn't at all like the way she – Mrs Bailey – went out of her way to prevent us from speaking to her blessed son."

"Did she?" His mother sounds upset, dubious.

"I thought I told you." She snaps the words out, as though his mother is some sort of a dunce. "She kept us – Dora and me – on the doorstep. And all the while he was in there, eating his dinner."

"Was he?"

The question is genuine, but Rachel Perry treats it as though it has been asked in sceptical disbelief. With more than a hint of exasperation, she says, "Yes, he *was*. Dora told me he comes back from the factory every dinner hour, which was why, after we'd finished with the Sergeant, we walked down to see his mother. We, that is Dora, knew he'd be there."

She makes the words sound like a charge.

His mother says, firmly now, "If you're hinting at what I think you are, I can tell you that you're quite wrong. Keith wouldn't harm a fly."

"Oh?" Flicker. "What makes you say that? How can you be so sure?"

"Because, Rachel, I know him and I know his mother."

The smile is dismissive. "And familiarity breeds content."

"I don't think you should say that."

"Really? Why not?"

"Because I have the feeling you're wanting to point the finger of blame, accusation – I don't know what – at that poor lad."

His mother is now sitting bolt upright in her chair, cheeks inflamed, eyes fixed on her guest.

"Poor lad, is it? Well, maybe. But I *saw* him." A pause, and now, when the flickering eyes steady long enough to meet his mother's gaze, he sees what looks to be a gleam of triumph in them. She has a point to prove. "He came blundering out into the hall while we were stood there on the step, saw Doreen and me, and tried to get back inside. I said to her – to his mother – 'Is that him?' and she said 'He's late for work, he can't stop now,' and more or less shut the door in our faces."

She allows time for the words to make their impression. Then, more slowly, and with unmistakable emphasis, she says, "But I saw the look on his face, Kay."

Drawing on the last of her cigarette, she crushes the stub in the ashtray, puts it on the ground beside her and takes her time brushing flakes of ash from her skirt. Only then does she look up, her gaze flickering between her two listeners.

They are silent.

Nodding to herself, as though she has won some important argument, she says eventually, "When we got back to Dora's bungalow I asked her what she thought. She agreed he looked mighty awkward. "'*Awkward*,' I said. He knows a damned sight more than he's letting on. Or is being allowed to say. Pardon my French, but there's no point in beating about the bush. Besides," she says, "he's definitely a few pence short of a shilling, wouldn't you say." But it isn't a question.

His mother shakes her head but still says nothing. Seeing the distress on her face, the troubled look as, chin in hand, she gazes down at the carpet, Peter wonders whether she may be thinking, as he now is, that Keith could after all be somehow responsible for Lorna May's death. Might it be so? And he remembers the occasion when the youth had lumbered after the girl; on that occasion she'd mimicked his clumsy movements. Perhaps there had been other such occasions? Perhaps he'd met her that afternoon he was out looking for bluebells. Perhaps …

"So," Rachel Perry is saying, "let me tell you what I did after Dora had given me a bite to eat. I took myself down to the woods. She'd have come with me but she had to go to some meeting at her church. Organizing aid for starving Germans." A short laugh. "Aid for that lot. I'd sooner let them starve. Not that I said as much to Dora. But I got her to tell me how to find my way, how not to get lost once I was in among the trees."

Another brief laugh. Her eyes go from mother to son, then are trained on the window. She frowns in concentration at what she is about to tell them. "Easier said than done. I was thrashing about for what seemed ages, I can tell you, didn't know where to roam, like the song says, but then at last I found the path Dora had told me about, the one that goes slap bang into the middle of the woods. It had to be the right one."

"It's the only one," Peter says. "It takes you to the hut where … " And he stops.

"You know it, do you?" She is looking attentively at him. "The hut?"

"Ronnie and me sometimes go there. Not often," he adds defensively, "but we've been a few times."

"Climb on the roof?"

"No," he says, "it's too dangerous."

"Too dangerous?" she repeats, incredulously. "Too dangerous?"

"Yes." He feels compelled to tell the lie, feels that in some way he may be helping Keith by the muttered untruth.

"Even though the overhang, the eaves don't you call them, are only about three feet off the ground, wouldn't you say? With a nice soft landing. Bushes and plenty of grass all around. Didn't you ever jump off that roof? *Ever*?"

He shifts uneasily. "Once or twice," he admits.

"Once or twice. Hurt yourself, did you?"

"You can get scratched by the brambles if you come down in the wrong place. And Ronnie once bruised his knee when he slipped off."

"Bruised his knee. Well, I never." The sarcasm is scorching. "I wouldn't call that much of an accident, would you? Not exactly a risk to life and limb. Not like getting your neck broken."

And when, slowly, reluctantly, he shakes his head, Rachel Perry, with a flicker of contempt says, "No, I thought not." Turning to his mother, she says, "Do you see what I'm getting at, Kay?" And, after a moment, "I'm sure you do."

His mother goes on looking at the carpet, saying nothing.

"I'm sure you *do*," Rachel Perry repeats.

And now, at this challenge, his mother does look up, her look troubled, wanting to say something, ready he hopes to challenge all these hints and innuendos.

But a knock at the front door prevents whatever words she may be preparing to utter.

13

"Ahoy there."

Face slightly flushed, eyes unnaturally bright, Sally Parsons stands in the porch, and though her smile dims as she sees that it is Peter who has opened the door, her high spirits dip only momentarily.

"Is Kay – is your mother in?"

Yes, he tells her.

"Alone?" She leans forward as she whispers the word extravagantly, and he detects on her breath a smell at once sweet and musky.

"Mrs Perry is here."

She straightens up, puzzled. "Mrs Perry?" Then, her eyes widening, "Good lord, you don't mean a relative of Lorna May?"

"Her mother."

"*No!*" She looks at him for confirmation, and when he nods, says, "Well, well. So she's finally surfaced."

As she speaks he hears the dining room door open and behind him his mother's voice. "Sally! This is a surprise."

"Ah, yes, the proverbial bad penny turning up just when you thought I must have finally rolled down the drain."

Standing beside him, now, hand on his shoulder, his mother says, "I was thinking no such thing."

"Kind of you to say so." The smile is guarded, perhaps sincere.

"Aren't you going to come in?"

Mrs Parsons, glancing down at her cream blouse and slim lovat-green skirt, says, "Am I presentable? I gather you have visitors."

"Just the one."

A moment's pause, and, looking up, he sees that his mother has placed her finger to her lips. Then she uses it to beckon Sally Parsons into the house.

As she steps into the hall and brushes past him, Peter notices the bottle she hands to his mother.

"Another peace offering?" His mother's laugh is off-kilter.

"If you like," Sally Parsons says. She reaches out, grabs hold of his mother's hands and briefly embraces her. "But I'm also celebrating. The house, thank god, is sold, and I'll be off in a couple of weeks' time. Trouble and Strife are still with Sandy's parents while I do the final titivating before we depart the scene."

"That's good news. Good for you, I mean."

"Yes, isn't it." The smile holds more than a trace of mockery.

His mother leads the way down the hall, then stands aside to let Sally enter the dining room ahead of her. She looks back at Peter, and he realises that he is not meant to join them.

He says, "Is it all right if I go round to Ronnie's?"

"Of course." She is smiling, grateful. "But back by bedtime. OK"

"OK." He waits until, following Sally Parsons into the back room, she shuts the door behind her.

So his mother and Sally Parsons are once again on friendly terms.

***

"Bloody 'ell."

They are lying on top of one of Farmer Connolly's haystacks, Ronnie listening to the slow unfolding of Peter's story. Walking up to school that morning, he'd told his friend about Mrs Perry's appearance the previous afternoon and how she'd stayed the night. Now he reports the damage to Lorna May's grave.

"Does she know who done it? Does old Lock-up?"

He takes a breath before rolling onto his side in order to face his friend. "She's been to see the hut."

Ronnie props himself up on his elbows. "So?"

"So she reckons anyone could jump off the roof without hurting themselves."

Ronnie flaps at midges dancing about their heads. "Well, you don't 'ave to be Rip Kirby to work that out."

"She thinks Lorna May *couldn't* have broken her neck, not jumping from that height."

"Yeh, we've seen 'er do that jump, didn't never bother 'er, did it. Didn't bother me, neither."

"Nor me," Peter says.

Ronnie looks quizzically at his friend, but says nothing. Neither of them is keen to admit that the dead girl's athleticism was far greater than theirs. She could outrun them, could scramble fearlessly up trees, and, as they know to their cost, was prepared to scale walls they'd never dare attempt.

Giving up on the midges, Ronnie says, "Mi mam seen Mrs Perry comin' up the road, this afternoon. S'pose that was after she'd been ferretin' about in the woods. Anyway, she reckons she don't look much like Lorna May. Sez she's got dark 'air for a start off."

"How did your mum know it was Mrs Perry?"

"Because she saw 'er go in your gate," Ronnie says. "And I'd told 'er what you'd told *me*, about 'er turnin' up at your mum's place yesterday afternoon."

"Oh, right."

Should he let his friend in on that odd moment the previous evening when Mrs Perry had rebuked him for calling her daughter Lorna May? "Lorna is – Lorna was – her name."

Not yet. He says, "Who do *you* reckon would have tried to scrub out her – Lorna May's – name?"

"Same person as scrubbed 'er out." Ronnie turns on his stomach, sneezes loudly as a cloud of straw dust hovers over his face, then once more rolls onto his back, wriggling his shoulder to get more comfortable. "Otch up," he says, "Give us some room."

Peter shifts a little. "You think she was *murdered?*" He tries not to admit to the thrill that has gone through him at Ronnie's words. After a moment, he adds, "You've said that before. It's not what the coroner decided."

But Ronnie says coolly, "Course she got herself murdered. Stands to reason. Mi gran reckons that the 'ut is a red 'errin'. Lorna May's body was dumped there, to make it look like she'd fallen off of the roof. And now this business with 'er name bein' got at. It means that 'ooever did it is lettin' us know it was meant."

"But that's mad."

"What is?"

"What you're saying. Someone kills Lorna May and makes it look like an accident, and then decides to show that her death *wasn't* an accident."

"Changed 'is mind, that's all." Ronnie eases himself down into his new position, sighing with pleasure. "Better like this," he says. "Now I can do me thinkin'"

Lying beside his friend, Peter can hear the ratcheting of nearby grasshoppers and, further off, Farmer Connolly's cows lowing contentedly as they are led up from the meadow into the farm's milking shed.

"Last year we used to lie on this haystack looking up for enemy planes," he says. He is trying not to think about what Ronnie has just said, fearing where it may lead.

"Yup." Ronnie laughs dismissively. "Never saw none, though, did we."

"And we won't now."

"Night-times was different. Saw plenty then."

"Yes," Peter agrees. In earlier years he had crouched with his mother beneath their steel table listening to German bombers as they thumped across the Midland skies. They were aiming, she told him, for cities to the west of their village, to Leicester, Coventry, Birmingham, and he tried to imagine how people living in those places must be hiding under beds or tables, or crouching in their garden shelters, or running for cover as they heard the low, rumbling sounds nearing and waited for the bombs to fall.

In their steel cave, lit by a single candle, elongated shadows stretching like water stains up the dining-room walls, the two of them would at length hear the planes returning, higher now, their engines a continuous drone as they made for the coast and then across the sea to Germany; and then would come the All-Clear, that weird, drawn-out-coil of sound as though a genie was being pulled protesting out its hiding place in the earth, a melancholy howl that seemed to make the house walls and the dawn air throb and shake, like the siren that tells Hoskins' workers the day is at an end, only in reverse. Once, standing at their front door in the dark after the bombers had apparently gone, he and his mother were startled to see two enemy planes come rumbling slowly across the sky toward them, then pass over their roof, so low that even in the dimly starred sky they could make out the crosses on the underside of the bombers' wings. He was so amazed, enthralled even, that only after they had gone, the last sound fading into silence, did he begin to shake. "Cold?" his mother had asked, putting a protective arm round his shoulders. His mouth was so dry that he couldn't answer her.

Now, as he and Ronnie lie staring up at the gradual thickening of evening light, he thinks of his mother's promise that with Mr Attlee in charge of the government, everything will be different. What would be different? he'd asked. You'll see, she said. Different and better. He couldn't imagine it. Except, of course, that his father would be coming home soon. Yes, that would be better.

"'Arrison," Ronnie says with sudden conviction.

Harrison? What does Ronnie mean?

"Could've bin 'im," Ronnie says, squinting up into the sky. "gettin 'is revenge on Lorna May fer scrumpin' 'is apples."

"Mr Harrison?" Peter pretends to consider it, but the suggestion is, he decides, absurd. "I don't think so," he says eventually. "We don't even know that he recognised her. I mean, we never heard any more about it. Not at school, not from the police."

"Well, 'e wouldn't want to look a Charlie, would 'e. But it don't mean 'e didn't know it was 'er. Could be the old bugger found 'er somewhere, maybe caught 'er at 'is apples again, did 'er in, and then dumped 'er body in the woods."

But he isn't serious. Poking Peter in the ribs, he says, "OK then, Sherlock. Tell us your suspect."

"Don't know," Peter says. "Mrs Perry thinks it was Keith."

"What, she *said* it?" Ronnie propped up on his elbows, is now looking down into Peter's face, his own expression registering genuine surprise, even shock.

"She didn't *say* it, no. But she was thinking it."

"'Ow do you make that out?"

"I'm telling you. She thinks Keith killed Lorna May."

"I don't believe it." Ronnie sits straight up.

"I told you she had her suspicions," Peter said. "Mum didn't want to go along with what she was saying. She and Mrs Bailey are friends, and Keith … " But he can't bring himself to complete the sentence.

Ronnie does it for him. "Keith's a Simple Simon," he says.

"I wasn't going to say that." Peter knows how upset, angered, his mother would be at such words.

After some moments, Ronnie says, slowly, "I don't reckon Keith would kill anyone."

"But he's gone after people who poked fun at him." Peter doesn't tell him about having himself once been hit by Keith. He has promised his mother not to talk about it. Instead, he says, "Remember that time he tried to get Lorna May?"

"*She* don't know that, not Mrs Perry." Ronnie looks down at Peter, who still lies flat on his back. "Not unless someone told 'er."

Struggling into a sitting position, Peter says, "Well, if anyone did, it wasn't *me*." He pauses. "He threatened to bash *us*, remember?"

"'Im and 'oose army?"

But Peter doesn't reply. Instead, he is yet again remembering Keith's words. Keith warning them not to go into the woods, or anyway not to go hunting for the bluebells he'd found. "Don't go looking for them, trying to nick them. I'll bash you. Both of you."

The flowers grew thickly at various places under the woodland trees, but by early May most had been picked by villagers, the remainder by gypsy women who with their families would arrive each year at Easter time by caravan and camp along Fox Spinney. Once there, the women and children dragged down hazel branches to make clothes pegs and bunches of bluebells gathered from forays into the woods intended for door-to-door sale. But the gypsies were gone by the time Keith had issued his warning, so his bluebells were safe from them.

"Don't go looking for them." That was the weekend Lorna May went missing. And it was Keith who, on the Sunday afternoon, had found her.

Was that a coincidence? Or does Keith know more about Lorna May's death than anyone suspects? Anyone except Mrs Perry, that is. Perhaps she senses that Keith is capable of violence, that it isn't just words with him, either. He might actually put his threats into practice. Could he have threatened Lorna May? But why? Well, suppose he'd come across her hiding in the woods when he went looking for flowers, and suppose she'd said or done something that had made him lose his temper? She'd think she was safe, she could outrun him easily. But suppose she'd tripped and Keith had caught her while she was down …

No, he thinks. That's wrong. She'd gone missing on Friday and it was the following afternoon when Ronnie and he had seen Keith coming up from the woods. He'd not said anything then about her. Still, she *could* have been hiding all that time …

"So?"

Startled by the question, he says, "So? So what?"

"So who did kill 'er?"

"Why couldn't it have been an accident?" He isn't going to bring up Keith's name, not again.

"Right. I've got someone." Ronnie scrambles to his feet. "Our German pal. Last act of Fritz before 'e goes 'ome. I don't mean 'e killed 'er. But suppose 'e went down to the cemetery and 'ad a go at the grave board."

"You mean Hans?"

"That's the one."

Peter looks up at Ronnie. "That's mad. He's miles away, isn't he. How's he supposed to get at her grave from where he's been sent? And anyway why would he do such a thing? He hardly knew Lorna May."

But even as he speaks he is remembering the scratch on Hans' cheek, remembering, too, the way the German's hand had gone up to the mark, even though he had at first claimed not to know he'd been scratched. "It is not bleeding." *And* he'd come running out of the field leading down to the woods.

Ronnie says, "Yeh, but 'e might not 'ave liked the 'erberts. And 'e'd not be the only one. Could 'ave been revenge. Nipped down and did it before 'e left and nobody noticed." He sighs. "Still, that don't solve the problem of findin' 'er killer. OK, I give up. I wouldn't mind seein' Lorna May's grave, though. We got time, won't take longer 'n fifteen minutes there 'n back. Wanna come?"

Peter, too, gets to his feet. "All right," he says.

***

It takes longer, of course. But some half hour later, when, in the summertime dusk, Peter tiptoes into the kitchen via the back door, he hears the sounds of women's voices coming from the front room.

Standing at the sink, he pours himself a glass of water, drinks it, refills his glass, and, as he does so, thinks about the wooden cross he and Ronnie have been to inspect. The damage was less than they had expected. Whoever had attacked it hadn't gone far enough to do more than scrape at her name, especially the three middle letters. Looking at the clumsy scratches Ronnie speculated that someone had come along while the work was in progress. "Scared 'im off good and proper. Reckon 'e scarpered and never 'ad a chance to come back."

"Who? Hans?"

"No. An evil ghost. They 'ave to be back underground before daylight."

Then, looking behind him, Ronnie had shouted, "Quick, *run*."

Peter, swinging round, saw nothing but rows of gravestones and, across the level grass, a small chapel.

"'Ad you there." Ronnie was laughing contentedly.

They run most of the way home, "like 'ans in trainin'," Ronnie pants, as they come thudding up the road and past the repaired crater.

Hans, Peter thinks now, swallowing the last of his water, then rinsing his glass out. But no, Ronnie's suggestion really is daft and so were the others he'd come up with as they'd walked down to the cemetery. Whistling Billy? But the tramp hadn't been around for weeks. Gypsies? But they'd left the village two months earlier and wouldn't be back until the autumn. As for Harrison, whose name Ronnie had once more spoken, the retired dentist could hardly drag himself along, and he'd never once been seen their side of the village, let alone near the woods.

Discounting one by one Ronnie's exuberant fantasies, and not wanting to admit his suspicions about Keith, he decides that the truth is, the truth *has to be*, that Lorna May died an accidental death. Nobody has killed her. She simply slipped off the roof of the woodman's hut, fell awkwardly, and her neck was broken.

***

"Stranger things have happened," his mother says. She has come up to his bedroom where he lies in darkness. The front door has opened and closed – Sally Parsons leaving, he assumes – and now, as she stands in the doorway asking how he and Ronnie spent the earlier part of the evening, he decides to tell her about their visit to the grave.

"Why on earth did you do that? Go there, I mean." Sitting on the edge of his bed, she speaks out of the gloom, her voice questioning, perhaps troubled, as she says, "I don't like all the speculation that's going on about the poor girl's death."

"Speculation?"

"People as good as pointing the finger. Claiming to know that there's a mystery about it, that she didn't die of natural causes."

Then, with a gust of anger, she says, "Why on earth can't they accept the coroner's verdict? Hasn't there been *enough* death and destruction. You'd have thought people wouldn't be in a mood to rake up more violent killings."

"But Mum, the damage to the cross."

He watches the outline of her body, as she sits there, chin in hand, still. Then she says, her voice full of sadness, "Stranger things have happened." A pause. "Tell me what you and Ronnie found."

He does, and when he finishes, she says, "From what you say it won't take much to make good the damage to the girl's name. Besides, there'll soon enough be a proper gravestone to remember her by. Whoever chose to attack the cross must be mad or wicked, but it doesn't mean – well, I don't know *what* it means. I suppose it could have been random. Someone horsing about. And even if it was meant, at worst some deluded person was wanting to do something spiteful. Someone who didn't like her."

She sits for a moment in silence. "But Peter, that's not the same as wanting to harm *her*, not wanting to have her out of the way."

"You don't think there's a connection between her death and the attack on her grave-board?"

" I won't believe it. Nor will I believe that Lorna May's death was … That it wasn't the result of an accident."

Registering the emphatic way she speaks the words, he himself is silent for a moment or two, then, lowering his voice to a whisper, he says, sure she must be thinking of Keith Bailey, "But Mrs Perry thinks Lorna May *could* have been killed."

Out of the dark, his mother says in her normal voice, "There's no need to whisper. Our guest has gone."

He struggles to prop himself on his elbows.

"Gone? Where? Back to London?"

"No." Her sudden, short laugh sounds one of relief. "Nowhere near as far," she said. "She's gone to stay with Sally Parsons."

"Really? Why?"

"Sally suggested it. She's packing up, getting ready to leave, and somehow, I don't quite know how, it came to the point where Rachel Perry was offering to help her scrub and clean and in return Sally was offering Rachel a bed for a few nights."

"So Mrs Perry's not going back to London?"

"Not yet. Not before she's seen some of the people she says may help her come to terms with her daughter's death. I think she's rather hoping she'll be able to talk to the coroner, and to the doctor who signed the death certificate, and then there are the police, the sexton … Old Uncle Tom Cobley and all."

She stops, slaps her thigh in self-rebuke. "No, I must not be … " She lets the sentence dwindle away. "I imagine she'll be gone in a week's time, which is about when Sally will also be gone. And meanwhile they'll be able to keep each other company."

"They're not much like each other, are they?"

His mother stands, moves toward the door. "You mean Sally Parsons is … " The quotation marks round the phrase that come next are unmistakable – "'upper-crust' and Rachel Perry isn't? More like Lady of the Manor and maidservant?"

As she stands by the open door, landing light illuminating her face, she is, he can see, smiling. "Now go to sleep."

He hears her as she goes downstairs, singing, and he knows that the surge of happiness he can detect in her voice is because they once more have the house to themselves.

And in the same instant he knows for sure that she doesn't like Rachel Perry.

Which suits him fine, because he doesn't like her, either.

14

Three days later, Friday, she is back again.

He comes in from school, and even before he hears her voice he sees the suitcase with its strap standing in the hall.

His mother looks up from the table where she sits facing Rachel Perry, a strained smile on her lips as she says, "We have a visitor."

"Large as life and twice as ugly," Mrs Perry says, swivelling in her chair to face him. "Always turning up where I'm not wanted, eh?"

Her eyes flicker over his face, then she turns back to his mother, who says by way of explanation, "Sally Parsons has had to dash off to Cornwall. Apparently the twins have been taken ill."

"She *told* me she got a telegram mid-morning," Rachel Perry adds, as he goes to stand by his mother.

"Want your tea?" his mother asks, putting an arm round him as she searches his face for evidence that he will understand the apology she is making for their lives being once more disrupted.

"I'll clear these cups away."

Rachel Perry makes to raise herself, but his mother says, "No, I'll do that." There is an emphasis in her voice, a note the other woman responds to by saying, "Don't think I'm not grateful for your help, Kay. I did offer to stay and mind the place for Sally, but she didn't seem keen on the idea." A faint smile, more a tightening of the lips, an expression that suggests a sceptical understanding of Sally Parsons' real motive. Her visitor is not one to trust. "So. Here I am again. Having to take advantage of your hospitality." She spreads her hands in a gesture suggesting the sad inevitability of her presence.

"Oh, well, one more night."

"I'm afraid it will have to be more than that."

The arm round his waist stiffens as his mother says "What?" Then, less harshly, "I mean, but why?"

Flicker, flicker. "The coroner can't see me until next Monday, Kay. And tomorrow I've got an appointment to meet the man at the *Chronicle*."

"The *Chronicle*?" This time his mother makes no attempt to hide her irritation. "Why on earth should you want to talk to *them*?"

She is standing now, the look she directs down at her guest one of disbelief, and, he can see, anger.

Rachel Perry meets his mother's stare, says with some hauteur, "Sally and I discussed it last night. We thought it the right thing to do. So today, once I'd got myself tidied up and out of Sally's hair, I took myself off into town. Coroner's office, then the newspaper office."

The eyes are withdrawn now, staring at the carpet beneath her feet. "As I think you know, Kay, I'm not satisfied with the explanation I've had about the cause of my daughter's death. We, Sally and I, came to the conclusion that there couldn't be any harm in my asking the local newspaper to – well, not investigate exactly, but to see if they can throw any light on what *I* think is a mystery."

It is defiant, even indignant. Someone is keeping the truth from me, she is implying, and I mean to find out who.

His mother gathers the tea cups and saucers together and takes her time in arranging them on the tray before she speaks again. Gripping the loaded tray as she goes to the door, she says over her shoulder, "This is wrong." Her voice is shaking.

"Well *I* don't think so," Rachel Perry says, as though to herself, but glancing up at Peter. "I think I'm entitled to an answer that will satisfy me, don't you?"

Embarrassed, he sits on the chair his mother has vacated, wondering what to say, but she solves the problem by asking him when the school holidays begin.

"Next Friday's the last day of term," he says.

"I expect you're looking forward to that." The words are formal, don't seem to require an answer.

He nods but can think of nothing to add.

After a lengthy pause, she says, "I don't suppose Lorna ever had the chance of a proper holiday. Not here."

Her eyes steady long enough to meet his, and it is as though she is challenging him to speak out.

Again he says nothing.

But his mother, who has overheard the words as she comes in with the tray on which she has placed bread and jam and a glass of milk, says, "The Herberts always did their best for your daughter." Her voice is under control now, her words uttered less as rebuke than to affirm the Herberts' worth.

She puts the tray in front of Peter, straightens up and, turning to Rachel Perry, says, "They may not have been used to children, but that doesn't make them ogres." It comes out as a formal statement, a plea for the defence.

Mrs Perry considers this. Then, "That's not what Sally Parsons thinks," she says. Looking at his mother then away, she adds quickly, "No, she didn't *say* as much, but you can tell what a person's thinking from *how* they say the words."

"And what did Sally say about the Herberts?"

His mother goes to sit in her hearthside chair.

Swivelling to face her, Rachel Perry says defiantly, "She said a good deal about them acting according to their *principles*." It sounds like a direct accusation.

In the act of lighting a cigarette, his mother says, "And what's wrong with that? What's wrong with acting according to your principles?"

He notices that she hasn't offered the packet to Rachel Perry, who now speaks with almost a simper. "It depends what those principles are, wouldn't you say?" Pause. "Mind you, I've got nothing against Dora Herbert. *She* seems nice enough, once you've broken the ice, that is."

The implication is that the man's ice can't be broken.

Reluctantly, he is sure, his mother does now offer a cigarette to Mrs Perry who, after a show of hesitation – "Are you sure you don't mind, Kay" – accepts.

For some moments the two women smoke without speaking.

The tension between the two of them is making him nervous. He says, "I didn't think newspapers worked on Saturdays. Not all of them, anyway. Not the *Chronicle*." The words fall awkwardly into the silence.

"This isn't work, exactly." Rachel Perry's eyes flicker over his face, and he knows she has seen through his ruse. He reddens, and now her smile once more becomes a simper. "The gentleman I saw suggested that we might 'conduct' an informal conversation. We've arranged to meet tomorrow lunchtime. He's coming over to the village."

"*Here?*"

"Don't worry, Kay, he won't be knocking on your door." Not sullying the purity of your home, she means. "He's going to take me to the Crown and Anchor. One o'clock, he said. He'll be waiting." Again the simper.

"And what are you going to tell him?"

His mother directs her gaze up to the ceiling, but he knows her outer calm masks some deep unrest.

"I'm rather hoping that *he'll* have something to tell *me*."

Rachel Perry sits at her ease, resting the elbow of the arm from whose fingers her cigarette dangles in the palm of the other hand, green jumper speckled with cigarette ash. "I gather from what he said that he knows most of the local police force. He implied they often pass him pieces of information for his newspaper."

"*His* newspaper?"

"The *Chronicle*. I don't suppose there are many staff. When I called in this afternoon he was the only one in the office, but then again that means he'll know most of what goes on. 'All the news that's fit to report.'"

" I still don't understand what you hope to gain by doing this."

"Don't you, dear?" Rachel Perry asks, slowly turning her head to look at his mother, who is still staring at a spot on the ceiling above her head.

Chewing his bread, Peter feels an edgy anticipation of danger. A thrill of something like fear runs through him. Rachel Perry is, he thinks, menacing his mother, or, if not her, then someone else, someone whose involvement in her daughter's death she seems to take for granted.

But she says, blandly enough, "If what he has to tell me helps me to be at peace with how poor Lorna died, I'll be satisfied."

"And if it doesn't?"

She shrugs. "No point in trying to cross that particular bridge until we come to it."

More silence. Stubbing out her cigarette, his mother says briskly, "Do you know where the pub is? I can walk up with you. I have to do the weekend shopping."

"The Crown and Anchor? Opposite the church? I'll be all right, thanks. Can't miss it."

His mother stands up, comes to collect his tea things, then turns to her guest. "Nevertheless I'd like you to walk up to the village with me, please." It is less invitation than order.

"Oh?" Rachel Perry for once seems startled, her eyes now focused on her hostess. "Why?"

His mother puts his glass, plate, and the jam jar on the tray, fiddles with the jam spoon. "I assume you'll be here for the Sunday meal?" Seeing the uncertain nod, she says "In that case, and always supposing the butcher has anything to sell, it will help us all if you can offer him

114

your ration card. That way we may even get a piece of meat larger than a matchbox."

Rachel Perry breathes out, laughing, relaxed now. "I see what you're driving at. And there was me, thinking you might want to keep an eye on me. Chaperone, don't they call it? Preventing an innocent woman from falling into the clutches of evil." The eyes resume their flickering, but more slowly. Despite her laugh, she isn't entirely at her ease. "The trouble is, Kay, I don't have my card with me."

And in response to his mother's look, she says, "True as I sit here. I've mislaid it. I've been moving about so much in London I can't keep track of even *my* few possessions. I must have left it somewhere, but I don't know where. Not a clue." She sighs. "Ever since finding out about Lorna I've been in such a whirl ... Sorry." The smile is candid, requiring forgiveness.

His mother says briskly, "Then we'll have to manage on scraps. Woolton pie."

"Tell you what. Why don't I pop down to that farmer over the road. The one you get your milk from? He may have something under the counter he could let us have. Most farmers do, don't they. Like as not, he will."

"Farmer Connolly?"

"That's his name, is it? Well, him, then."

"No," his mother says firmly.

"If it's a question of money, he'd let you have anything on tick, wouldn't he? He knows you."

"No," his mother repeats, reddening, "it's not that."

But it is, he knows. Money is in short supply. An extra mouth to feed means more of what his mother calls scrimping and saving. A year previously she'd followed the example of other local women who use the notice-board in the village newsagents to advertise for work. Hers, which he'd read one morning as he passed it on the way to school, stood out among the offers of cleaning or child-minding, or knitting and darning.

Qualified French teacher Mrs K. Howard, BA,
willing to undertake home tuition.
Reasonable hourly rates.

But whatever hopes she may have had of raising what she called "the wind" were soon flattened. She was offered an hour a week tutoring the two daughters of an Ashton bank manager, and fortnightly visits to the wife of a local doctor, whose lessons proved to be, so his mother admitted, "a pain in the neck. She can't remember anything from one class to the next."

"Why does she want them?" he asked.

"Because after the war, so she says, they'll be off on their travels again and she'd like to be able to communicate with the natives. Fat chance. She can't even say 'Bonjour.' It sounds more like *bojer*."

For a while they used the term in mock-greeting to each other. "*Bojer*, Mum." "*Bojer, Pierre*."

But then she put a stop to it. "I don't like to laugh at the poor woman, especially when I'm taking her money."

For the money this tuition brought in was a help, though a very little help, in supplementing her husband's army wages, which, when paid to her by the War Office, were, she said, "barely enough to keep a mouse in crumbs." And though she always laughed when she spoke the words, he guessed from the care with which she counted out cash each Friday evening that there was only just enough of it to last from one week to the next.

But also, as she sometimes says, she doesn't think it right to take more than her fair share of foodstuffs.

"At least rationing means that everyone gets fed," she had explained to him more than once.

So the suggestion of a visit to Farmer Connolly is turned down.

Rachel Perry shrugs. Suit yourself, the shrug implies. But aloud, she says only, "I'll be happy to pay for my share of the food, Kay. I'll let you have something tomorrow."

And what can his mother say to that, except "I wouldn't hear of it."

With which words, uttered smilingly to show she means what she has said, she gathers up the tray and goes out to the kitchen, and as she goes he hears the knock at the back door which means that Ronnie has come to collect him for their game of cricket.

15

The rattle of the letter-box comes as he is finishing his breakfast.

A moment later his mother is standing in front of him, smiling, happy, waving two letters above her head.

"Ta ra, ta ra." she says, and, when he looks enquiringly at her, "the Post Horn Gallop. Speeding the good news on its way."

"How do you know it's good news?"

"Because," she says, holding one of the unopened envelopes out for his inspection as she sits opposite him, "this is from your father. And, who knows, it may contain his demob date. Telling us he'll be home immediately, if not sooner."

She lays the letter aside.

"You're not going to open it?"

"Not yet. Let's get the unimportant one read first."

"How do you know it's unimportant?"

"Anything is unimportant compared to your dad."

She is still smiling but her voice has become serious.

He watches her as, having looked quizzically at the postmark, she reaches over and takes his knife, licks the smears of jam from it while winking at him, uses a thumb nail to prise up a corner of the envelope's top flap, then inserts the knife and carefully slits the envelope open.

A single piece of paper falls from the inverted envelope.

"What's this?"

She is staring, puzzled, at the bottom of the cheap sheet of notepaper. "Sally?"

Raising her eyes, she looks across at him.

"Letting me know all's well with the twins, I suppose."

She begins to read and as she does so her expression changes, the laughter lines are replaced by a frown, followed by a sharp hiss of intaken breath.

"Good morning, both."

Rachel Perry has made herself up more carefully than usual. In place of her green jumper she is wearing a white, short-sleeved blouse, open at the neck to reveal a necklace of blue beads. Carefully combed hair is pulled back behind her ears, on the lobes of which are gold clasp earrings. She brushes an imaginary crumb from her cherry-coloured skirt, buttoned at the side, before lowering herself on to the chair at the head of the table.

"Couldn't ask for better weather," she says, looking appreciatively out of the French windows, then at each of them in turn.

Her gaze steadies as it takes in the envelope his mother has discarded. "Fancy that," she says, studying the postmark. "Cornwall. Well, I never."

"It's from Mrs Parsons," Peter says and at once realises he shouldn't have done so. His mother is staring at him, the almost imperceptible shake of her head warning him to say no more.

"Really?" Rachel Perry seems only mildly interested. Then, as though remembering her manners, she asks, "Everything all right is it? The twins aren't worse, I hope."

"No, *they're* fine."

Has he imagined the faint stress on the word?

"That's good." Rachel Perry smiles complacently. "So even if Sally didn't go on a wild goose chase she's got nothing to worry about." The gaze is now directed to his mother. "I suppose that's how she found time to write so soon after her arrival."

"It's only a note."

"No, well, she wouldn't have been able to write a full letter, would she, not if she was going to pop it in the post to get the evening collection. She couldn't have got to – where is it, Padstow – until tea-time."

His mother stands. "Tea?" she asks her guest, who says, "If you've the milk to spare"

"I collected a pint from the farm earlier."

No, he isn't imagining that, the new edginess in her voice.

He watches his mother scoop up Sally Parsons' letter, push it into her apron pocket, then leave them.

While she is out of the room Rachel Perry looks around her as though seeking for something to say, then makes to glance at the still folded *Daily Herald*.

But she seems on her watch when his mother reappears.

As her tea is put in front of her, she says, "It must be nice to get letters." She makes the remark sound somehow absent-minded, wistful.

Before he can stop himself, Peter said, "'Letters and me don't agree.'"

Then, as both women look enquiringly at him, "I remember that's what Mrs Perry said."

"Well, you are a sharp one," their guest says, smiling as though in approval. But the stilled intensity of her gaze suggests otherwise.

He pushes himself up from his chair. The earlier mood of breakfast happiness between his mother and himself is now dispelled.

"I'll do my washing up," he says.

"And then?"

His mother makes no attempt to smile. Whatever is troubling her, whatever Sally Parsons' letter contains, must, he knows, relate to the woman sitting opposite her, staring intently.

"I could come up to the village with you," he says, going to stand beside his mother. "Help carry the shopping."

Cheer up, mum, he wants to say. And when, as though in response to his unspoken words she puts an arm round his waist and draws him to her, he adds, "This afternoon me and Ronnie want to go up to the rec. to watch the cricket match. Geoff Rice is playing."

"Geoff Rice? And who might he be?" Rachel Perry asks. Teacup half way to her lips, she is pretending an interest he is sure she does not feel.

"One of the men who went on the Dambusters raid."

If he is expecting the information to impress her, he is wrong.

"Well, at least he lived to tell the tale," she says, sighing extravagantly. "Lots of those who fought didn't. Like my hubby."

He looks uncertainly at his mother who, with a faint lift of the eyebrow, indicates that he'd better be leaving them.

So he does.

***

Walking up to the village through stubble fields where stooks from the first hay harvest stand all around and a dry, warm scent of chaff is stirred up by every step they take, he wonders how to ask about Sally Parsons' letter. What had it contained that so disturbed his mother?

"Did you have time to read Dad's letter?" is the best he can do.

"I wasn't in the mood. I'm saving it until this evening."

"Did Mrs Parsons have bad news, then?"

A moment's silence as they tread side by side across a final strip of meadow, then turn to wait for Rachel Perry, who is labouring along some twenty yards to the rear.

"I'd rather not say," his mother finally tells him.

She speaks quietly, and as quietly adds, "Something I'd rather have not known about. Though I suppose Sally thinks she's doing her duty."

He waits for a few moments, until they are in the narrow twitchell that will bring them out onto the village's main street, then, knowing their guest is still some way behind, tries again, whispering the words. "Is it anything to do with Mrs Perry?" Silence.

So it is, he thinks, as they walk along the road to the parade of Co-op shops. But what?

***

The church clock on the tower overlooking the cricket ground begins to strike 7 o'clock as the match ends.

Batting second, Stonely have won by six wickets and Geoff Rice is seventy-six not out when the teams come off. "A hero in the skies and at the crease," someone in the crowd calls out, as Rice, walking back to the small green-painted pavilion, modestly raises his bat in acknowledgement of applause that comes from all round the boundary. Most of the village, it seems, has turned out to see the man made famous by one night of daring.

"What you reckon," Ronnie asks, as he and Peter make their way down the fields to home territory. "Geoff Rice for England?"

But he is laughing. Len Hutton is his hero no less than he is Peter's, and this morning he has learnt that before the end of the season he is to be taken to what he calls a proper cricket ground, to watch Yorkshire play. "Mi mam's goin' up to Leeds to see 'er brother and 'e's takin' me to 'eadingly."

"Leeds? That's miles off. How do you get there?"

"We're bein' fetched in 'is motorbike and sidecar," Ronnie says, adding as an afterthought, "Shame you can't come."

"When my dad's home I expect he'll take me to plenty of matches."

"When'll that be?"

"Soon."

"You 'ad word, then?"

"Mum has."

They part then, before Ronnie can ask further questions.

***

As he pushes through the back door he is about to call out that he is home, but hearing voices coming from the dining room, creeps to the adjoining door into the hall. It stands ajar and from there he can hear them both clearly.

"You told me that Sally received a telegram."

"No, dear, I said that that was what she told me."

"I really don't see the difference."

"Don't you, dear?"

Rachel Perry sounds like a teacher explaining something to a dull pupil. "It's true I was upstairs when she called out to say it had been delivered, but I heard no knock on the door, nothing at all to suggest it had come."

His mother's voice then, irritated. "Just because you didn't *hear* doesn't mean it *wasn't* delivered."

"Maybe, maybe not." A pause. "But I happened to notice that she had a suitcase already packed."

"You noticed that while you were still upstairs, did you?"

The brief silence is broken by Mrs Perry.

"And what's that supposed to mean?"

"It means that if you're right and Sally was for some reason planning an excuse to go away, she'd not have left her suitcase on show, would she? Where was it? In her bedroom?"

For the first time the other woman's voice, when she speaks, sounds less than certain. "I don't see it matters where the suitcase was."

"I think it does," his mother says.

Behind him, the back door, which he'd not shut when he came in, bangs shut.

By the time his mother comes into the kitchen he is standing at the sink pouring himself a glass of water.

"Peter! Why didn't you let me know you were home?"

He waits until he has drunk some water before saying, "I was just going to."

"Did you enjoy your afternoon?" She looks distracted, her face flushed.

"Yes, thanks."

"And you ate the food, I hope." Her smile aims for reassurance, but her eyes are troubled.

He holds up the tin box which had held sandwiches and a slice of cake, shakes it to show it is empty.

The kitchen door is pushed wide open, framing Rachel Perry.

"Early as it is, I think I'll go up to my room," she says to his mother's back. "Good evening, Peter."

The voice, the expression on her face, suggest wounded dignity. "Your mother will tell you that I shall be moving out early tomorrow morning."

And with that she pulls the door shut and they hear the tread of her feet on the stairs.

His mother puts a finger to her lips, cocks her head and waits for several seconds.

After which, nodding as though satisfied, she blows out her breath and, keeping her voice low, says "She's taken work at the Crown and Anchor. Barmaid and other duties. She gets bed and board." Silently, she mouths the words *thank goodness*.

For some moments she stands, looking over his shoulder, until the flush on her face has faded. Turning back to him, she brings her hands together in a gesture of prayer, fingers to her lips which she eventually allows to part in a silent smile.

"Was it the letter?" he whispers.

Silent still, she nods, before mouthing *I'll explain later*.

And with that he has to be content.

PART THREE

16

Rachel Perry does indeed leave early next morning.

He is still in bed when he hears the front door open and slam shut.

A few minutes later there is a creaking of stairs and his mother comes into his bedroom. She crosses to the window and draws back his curtains. Light blares in.

"Well," she says, turning to him, "we've got the house to ourselves again." A slight pause. "Yippee."

Raising himself onto his elbows, he tries to read the expression on her face. Relief, certainly. But something else, too, some suggestion of guilt, or is it guilty pleasure.

"Did she – did Mrs Perry have some breakfast?"

"She asked for and was given a cup of tea."

It is oddly formal. Why does she so dislike Rachel Perry? He knows why *he* does. He doesn't like the fact that she makes his mother uncomfortable and, more than uncomfortable, on edge, sometimes downright irritable. But why is that? It started before the arrival of Sally Parsons' letter, though whatever is in that letter has certainly sharpened his mother's dislike of the other woman. Sooner or later, she will, he knows, explain. And he'll then tell her why Lorna May's mother always makes *him* feel uneasy. Those flickering eyes, the way she has of somehow both looking and evading contact until, suddenly, she'll fix her gaze on you, a stare, one full of – concealed anger is it? – and yet perhaps an appeal or an attempt to search you out, as if she is trying to decide whether you understand her at some level below the actual words she uses. But no, he can't think what it is, what that look *really* means.

He says, intending it as a joke, "No ration book, no breakfast."

"Ah, I'd not have begrudged her that," she says. "But work at the Crown and Anchor begins early. Nine sharp, so she claims. Cleaning duties, and then, apparently, she's rewarded with a full breakfast before bar work."

"On a Sunday?"

"A publican's work is never done. Like a mother's." Suddenly gay with laughter, she pulls the bedclothes off him. "Now then. Rise and shine."

"What was in Mrs Parsons' letter?"

"I'll tell you about that over breakfast. All that's fit for your ears."

She winks and then, with a near conspiratorial lift of an eyebrow, leaves him and he hears her run downstairs. A moment later her voice comes up from the kitchen. She is singing. *"Meet me in St Louis, Louis, Meet me at the fair."* He pictures her waltzing round the small kitchen as she sings. *"Don't tell me the sun is shining anywhere but there."*

But looking out of his window he can see that the sun *is* shining elsewhere. And now he is wondering not merely about Sally Parsons' letter, but about his father's.

***

The church clock is striking nine o'clock as, fully dressed, he stands at the head of the stairs, about to make his descent.

What stops him is a banging on the front door.

Mrs Perry returned for something she's left behind? He pauses, listens as his mother opens the door.

No, it isn't Mrs Perry.

"Kay, I'm so sorry to disturb you on a Sunday morning … "

"Maureen. What is it? Come in, come in."

By the time he enters the dining room, Mrs Bailey is sitting across from his mother, who is pouring tea for her guest and herself.

"You don't mind Peter being here? He's not had his breakfast."

Mrs Bailey, dressed in her district nurse's uniform, half-turns to him. "Hello, Peter," she says, distractedly. Then, "No, of course not. He'll hear soon enough, anyway."

She raises the cup his mother had passed her, takes a sip, then carefully replaces the cup in its saucer before she says, "Is your guest – is Rachel Perry still with you?"

Peter slides onto his chair and reaches for the cereal packet as his mother says, "No, she is not."

The emphatic denial seems at first to startle Mrs Bailey. But then she says, "In that case … "

A pause, as though, he thinks, she is hesitating whether to say more. Lowering her cup, she says with sudden vehemence, "I think she must be behind it all."

"Behind all what, Maureen?" His mother looks apprehensive.

"Something very unpleasant happened yesterday afternoon."

Another pause, then the words come with a rush.

"A man came knocking on our door. A journalist or reporter, he said that he works for the *Chronicle*."

"Oh, good heavens," his mother says, a hand going to her mouth.

"You know about this, Kay?" The question is sharp, almost accusatory.

"No." His mother shakes her head. "But I think I know what you're going to tell me." And looking at Maureen Bailey she says slowly, "Rachel Perry arranged to meet someone from the *Chronicle* yesterday. For lunch."

"And why should she want to do that?"

Fiddling with the top of the jam jar, his mother says, reluctantly, "She told me she'd been to the paper's offices on Friday, and that she was due to meet a reporter yesterday. They were planning to talk about her daughter's death. I'm afraid she's persuaded herself that it wasn't an accident."

She looks up, her gaze meeting Mrs. Bailey's.

"I'm so very, *very* sorry, Maureen."

"According to this reporter, she's as good as accused Keith of being … of being behind it."

Mrs Bailey's voice is shaking with anger.

"Is that what he … the reporter told you?"

Sitting straight up now, she is watching Mrs Bailey's face.

"James Morgan is the man's name. He didn't *tell* me what Rachel Perry had said, he didn't *say* anything about accusations, but he certainly let me know that 'some people' in his words 'harbour suspicions.'"

Peter tries to swallow cereal without crunching the flakes, but a fit of spasmodic coughing makes his mother half-stand, reach to where he sits, and slap him on the back. She smiles at him abstractedly. "All right?"

He nods. "All right."

She sinks back into her chair. To Mrs Bailey she says, "What exactly did this man, this James Morgan, want from you?"

"A friendly chat. That was how he put it. Friendly my backside."

Mrs Bailey drinks her tea, and returns the cup, rattling, to its saucer.

"How dare he bother you on a Saturday afternoon."

"Oh, he was full of apologies. Just passing, hoped I'd not mind if he asked me a few questions about anything I knew to do with the girl's death, and was my son available for comment. I told him I'd nothing to say, ordered him off my doorstep, and shut the door."

"Good."

"No, *not* good, Kay." Mrs Bailey shakes her head, repeats, "*Not* good. I've been awake all night worrying about what I said, what I did, wishing I'd not slammed the door in his face. You know what reporters are, know how they can twist a story."

His mother says, intending the words as reassurance, "But there's nothing to twist."

A brief, sardonic laugh. "Wait and see."

"Maureen," his mother says, "If there's anything I can do to help, you know I will."

"I know," Mrs Bailey said, her voice softer now. "I know. I can't share this with Keith, poor lad."

From where Peter sits he can see the lines of suppressed sadness tugging at the corners of her mouth, and when she speaks again her voice is full of such sadness.

"If that man comes to see you, Kay, you won't say anything to him, will you? He's trouble, I can tell."

"Of course I won't."

With something like a return of spirits, Maureen Bailey says," I suppose I should at least be thankful that Rachel Perry is off the premises."

"She's not left the village, though. She's found work at the Crown and Anchor. That was where she met this reporter, James Morgan, yesterday."

"And where she dripped poison in his ear. She must have put him up to it."

His mother says, resignedly, "I wouldn't be surprised."

"Of course she did. How otherwise would he know where I live? Besides, it's the kind of thing she does."

Peter watches his mother flash a look at Mrs Bailey. "What kind of thing?"

"Yesterday, I had a letter from Sally Parsons."

"*You* had a letter from Sally." She stares at the other woman. "Maureen, *I* had a letter from Sally. Let me guess what she told you. She gave you a warning, didn't she? A warning that Rachel Perry isn't to be trusted, that she's been spreading lies about us."

Mrs Bailey says, "And about the Herberts, don't forget them. Not so much Mrs H. – Dora – as she calls her, but she's got it in for him, all right. She claims she has evidence that the husband is some sort of … " She looks at Peter, amending whatever word she'd been going to use to "danger."

"I'm not going to repeat what she said to Sally concerning me," his mother says. "Nor what she said about you, Maureen. But it was very, *very* unpleasant."

Mrs Bailey looks at his mother. "My god," she says, "what's going on here?"

***

Only later that morning, as they walk home from church, does he think to ask about the other letter that she had waved at him the previous day.

"The other letter?" They are in the twitchell leading to open fields and she stops to look about her, as though trying to recollect where she is.

"Dad's."

"Oh." her face clears. "Only a note, I'm afraid. He's still hoping to be with us soon, but he doesn't know when."

There is a moment's silence as they listen to larks far above their heads and, further down the sky, watch a large black bird circling above the bottom field. "Must have seen something it fancies for its supper," she says, pointing, before retracting her hand, she places it on his shoulder and squeezes. "So without your dad it's us two alone against the world for a bit longer. Can you manage that?"

"Yes," he says, "I can manage. Promise."

And in the years to come he will have cause to remember the words. I can manage. Promise.

17

Term is over, the school year at an end.

Miss Wheelock, in her blue cardigan and black skirt, grey hair in its accustomed bun, spectacles flashing to all corners of the school hall *cum* dining room, stands on stage to offer her best wishes to those who are leaving and assure the others that she looks forward to seeing them again in September. There is a blessing, "May God keep you safe," followed by the singing of "Onward Christian Soldiers"; then they are free to go.

In the kitchen he reads the note his mother has left for him: *Sandwiches under breakfast bowl. Apple pie in tin.*

"Out of the blue," as she put it, she has been asked during the last week of term to give a conversation class in French at the local girls' grammar school, and today is no exception.

He'd sat beside her the previous evening as she made the pie, watched her roll and knead the dough into pastry on their large bread board, then spread a layer of it on the bottom of the pie dish she'd got him to grease with a mixture of lard and margarine, after which she arranged the sliced apples, some tin-tack cloves and a tiny sprinkling of sugar, all she could spare from their ration, scattered a few tablespoonsful of water over the mixture and, having wetted the rim to make a seal, closed the pie with another layer of pastry, careful first to position in the centre of the dish the china blackbird she used to keep the pie crust from collapsing, pressed down the edges of the pastry with her thumbs, and trimmed the pastry hangovers with a small, serrated knife. Finally, having pricked the pastry lid all over with a fork, she'd reversed the knife, and with the back of the blade indented the pastry edging at regular intervals, brushed milk over the cover for a glaze, then "into the oven with it."

And into the oven the pie went.

He loves watching her prepare food. Her movements are so deft, fluent, her fingers so lithe, nimble. She appears never to hurry but to have the skill of a magician, a proper one, unlike the old man who comes to entertain the school each Christmas and whose tricks are so clumsily managed that, to Miss Wheelock's embarrassment, everyone laughs at his performance. "Professor Dexter," he calls himself, but behind his back they all call him "Old Cack-Hand".

**

He has only just carried his food through from the kitchen when he hears his mother's key in the front door and a moment later she comes into the dining room.

"You look posh," he says.

Over a white blouse, buttoned high, she is wearing the dark-blue jacket she usually reserves for church, as she does the pleated grey skirt he'd watched her sponge and then iron the previous evening while she waited for the pie to bake. "Did it work?"

She had told him that today she would be "dolling herself up," as she put it, because she was due to be interviewed by the school headmistress about further teaching from September.

She smiles distractedly. "I think so."

He is puzzled. "Don't you want to teach?"

She sits facing him. "It isn't that. Peter. Something rather dreadful has happened."

His heart seems to stop. "Dad?"

"No, not Dad, thank goodness."

She reaches into the bag in which she carries books intended for her teaching work, draws out a newspaper. "You may as well know. It will be all round the village. Front-page news."

He stares at the newspaper, then at his mother. "Read it," she tells him. "It's today's *Chronicle*."

He looks at the newspaper spread in front of him, takes in the headline, **Grieving Mother Wants Questions Answered About Daughter's 'Mysterious' Death,** sees the name "Our Reporter, Simon Morgan," and reads on.

Rachel Perry, mother of deceased schoolgirl Lorna Perry, has spoken to the *Ashton Chronicle* about her distress over events surrounding her daughter's tragic death, which occurred earlier this year and was reported in our newspaper. Lorna, an evacuee from London, lived with a local couple, Mr and Mrs Arnold Herbert of Stonely. They had agreed to take the little girl in at the outbreak of hostilities. In May of this year, Lorna went missing. Despite a widespread search, her body lay undetected for up to forty-eight hours in Stonely woods, before it was discovered by a youth, a close neighbour of the dead girl. The police were called and the girl's body taken to Ashton General Hospital where a doctor certified the cause of death as resulting from a broken neck.

Inquest

As required by law, an inquest followed, and after the coroner had decreed that Lorna had fallen to her death from the roof of a disused hut in the woods, the body was released for burial, as the *Ashton Chronicle* reported at the time. The funeral took place at the Methodist church where Mrs and Mrs Herbert are regular worshippers. The girl's body was then taken to the local cemetery for private burial.

He looks up, sees his mother watching him intently. "This is all right, isn't it," he says.

"Read on," she tells him.

Mother's Grief

Because she had been bombed out of her home in London and was forced to live in temporary accommodation, Mrs Rachel Perry could not be reached by those who had the responsibility of caring for Lorna, nor by the relevant authorities. It was a matter of chance that a Police Notice reporting her daughter's death came to her attention. Mrs Perry at once journeyed to Ashton and contacted Mr and Mrs Herbert as well as others who had known Lorna. Speaking in a personal capacity, Mrs Perry says she regrets that certain lines of enquiry concerning her daughter's death have not been pursued.

"Lorna was an agile girl and tall for her age," she told our reporter. "The overhang of the roof from which she is said to have fallen is no more than two and a half feet from the ground and was regularly used by local children to jump from. Moreover," she went on, "why did it take so long to discover her body, given that it was in a spot often visited by locals – adults as well as children? And above all, why was her grave desecrated?" This last is a reference to the fact that the temporary wooden cross marking Lorna's grave has indeed been defaced, her name having been scratched out with some sort of implement. "When I asked local people about this," she concluded, "I received no replies. It is as though a wall of silence has been built around my daughter's death. But I want answers."

No Answers

Mrs Perry, who is for the time being living and working in the village of Stonely, would be pleased to hear from anyone with information that may help her. The police say they have no plans to reopen the enquiry into the cause of Lorna Perry's death, and locals whom this reporter has approached have declined to be interviewed, including the mother of the youth, Keith Bailey, who made the discovery of Lorna's body. Mrs Bailey also made clear that her son did not wish to be approached by the press. Mrs Perry can be contacted through this newspaper, or at her place of work, the Crown and Anchor, Stonely.

He finishes his reading, looks at his mother enquiringly. The adult Peter Howard will have good reason to understand the ways of journalists, their innuendos, the half and quarter lies that can ruin a reputation, even destroy a life. But now he is merely puzzled. Why is his mother so troubled by the report?

"What that's done is to put Keith in the firing line." She pulls the newspaper toward her and reads, "'Mrs Bailey made clear that her son did not wish to be approached by the press.' As though the poor lad – the 'close neighbour' – has something to hide. And his mother, too. She'll be horrified."

***

As she is.

Nor is she the only one. Later that evening, when he comes in from a lengthy session of cricket with Ronnie, he finds a meeting in progress in their front room. As well as his mother and Mrs Bailey, who are sitting on upright chairs, there is a third woman, Sally Parsons, occupying a place on the sofa.

"Hello, Peter," the last of these says, as he pokes his head round the door. "Don't look so amazed. I'm not a ghost. I got back from Cornwall late this afternoon. Your mother will tell you all about it."

Meaning that he should withdraw and let them get on with their discussion.

So he does.

But when, half an hour later, his mother breaks off from the meeting to run upstairs and wish him goodnight, he asks "What's happening?" and then, "How did Mrs Parsons come to be here?" Sally Parsons has, he is told, been intending to return to Stonely as soon as she could leave the twins, there being so much left to do before she can quit her house. No, she'd not had wind of the piece in the *Chronicle*, but she feels, with the rest of them, that Rachel Perry is … and here his mother pauses before blurting out … "She's a menace, that woman. And we're having a council of war. Trying to decide how best to deal with her. Something has to be done."

And with that she is away and he hears her run swiftly downstairs to rejoin the others.

Deal with her? Deal with Rachel Perry? What does his mother mean?

He will have to ask her in the morning.

How long the meeting goes on he can't be sure, but for a long time he can hear the murmur of their voices in the room below.

18

"Aye up," Ronnie says, "there's Keith."

The first week of their school holidays and they have just returned from Ashton where, among school friends and others of their own age, they spent the morning watching an Abbott and Costello film. Watching rather than listening to, because the soundtrack was rendered largely inaudible by an unceasing chorus of cries and yells, although the hubbub had been temporarily silenced when the film jerked to a halt and the cinema manager, in black-and-white suit and black bow tie, strutted down to the front of the auditorium. The film would only recommence, he announced, if and when they shut up. Meanwhile, behind him, the action lurched unaccountably back to life, and Abbott, dressed as a marching-band musician strapped into a vast bass drum and therefore unable to see where he was going, made steady progress toward a large manhole into which, and to the accompaniment of the audience's joyous approval, he disappeared.

Now, early in the afternoon, as they walk down to the woods, Peter acts out Abbott's bass-drummer's strut, while Ronnie, ahead of him, swings his arms in swaggering pretence of the drum major, as comprehensively failing to catch a stick he hurls into the air as had Costello the gleaming baton which arrowed down onto a hapless bandsman's head.

But then Ronnie, bending to retrieve his stick, draws Peter's attention to the figure shambling into view.

It stops, begins to turn away, then, as though unable to escape, stands by the hedge at the field bottom, waiting for their approach.

As they come up to him, Keith ducks his head and swings a shoulder round so that they can't see his face.

"Aye up, Keith," Ronnie says. "Awright?"

Keith grunts.

"Summat doin'?"

No answer.

"Have you been to the hut?" Peter asks.

It's where the two of them are heading. Until now, the death of

Lorna May has, for all their bravado, prevented either from taking turns at jumping off the overhang from which she fell. "Go on, don't be so mardy," Ronnie had taunted Peter a few days earlier when they'd been down there, "don't be so bleddy nesh. We've done it often enough. It's easy."

"All right," Peter said, gazing at the dilapidated structure, "you go first."

But Ronnie wouldn't.

Of course it wasn't dangerous, and yet …

But this afternoon, as they walk down to the woods, they vow to each other that they will not only once more clamber up onto the gapped roof, but that they'll jump off. "Red berets," Ronnie says, "landin' in enemy territory," though now that the tall grass has been flattened by the feet of so many visitors who have come to inspect the spot where the evacuee died, they can no longer wriggle through the undergrowth on their stomachs, intent on taking Fritz by surprise.

Ronnie edges round, trying to peer into Keith's face.

"Bloody 'ell, Keith. What's 'appened?"

There is concern as well as surprise in the words. "'Ow'd you come by all that?"

Then, more gently, "Show Peter. 'Ee ain't gonna 'urt you."

Slowly, Keith raises his head and Peter sees the heavy bruising round his eyes, the blood crusting below his nostrils, the split lip.

A thrill of fear goes through him. Perhaps there *is* some force at work here, some evil spirit that rouses itself to maim and, even, kill.

But this is followed by another thought.

He looks at Keith's stained blue overalls, the cracked leather shoes.

"Shouldn't you be at work?" he asks.

Keith hangs his head but says nothing.

"Yeh," Ronnie says, not unkindly, "it's Friday, this is, Keith. You ain't due for a day off yet, not by my way of reckoning."

All around them are the deep musty smells of grasses, cow parsley, Queen Anne's lace, the rusty chirr of grasshoppers, the movements of ragged-looking butterflies.

But Keith's face, the blood and ugly bruising, his bent, dejected stance, take the warmth out of the day.

"I'm not goin' back to work," Keith says, and with that he turns and begins to plod along the path toward the fields and his home.

***

That meeting puts an end to their plans. In silent agreement they take a path round the woods that brings them to the spinney. This afternoon they have it to themselves. Whistling Billy's tin bath is in its usual place under the hedge, sacking stretched across it, but there are undisturbed leaves strewn over the sacking and a spider has stitched a web between one frayed corner and a hedge twig.

The tramp, it seems, has been gone for some time.

"Reckon the gyppos put a spell on the 'ut?" Ronnie asks.

Peter does not answer.

"Or maybe the ghost of Lorna May," Ronnie says. "Perhaps she's 'aunting the place."

***

And when, many years later, Peter thinks back to the summer of 1945, it occurs to him that Ronnie had in a way been right. The unappeased spirit of the girl *was* haunting the woods. And more than the woods, if it came to that. Something bad had happened, something which his adult, rational mind didn't want to call evil, but for which he struggled to find a word that would make sense of what took possession of people in Ashton and Stonely at that time. You could say that some malevolent power had been set loose. But you could as well say that this was not confined to a small, rural area of the English Midlands, any more than it was a unique phenomenon of the time when wickedness – Auschwitz, Babi Yar, Hiroshima – provided all the evidence anyone could require of the insufficiency, the frailty, of light, warmth, kindness, against the world of night. How weak and little is the light. Let not our naïve labours have been in vain. Who, though, is to reward these labours, to justify them, to vindicate them? Are they bound to be naïve? Would you abandon them if you knew more? Maybe, maybe not. Even if the world should end tomorrow, I would still plant my apple tree.

***

Peter arrives home for tea, planning to tell his mother about the meeting with Keith. But she already knows.

"He was attacked by workmates," she says. "Maureen knew

135

something was wrong when she found he hadn't been home for his dinner. She found him lurking in the garden, bloody and bruised, and managed to drag the story out of him."

Mrs Bailey, it appeared, who had been out on several duty calls, left Keith's food waiting for him, only to discover it still there, untouched, when she arrived home in the middle of the afternoon, which, Peter thinks, would have been not long after he and Ronnie had encountered Keith at the edge of the woods.

"What were you doing down there?" she asks suspiciously.

"A walk. We didn't go to the hut."

He is grateful that he doesn't have to lie. "We met Keith before we got into the woods. He'd been in a fight."

Her voice shaking with sudden anger, his mother bursts out, "That damned woman. And that stupid, *stupid* man."

"Man?"

"That journalist. Look at what he's done."

She reaches down beside her chair, picked up a newspaper, and held it up.

The Ashton Chronicle.

"What's his name." She stares hard at the front page, then hurls it down in disgust. "Morgan, that's it."

Once more retrieving the paper from the floor beside her, she looks at it as she says, "not content with last week's story about Lorna May, he's now written a follow-up. He's claiming that '*members of the public*' – unnamed of course – are '*demanding that the police reopen their inquiries into the little girl's mysterious death*' as he calls it. *And* he singles poor Keith out. 'The person who claims to have found the body.'"

She jumps up from her chair, the newspaper clutched in her hands as though she wants to rip it to shreds.

"Goodness only know where this will all end," she says, coming to stand beside him as he sits over his tea.

He is shocked, not merely by the depth of her anger, but by her words. "Where will what end?"

"You can't simply put this back in its box, you know." A deep breath, then, "Sorry, Peter. I don't mean to be angry with you."

"I don't mind," he says, though he does.

"Ah, my love." There is a wealth of sadness in the way she says the words.

She retreats to her hearthside chair, sits, reaches for her cigarettes, trying to smile at him, though there is no trace of happiness in her smile.

Tilting her head back as she exhales the smoke, she says, as if to herself, "You'd have thought they'd have had more sense. And if *they* hadn't then you'd have thought someone would have intervened. Damned bullies." Her voice is thick with anger.

"Bullies?"

"What else can you call them? The men who work at Hoskins. Those of them who go to the pub for a pint on Friday dinner time. This time apparently they took Keith with them. They were planning to celebrate someone's birthday, so he told his mother. Some celebration!"

She pauses, draws deeply on her cigarette, then stubs it out, twisting until the paper bursts and tobacco shreds spill across the ashtray.

"No doubt Madam Perry let them know what *she* thought about the piece in the *Chronicle*. I gather she made sure to read it out to them, probably after they'd had more than enough to drink. You can just see her drawing attention to Keith's name, can't you, then mentioning her suspicions … And, oh, you can guess the rest."

Peter says, hesitantly, "But it doesn't make sense. If Keith … " – he is going to say "killed her, Lorna May, " but changes it to – "hurt her, well, he wouldn't have wanted anyone to discover her body, would he?"

His mother, who has been staring at the carpet, lifts her head. "Of course, he wouldn't. And as for 'interfering' with her, which is apparently what at least one of the men who laid into him accused the lad of doing, it's unthinkable. 'Interfering.' It's the kind of thing she *would* say. But we know, don't we, that Keith wouldn't harm anyone."

He looks at her, realises she is studying his face, expecting him to agree. Is she remembering, as he suddenly is, an occasion the previous year, wintertime, when, as he came home from school, he stood outside his gate to watch the sunset spread a deep crimson flush across the darkening sky.

Keith, who had been ambling up the road, stopped beside Peter and followed the direction in which he was staring.

"What d'you reckon?" he asked. His voice is full of awe, or was it dread.

"It looks as if the sky's on fire," Peter told him.

"It's a bomb, that is. The Germans are bombing Ashton."

Thinking Keith was joking, Peter laughed.

The next moment, Keith's swung fist caught Peter a glancing blow on his mouth. "Don't you go laughing at me," he said, his face fixed in an angry grimace, his teeth set. Then he lumbered away to his own house.

As she smoothed Vaseline into Peter's cut lip, his mother said, "We'll not let Maureen – Mrs Bailey – hear about this. She has enough to worry about. There." She examined the lip. "It's a bit swollen but you'll live," she said, before adding that "poor Keith", as she called him, would by now be feeling sorry for what he'd done. "He means no harm. He probably thought you were mocking him."

Lorna May made mock of Keith, he thinks now, but doesn't say. He does, though, remind his mother that he and Ronnie had seen Keith coming up from the woods the day before Lorna May's body was discovered.

"I know," she says, sighing. "That *is* awkward, I admit. It could be very awkward if anyone ever finds out about that and wants to make something of it."

***

Someone does.

There is rain at the weekend. Scurrying with his mother to the village shops on Saturday morning, Peter catches a glimpse of Rachel Perry swabbing down the front steps of the Crown and Anchor. She gives no sign of having noticed them, although from the resolute way his mother stares ahead Peter is pretty sure the two women have caught sight of one another. Risking a backward glance, he sees that Lorna May's mother is resting on her knees, staring after them. Too far away to see the expression on her face, he thinks she may be smiling.

An hour later, when they return in a lashing squall, wet, depressed by the prospect of spending the weekend indoors, they find Ronnie waiting for them, sheltering in the porch.

"Cricket's been cancelled," Peter tells his friend. A blackboard propped outside the village ground had announced that the afternoon's match against Earl Shilton would not now take place.

"I could 'ave towd you that." Ronnie is disconsolate.

As she pushes her key into the front-door lock, Peter's mother says, "Are you on your own, Ronnie?"

Peter knows that his friend has been left with his gran while his own mother is away for the weekend.

Ronnie nods. "But that ain't it," he says.

She pushes the door open. "Well, let's all get in out of the rain."

In the small kitchen, watching Peter towel his hair as she pours them both glasses of water, Ronnie says, "That bloke from the *Chronicle.*"

Pausing in the act of stowing the vegetables she and Peter have carried home, his mother says, sharply, "What of him?"

"He come to my 'ouse this morning. With another bloke. Another on 'em."

She stares at him. "Another reporter?"

And when he says yes, she demands to know more. "What did he want. What did *they* want? And who was this other reporter? Did he say?"

"Calls himself Lewis Grant. Wrote it down for me. And they give me this." And Ronnie digs a hand into the pocket of his shorts, then, turning his fist palm upward, he opens it to reveal a half-crown wrapped in a scrap of paper.

She is stock-still, eying him. "Why should they do that?"

"Asked me what I knew about the weekend Lorna May went missing. I said I'd already towd Sergeant Lock-up and the officer at Ashton all I know – same as Peter."

He drinks some water.

She reaches down into a cupboard, comes up with the biscuit tin, offers ginger-nuts to them both.

"And that satisfied them?"

"They said if I remembered owt else to let 'em know. I'd find 'em at the newspaper place in Ashton."

"I wonder what they were really after," she says, her voice troubled, her expression wary. "Were they planning to see anyone else, did they say?"

"Dunno. They come in a car. The other bloke was driving. Lewis Grant. Said 'e was from the *Morning News.* According to my gran that's a proper newspaper. Gets all over England."

Peter sees the agitation on his mother's face. "You boys stay here," she says. "I'm going to run up to Maureen's. She needs to know about this new reporter who's sniffing around. If she hasn't already discovered."

"She ain't there," Ronnie says. "She went off on 'er bike a bit ago.

P'raps they seen 'er before they come to our 'ouse. They'd been talkin' to the 'erberts, that's for sure."

"You know that?"

"That's why they come across to our 'ouse. Mrs 'erbert towd 'em Peter and me 'ad been around when Lorna May went missin' and that we knew what was goin' off."

"Ronnie, what do you mean?"

He flinches, taken aback by her sudden vehemence.

"You know, Mrs 'oward. Keith findin' Lorna May on Sunday after he'd missed seein' 'er the day before." He is trying to order his words, wanting, Peter knows, to placate her, and at the same time determined to report accurately all he'd said to the two men. "And the 'erberts not bein' at 'ome because they'd gone to London to look for 'er. Lorna May."

He pauses once more. "And all the rest."

But it isn't the rest that concerns her.

Nor, Peter realises, growing suddenly wise, will that be what interests the man from the *Morning News*.

19

Ronnie is right.

Maureen Bailey is not at home, Peter's mother reports when she returns from a brief visit to her neighbour's.

"I had to speak to Keith through the letter-box," she tells the expectant boys. "And even that took some doing."

She watches them as they sit at the table, counting cigarette cards, of which Ronnie holds by far the larger number, before she adds, "He wouldn't open the door. He told me his mum had made him promise not to let anyone in while she was away."

"He doesn't want anyone to see his face," Peter suggests.

"I think it's more than that."

She goes to the French windows, stands looking out at the garden, then swiftly turns back to them.

To Ronnie she says, "You don't know whether those men managed to speak to her?"

"Dunno Mrs 'oward." Still rattled by her earlier display of anger, Ronnie is wary of displeasing her again. "The 'erberts might know."

"Yes," she says, moving toward the door, "of course. Why didn't I think of that. I ought to go across the road and ask them."

Then, pausing on the threshold of the dining-room to smile at Ronnie, she says, "I'm sorry for snapping at you."

"That's awright," Ronnie says graciously.

"Mrs Bailey and Keith." She raises her hands in a gesture that is both apology and explanation. "I'm worried for both of them," she says

"What do you want to ask the Herberts?" Peter asks her.

Hand on the door knob, she shakes her head, mutters some words he doesn't catch.

He looks at Ronnie enquiringly, but his friend hasn't understood her either.

"Sorry, Mum, I couldn't hear."

The words coming out in a rush. "I need to ask them if they know whether those men have talked to Maureen, whether she knows that they're here making trouble for Keith."

"Is that what they're doing?"

"Oh, Peter, yes," she says. "*Of course* that's what they're doing." Then, with a tight smile, "*They* may not see it like that." An abrupt shake of the head. "They've probably convinced themselves that they're simply in pursuit of the truth."

She comes back to the table, puts a hand on his shoulder. "That's how they – that's how reporters – like to dress up what they do. But believe me, they mean trouble, no doubt about it."

She looks across at where Ronnie is setting out his teams of cards.

"Half-a-crown's a lot of money," she says.

"I never towd 'em owt," Ronnie says, looking up.

"I wouldn't blame you," she says.

"I didn't, though."

"Good." She is about to leave the room when there is a knock on the front door.

"I'll deal with this," she says, over her shoulder. "You two stay here. And if it's those men – those reporters … "

A moment later they hear the door being opened and Sally Parsons' voice. "Good heavens, Kay, you look as though you want to brain me. I'm not a Kraut, you know. As always, I come in peace." A laugh follows, more perhaps a nervous exhalation of breath.

His mother's voice then. "Sally. Yes, friend, not foe. I'm glad you're here, *very* glad. There's something I need to tell you."

And the boys hear the women going into the front room and its door firmly closing behind them.

"What's goin' off now?"

Ronnie looks enquiringly at Peter, who himself wonders at the resumed friendship between his mother and Mrs Parsons. The frosty exchanges of earlier weeks have melted into a new warmth.

Having pocketed his cigarette cards, he goes to stand at the French window.

"It's stopped raining."

"So?" Ronnie is still shuffling his own cards into order.

"So let's go out."

As he and Ronnie make for the front door, Peter calls out a farewell to his mother, then wrenches open the front door.

Hand raised, about to knock, Maureen Bailey stands in the porch.

"Is your mum in?" The words come in an urgent rush.

"In the front room. Mrs Parsons is with her."

From behind him, his mother says, "Maureen, I thought I heard your voice. Sally is here, come and join us."

Mrs Bailey, eyes enlarged and glittering behind her spectacles, has already stepped beyond him.

"Kay," she says, her voice scarcely under control. "My god, listen to this."

***

What Peter himself hears from his mother as they sit at tea is, he realises, by no means a full account of all that has been going on, but as much as he needs to know. Mrs Bailey had been in when the two men – Morgan and the reporter from the *News*, Lewis Grant – called, and in no time she guessed that their questions to her were prompted by Rachel Perry. Rachel Perry believes that Keith is responsible for her daughter's death, and the reporters let slip – accidentally on purpose – that she is building a strong case to take to the police.

"I know the *Chronicle* said that the police had no plans to reopen enquiries into the death," Peter's mother now tells him, "but Rachel Perry's been allowed to see the medical report about her daughter, which says that Lorna May could have been dead for as long as forty-eight hours before her body was discovered."

Peter swallows the last of a rock cake.

"Two days," he says, thinking about it. "So Lorna May could have been lying dead even before Mrs Herbert asked me whether I'd seen her."

"Or soon after. Or, of course, she could have died later that day. The report isn't precise. 'Could have been dead for as long as forty-eight hours' doesn't mean that the death *had* to have occurred on Friday. It could even have been a day later."

"On Saturday?"

"Exactly."

He doesn't at first realise why she is staring at him.

Then he does. "Oh," he says. "You mean when Ronnie and I saw Keith coming up the fields on Saturday afternoon … " He stops, tries again. "You think … " And again he stops.

"It isn't what *I* think," she says, head now lowered, held between hands whose elbows rest either side of her empty plate. "It's what anyone else may think."

"But what difference does it make?"

Over her shoulder he notices raindrops splattering against the

French windows, hears a distant rumble of thunder, a sound that now, unaccountably, reminds him of the noise made by the steamroller Hans drove slowly backward and forward as he flattened rock into hardcore.

Hans. Hans running up the road, Hans reaching to touch the scratch he claims isn't there. But then, he thinks, the defaced name on the wooden cross. That couldn't have been the German's doing.

"This is a terrible mess," his mother says, standing. She looks at him, long and hard. "Now that you know so much, I think you need to hear what happened when Maureen went to confront Rachel Perry."

She moves toward the door. "I'll put more water in this pot," she says, then, matter of factly, "and while I'm doing that you can read your dad's latest – here."

She fishes out from her cardigan some sheets of paper, which she inspects before retaining the last one, hands him the rest, and he bends to his father's hand-written letter.

"So Dad'll be home by the end of the year," Peter remarks as some minutes later she comes back in carrying the refilled teapot.

"Fingers crossed he will. The men are obviously bored out of their wits with nothing to do."

"He says he's giving drawing lessons."

She pours herself a cup of tea. "To the few who are interested." She looks at him, says semi-seriously, "The War Office will have a mutiny on their hands if they don't get a move on. An army with no one to fight. It's asking for trouble."

"You said you'd tell me about Mrs Bailey's going to see Rachel Perry."

"So I did. Sorry. It was after that pair of scandalmongers had left her. Which wasn't before they'd threatened the poor woman, told her if she didn't let them speak to Keith they would go with Rachel Perry to 'lay certain facts before the police.' Goodness knows what 'facts' they have. But it's easy to see what they're up to. Trying to frighten Maureen into agreeing to let them get at her son."

"Was Keith there? Was he in the room?"

"No. She'd taken the precaution of bundling him out of the way before she let them in, but she thinks he must have overheard some of what was said. According to his mother the lad is in a dreadful state, thinks he's going to be arrested for … Well, I don't know what. And what Maureen has done won't, I'm afraid, help matters."

Because as soon as the men left her, she now explains, and after Mrs Bailey had spent some time trying to calm Keith and told him that on no account was he to answer the door to anyone while she was gone, she got on her bike and pedalled up to the village.

Needless to say, she found Rachel Perry leaning over the back bar at the Crown and Anchor deep in conversation with Morgan and Grant. They broke off as soon as she appeared, and, so Maureen Bailey claimed, the two men looked like little boys caught with their fingers in the sweet jar. Not Rachel Perry, though. "'Bold as brass,' according to Maureen, wanting to know whether she'd come for a drink or to apologise for her son."

At which, Mrs Bailey had, so his mother says, admitted falling into a rage, telling Rachel Perry that she was a liar and that Sally Parsons had even written to "warn Maureen and me about her poison tongue."

She pauses, looks at Peter. "Sally and I, as I suspect you realise, haven't been getting on all that well, although skies are clearing. Sally seems to be getting over whatever was making her difficult. As a result I think she may have said something to Rachel Perry about the pair of us having patched up our friendship and Rachel Perry took that as an incentive to rip it up again. She has that kind of cunning about her. Or do I mean spite? Say something nasty about me and worm her way into Sally's good books. And why stop at me, when there's my friend Maureen Bailey? Another name to blacken. Mother to a child killer."

Again she pauses, this time for breath.

"I wish Maureen hadn't blurted it out, though. As it was, the Perry woman told Maureen that Sally herself was a liar – and worse." A pause. "Oh, you may as well know. Sally is apparently someone who chases after anything in trousers."

He doesn't really understand and anyway he isn't interested.

"But why did she want to be nasty about you?"

"She's a nasty piece of work. And she may have decided that her welcome here was lacking in … well, in the red-carpet treatment. No offering her the fat of the land."

"No begging Farmer Connolly for a special treat."

She looks at him, eyebrow raised.

"I'd forgotten that," she says. Then, dismissing it with a wave of her hand, she says with an angry little laugh, "But she smoked enough of my cigarettes."

Saying which, she reaches for her packet.

"You'd better hear the rest of what Maureen told Sally and me," she says. "Poor Peter. In your dad's absence you'll have to be the sounding board."

There is a good deal he has to hear from a mother who, as an adult he comes to understand, must, despite her friendship with Mrs Bailey, have experienced days and weeks of lonely endurance, and who inevitably turned to a son not surprisingly unable to intuit all her frustrations, sexual, social, emotional, though what she tells him on this occasion both alarms and intrigues him.

Grant, the man from the *News*, had apparently intervened between the two women. He gave Maureen Bailey details of the case he and Morgan were beginning to build and which they planned to publish at the time they allowed the police access to their 'findings'.

This was what they intended to say. That Lorna Perry was unhappy at the Herberts, that Mrs Herbert, while appearing to be under the thumb of her husband, made the evacuee's life miserable by treating her as a dogsbody, that as a result, and as some villagers could vouch for, Lorna Perry sometimes ran away, that on the Friday night of the weekend when her dead body was discovered in the woods she must have decided to hide in the hut outside which she was found, that Keith discovered her there the next day, Saturday, that something she said or did enraged him and prompted him to assault her, and that in what followed her neck was somehow broken. Keith then panicked, left her in the woods, and, when he had worked out some sort of a story, returned the next day, and claimed only then to have stumbled across the body.

"Of course," his mother says, draining her teacup, "Sally and I tried to reassure Maureen they'd never dare to put all that into print, and that even if they took their story to the police they'd be told it would never stand up in a court of law. Unfortunately, poor Maureen has convinced herself that Keith will be arrested and – who knows what will come of it all?"

When she speaks next, her voice is full of foreboding. "I'm afraid that matters are getting out of control."

She turns, looks out at the rain, then back to her son.

He says. "What about Lorna May's name?"

She frowns at him, then, realising what he is referring to, says with a shrug that is half-despair, half-contempt, "Oh, easy enough to claim that Keith could have gone down any time and scraped away at it."

"But why?"

"You mean how would the reporters explain his actions? Easy. Someone not in his right mind trying to pretend that his victim never existed. Or a guilty man, who being half crazy, thinks that in wiping away Lorna May's name he's wiping away his guilt." A thin smile. "Any twopenny halfpenny mind-reader could give you a plausible explanation for why *that* was done." Her face resumes its brooding expression. "All of them pointing to Keith's guilt."

"*You* don't believe he did it, do you?"

She looks at him, opens her mouth to speak, then slowly, silently shakes her head, though the expression in her eyes suggests far less certainty.

PART FOUR

20

Keith doesn't go back to work.

On Monday, Peter and Ronnie come upon him at the bottom end of Connolly's field, where, beyond the stile, the path to the woods begins. Sullen and silent, he is propped against the stile-post as they approach, looking away but plainly alert to their presence, almost as though he is on guard, intent on denying them the right of way.

"Aye up, Keith," Ronnie says, determinedly cheerful. "Good weather fer sunbathin', this is."

Keith mutters something they can't understand.

"Come again," Ronnie says, taking a step forward.

Still not looking at them, Keith says, audibly this time, "I said 'Keep off.'"

"Keep off what? Can't keep off the grass, Keith. There ain't nowt but grass where we are. Look for yersen." And Ronnie swings an arm expansively to indicate the length and breadth of the meadow as well as the grassy sides of the path where Keith stands.

"Keep *off* me, will yer."

The words are followed by a choking sound. Peter and Ronnie look at each other. They've been planning on going into the woods, drawn yet again to the hut and the mystery of Lorna May's death; but Keith's brooding presence rules that out.

Shrugging, baffled, defeated of their purpose, they turn and walk back up to the top of the meadow, following the imprint their feet have made in dew-wet grass as they'd sauntered down to the lonely figure against the stile.

When they turn for a look before exiting to the road, they see him, in his sweater and baggy grey trousers, still propped immovably against the stile-post, head slumped between his shoulders.

It's the same the next day, and then, on Wednesday, when they decide to walk down to the spinney to see whether Whistling Billy has returned, Keith comes shambling up the road toward them.

They are still some distance away when he catches sight of the boys. He steps out into the road.

But he hasn't looked behind him and nearly goes under the

wheels of the baker's van whose driver blares his horn as he brakes and skids to a halt. Taking no notice of the man's furious yells, Keith reaches the far side of the road and continues his clumsy progress, averting his head in response to Ronnie's cry of "nearly got yersen squashed then, Keith. Could've ended up like strawberry jam."

***

That afternoon, over tea, Peter tells his mother about Keith. "He's not at work. We've seen him down the bottom of Connolly's field, and this morning when he saw us coming he dodged across to the other side of the road and nearly got run over."

"Poor Keith," she says. "I know his mother hopes he'll go back to Hoskins once the bruising has gone."

"What do you think?"

She lifts troubled eyes to his. "I hope she's right. But … " She leaves the sentence unfinished. "I'm afraid he's made enemies in the village."

"Will the police come here again? Do you think they'll want to ask Keith more questions?"

"I hope not. But his mother's worried about that. And if I were in her shoes, I'd be worried too."

She stops there.

"Why?"

She looks away, surveying the carpet as she says, "Who knows what he might say."

She looks up then. "In tight spots people sometimes blurt out things they don't mean, 'incriminate themselves', as crime reporters love to say, and given Keith's state of mind there's no knowing what he might or might not let slip. Even someone as innocent as Keith could say something that will point in the wrong direction."

Let slip, he thinks. *Innocent*. What can she mean? He studies his mother's face. He is beginning to suspect that she fears Keith knows something about Lorna May's death the youth hasn't let on. The suspicion becomes a thrill of guilty excitement, something to share with Ronnie if not with her.

And yet. Is it likely that Keith could harbour secrets, let alone guilty secrets? He doesn't think so. But then …

***

When Peter Howard, beginning to scratch a living as a free-lance writer, makes it his business to recall all he can of the summer of nineteen forty-five, he sets himself to jot down notes about that time. Is there enough for a story? He thinks there is. But how to explain the sequence of events that led to a conclusion which even now, so long after they occurred, leaves him bewildered, grieving, angry, too, over the follies of so many who were involved.And as he broods over that question, so, inevitably, the memory of his mother's anxious insistence on Keith's "innocence" comes back to him.

Keith's "innocence." He knows now as he hadn't then known that when his mother stressed the word, as she often did, she didn't so much mean that Keith was guileless as that he was lacking in the wit to keep out of trouble. Not ingenuous but simple. Simple Keith. And thinking that, he realises yet again the extent to which Keith's presumed guilt was, as that summer progressed, increasingly fixed in people's minds.

Keith might not have intended to kill Lorna May but that didn't mean he hadn't in some way been the cause of her death. So at least the villagers had decided, some of them, prompted by Rachel Perry, that nasty piece of work, as his mother had called her, rock-hard certain that Keith Bailey was a killer.

He makes more notes then lays them aside and turns to other work. Four thousand words his agent has secured him for a colour supplement feature on a newly fashionable novelist, Jed Berkely, whose three books Peter has read with decreasing attention. They are, he is sure, essentially trashy. The loves, lusts and money-laundering of metropolitan high-livers mostly out of their minds on designer drugs and cocktails with names more suited to tropical fish. His agent has urged caution. "Tickle him with the dagger, don't shove it between his ribs."

But the evening after he has talked to his agent, sitting in a local pub with a friend of his, a doctor, he finds himself talking about Lorna May's death. He explains the sequence of events, the discovery of the girl's body, and asks, could it have been an accident?

"Just about possible," his friend says.

"You could fall from a height of two or three feet and break your neck?"

"You could. You could die simply by falling over. It's been known. But it's less likely when you're young. The bones are still green, they bend. Why are you so interested?"

Peter repeats in more detail the facts as far as he can remember them.

When he finishes, the doctor says, "Open verdict, that's as far as a coroner could go with that. If there was neither incriminating evidence nor some sort of confession I don't see anyone could know exactly how she died. You might have your suspicions, but suspicions are like conspiracy theories. Easy to come by, bloody hard to prove. Now, if there were physical signs – bruising round the neck, evidence of a struggle – then you might want to order a criminal enquiry. *Was* there anything like that?"

Peter tries to recall. Was there? No, he doesn't think so, but then neither the doctor who'd been summoned nor the police who'd carried out the investigation had cause to think there was anything suspicious about the girl's death. Added to which, it was 1945, Victory in Europe had just been celebrated, people were desperate to get the war behind them, to return to peacetime ways, and who, to be honest, was going to bother overmuch at the death of one stroppy girl evacuee?

"That's pretty brutal," his friend says. "Still, going by what you tell me, I'd say the coroner was right to put her death down to natural causes."

It is only later, after he's left the pub and as he walks the short distance to his flat, that Peter finds himself remembering the scratch he'd seen on the cheek of the German POW. Hans. Hans of Hamburg. Hans the footballer. That scratch could, couldn't it, have been made by a girl fighting for her life? In the days following the discovery of Lorna May's death, he'd not allowed himself to consider that possibility, or rather he thinks he'd not wanted to confront it, but now, all these years later, it once more surfaces. And as it bobs up so do the doubts. The mysterious attack on the girl's name. Who on earth was responsible for that? Not Hans, that much was certain. He'd already gone from the village. So who?

And as he remembers that, yet another memory comes and with it, in a trice, the realisation of who was almost certainly responsible for defacing the wooden cross, and he is profoundly glad that he hasn't told his friend about the incident which united the village in its belief that Keith Bailey was a killer.

Indoors, he draws toward him the notes he'd earlier that day pushed aside. *What do I really know?* he writes. Then, crossing the words out, he writes beside them, *How do I make sense of what I remember?*

21

On Friday morning, Peter and his mother catch the bus into Ashton.

The previous evening he'd sat at table with her as she went through her ration book reckoning up her clothing coupons, then shook out from an old cake tin the metal disks which, put into separate piles of brown and silvery-grey, represented her Co-op savings, before she decided that, yes, she had enough coupons and disks to buy a dress for herself and, for him, a coat to replace the one he'd grown so far out of that, as she said, laughing, "It really does fit you to a T. Time for one that lets your arms swing free."

In the event, she can find no dress that suits her. Ashton's high street shops, including the Co-op store on which she'd set her hopes, are more or less empty of what, as they sit in a British Restaurant eating without pleasure heaps of powdered potato – *Pom* it's called – and baked beans, she refers to as anything wearable, let alone bearable.

"Never mind," she says, with determined gaiety, brown eyes aglow. "We've got you a raincoat, and now the war's over the shops will soon be full again. You wait. By the time dad gets home I'll be decked out like the Queen of Sheba."

They themselves are home soon after midday.

As they step down from the bus stop not far below their house, a grim-faced Mrs Herbert emerges from her bungalow. She is dressed in what his mother calls her "battle-uniform," the black coat and hat worn for Sunday attendance at Methodist church. His mother is preparing to speak, when, with no more than a curt nod in response to her friendly wave, Mrs Herbert crosses the road in front of them and marches up Mrs Bailey's drive.

"Goodness," his mother says as they turn into their own gate. "She doesn't look as if on pleasure bent. I hope nothing's wrong."

But there is.

***

Because that afternoon, when he comes in for his tea, he finds Maureen Bailey sitting opposite his mother in the dining-room. The two women, who are talking in urgent near-whispers, make no attempt to break off their conversation as he pushes open the door. Mrs. Bailey does no more than glance briefly in his direction before she carries on with what she is telling his mother.

"Do you mind Peter hearing this?" his mother says across the stream of her visitor's words.

"Oh, I expect it will soon be all round the village," Mrs Bailey says. Shoulders slumped, she looks utterly dejected.

"Mrs Herbert has been complaining about Keith's mooning about the cemetery," his mother says, as he takes his place at table. "Apparently she found him there this morning when she and Rachel Perry went to put some flowers on the grave."

Mrs Bailey says, "My son's at a loose end, everybody knows that. I can't get him to go back to the factory. He won't go, even though I've had a letter of apology from the manager, promising that there'll be no repeat of last week's bullying."

Straightening her back, she says, "Those *fools*. First of all choosing to swallow rumour and innuendo, and then going for Keith the way they did. He's terrified of them."

"No wonder." His mother reaches out a hand to touch her friend's arm.

"When Keith got this job I thought it would do him so much good. He was thrilled to have it. But now... "

She takes off her spectacles, peers at them, then rubs them on her cardigan sleeve. Without them, her eyes look naked. "What's the *matter* with people! Why can't they see that Keith ... "

She puts her spectacles back on and now her stare is one of bewildered helplessness.

"What's the matter with people?" she repeats dully.

Peter says, "We met Keith coming up the road yesterday morning. Ronnie thought he might have been to see if Whistling Billy was back, but perhaps he'd been down to the cemetery."

He doesn't quite know why he's offered this information, perhaps to suggest that Keith's movements are nothing unusual, his behaviour in no sense odd. Though of course, it is.

Mrs Bailey says, her voice now urgent with exasperated anger, "What does it matter *where* he goes to be on his own. He simply wants to be out of harm's way, he's not looking for trouble."

"But Mrs Herbert obviously now thinks it could have been Keith who tried to deface Lorna May's name," his mother tells Peter.

"And she's as good as warning me against letting him go near the cemetery. In case he repeats his act of 'interfering' with the girl's cross."

So that's it. That's why Mrs Herbert paid her visit to the Baileys.

"Did she actually make that accusation?" his mother asks.

"She didn't go that far. But it was what she was thinking. No doubt Madam Perry urged her on."

She finishes her tea, stands, her nurse's uniform looking crumpled and, he thinks, as dishevelled as her hair.

"I'd better be getting back," she says. "Keith will be coming in soon, as though he's spent all day at the factory. I'll have to get him something to eat."

"Poor lad," his mother says. "And poor you," she adds.

Mrs Bailey manages a bare smile of acknowledgement, and precedes them along the hall; but pausing at the front door, she says wearily, "How on earth I'm going to explain to him he ought not to go into the cemetery again, I'm blessed if I know."

She opens the door, stands in the porch. "Well," she says, lifting her hands in a gesture that suggests a weary bafflement and yet resolve, "I suppose I'll find a way."

They wait until she has reached the bottom of their short drive and then his mother waves and closes the door.

22

"Look!"

VILLAGE HIT BY SECOND TRAGEDY

He takes the words in at a glance. "That didn't take long," he says.

"Oh, they had all yesterday to work on it."

Fresh home, his mother is dressed in what he thinks of as her teaching uniform, the dark blue jacket and grey skirt she habitually wears when she goes to give French tuition to the daughters of the bank manager she doesn't like. But it isn't so much the dress that holds his gaze, it is the expression on her face, in her eyes.

Though the effort to explain simple rules of French grammar to the manager's daughters amounts, she once told him, to a labour that would have defeated even Hercules, she also admits that she quite likes their bouncy candour, their untroubled confession as to the thickness of their own skulls. "You couldn't drive a six-inch nail into mine," one of them had told her, having failed for the umpteenth time to grasp the need for noun and adjective to agree. It isn't that which can explain her fury.

He looks back at the newspaper.

The Morning News. It is dated Monday, 30th July. This very day.

VILLAGE HIT BY SECOND TRAGEDY

Last Saturday, the small Leicestershire village of Stonely was coming to terms with the second death in recent months of one of its younger inhabitants. First, as reported in the *Morning News*, came the unexplained death of eleven-year-old Lorna Perry, whose body was discovered in woodland below the village in early May. Cause of death was a broken neck and it was assumed the girl had fallen from the roof of a disused woodman's hut near where her body was found.

Now, another death has stunned this quiet village. The body of sixteen-year old Keith Bailey, who discovered the dead girl's body in May of this year, has been found lying beside one of the tracks in Ashton's marshalling yard.

Suicide or Misadventure?

The body was found by signalman Jack Knowlson early Sunday morning. According to Mr Knowlson, he was going on early duty when he at first saw what he thought was someone asleep beside one of the tracks. Speaking to our reporter, Knowlson, a married man with two children, said that as soon as he examined what he thought might be someone sleeping off the effects of the previous evening's over-indulgence he saw signs of massive injury to the head and face. Although the body was still warm, he could detect no signs of life. "I was shocked it could have happened so near to where I worked," Mr. Knowlson said. "He must have walked into the path of one of the shunters. There's a lot of activity in the yard both day and night. But we've got notices everywhere warning the public not to go near the tracks."

Mysterious

It seems that for whatever reason, Bailey chose to ignore the warnings. Jack Knowlson summoned aid and a doctor and ambulance were soon on the scene. Keith was taken to Ashton hospital where he was confirmed dead on arrival. One of the nurses on duty recognised the body as that of the son of Maureen Bailey, a district nurse. She was sent for and identified the body. Mrs Bailey was too upset to speak to our reporter, but according to a neighbour Keith had been observed behaving strangely over the past days. "It was as though he had something on his conscience," the neighbour said. As with the death of Lorna Perry, a Coroner's inquiry will be required before the body can be released for burial. And then, perhaps, Stonely can at last return to the quiet ways of former years.

"Who do you think the neighbour is?" he asks his mother.

She raises her shoulders in an impatient shrug. "Who knows? Not me, not Sally Parsons."

Looking directly into his eyes, and, he knows, wanting an answer to her question, she asks him, "Could it have been Ronnie? That man Lewis Grant gave your friend money to spill the beans on anything that took his fancy."

"Ronnie wouldn't do a thing like that," he says, speaking with more confidence than he feels. "How about the Herberts? They were complaining to Mrs Bailey about Keith hanging about the cemetery."

"It's possible," she agrees. "Anything's possible. My poor Maureen," she says. And, with bitter vehemence, "And *she'll* be enjoying all this, of course."

He doesn't need to ask who his mother means.

***

The previous day, Sunday, had been one of constant disruptions, during which Peter saw little of his mother. She was in and out with barely enough time to tell him more than the bare bones of what had happened. Most of the story he pieced together from her occasional snippets of information. The discovery of Keith's body, Mrs Bailey being driven to hospital to identify her son, her return and request that his own mother be with her; the "informal" police visit; Mrs Bailey's emotional exhaustion, the arrival of a doctor who had given her a sedative, ordered her to bed, and left instructions with Mrs Howard to call him if she thought it at all advisable. (He took for granted that she'd stay with her friend.)

But in the few impassioned words his mother spoke when she looked in at lunchtime to check that Peter was back from choirboy duties, she paused long enough to give voice to her own grief. "A good, good woman," she said of Maureen Bailey. "She didn't deserve this."

Unspilled tears trembling on her lower eyelid, the intensity with which she spoke leaving him abashed. He hadn't known you could feel like that about someone who didn't belong to you.

Partly to cope with his own embarrassment, he asked her about Sergeant Locker and the detective who she'd told him were then on their way from Ashton. "I'll tell you later," she said. "I need to get back to Maureen." And off she went.

***

That evening, Mrs Bailey now in bed and his mother having promised to call in again later to monitor her condition – "She's out on her feet, poor love", – she told him over a scratch meal that it had been the plain-clothes policeman, Derek Humphreys, who asked most of the questions. "He was the detective who'd been with Sergeant Locker when the police took statements at the time of Lorna May's death, remember?"

Peter did remember.

"Well," she said, "he took the lead."

His mother had been expecting Mrs Bailey to make brief answers

– yes and no. But her friend surprised her by answering the policemen's questions at length. Talking, his mother said, seemed to help her. It certainly allowed her to voice her deep rage at the beating Keith took at work and at the "low thugs, the cowardly bullies" who had left his face and body covered in bruises. Naturally those who beat him up claimed to have found their excuse in the article about Lorna May that had appeared in the *Chronicle*.

Had the two policemen seen that? Yes, they said, they had. Then they could surely understand why following its appearance and then what he'd suffered from his workmates, Keith wouldn't go back to work, why he had become more and more withdrawn.

"Withdrawn?" Humphreys had asked.

Keith, Mrs Bailey explained, had taken to going on long, lonely walks about the village, often disappearing from home for hours at a time, and only coming in for his food at irregular intervals.

When she finished her account of her son's roamings, Humphreys said, "We heard he'd been seen in the cemetery where that little girl, Perry, is buried."

Maureen had fired up immediately. "Is that against the law?"

"No," Humphreys conceded, "but it's slightly unusual, wouldn't you say, for a young lad to go wandering about such a place?"

Peter's mother looked at Peter. "You can guess what he meant. That no one in his right mind would want to spend time in a cemetery. I'm glad he didn't say that but of course Maureen knew what he had in mind and she was furious. So before she could make some remark she might have regretted I jumped in and told them that people often went into the cemetery to be on their own for a while, away from the hustle and bustle of daily life. Stonely a place of hustle and bustle, I could see them thinking. It was what your dad would call 'waffle' but it was the best I could do and we all calmed down after that."

There had, however, been more trouble when Humphreys asked the inevitable question.

When had Mrs Bailey last seen Keith

"On Saturday evening," she told them. He came in at about eight o'clock and soon after he'd eaten his supper she'd made him a mug of Horlicks which he drank before going upstairs. She heard him go into his bedroom and shut the door. Later, when she herself went to bed, she saw his light was off.

"He wasn't one for reading," she had told the policemen.

"She actually blushed when she said that, it must have been so *awful* for her," his mother told Peter.

"They already knew that Keith was a bit … " He doesn't say the word. "I mean Sergeant Locker must have known, and he'd have told the other policeman."

"Maybe, but I saw them exchange glances. It was as if they'd trapped her into giving away some dreadful secret about Keith. And *of course* she saw the look that passed between them. *She* realised what she'd done, though she'd never intended to."

"You think they might want to blame Keith for Lorna May's death?"

"I've no doubt about it. And I've also no doubt they think everything points to the lad's guilt."

She sat silent for several minutes. Then, "Well, he's out of harm's way now. It's his mother we need to protect."

"Protect from what?"

"Rumours, whispers. People telling each other that Keith killed himself because he couldn't stand the guilt of what he'd done to Lorna May."

"His death could have been an accident."

"I know, I know, Peter. But that's not what people will be thinking."

He wondered whether to remind her of the moment when Keith had stepped into the road and nearly been hit by the baker's van, but before he could open his mouth she said. "And that's not the worst of it. Those who say he took his own life will also be keen to hint that his mother must have known all along that he killed the girl and was covering up for him."

She was right, of course she was. He himself had wondered about that. Keith's death could hardly have been an accident. He must surely have known what he was doing, tiptoeing out of the house in the middle of the night in order to make his way to the shunting yard. Finding the path through the woods had to be something he intended. And then stepping beyond the woods and into the yard itself, as busy by night as it was by day. You didn't need to be able to read warning notices to know how dangerous the sidings were. Keith would have *heard* the cofflings, the shrieks of engines letting off steam, the pig-squeal of brakes being applied. And because the arc lights were switched on now that the war was at an end, he'd have *seen* the incessant toing and froing of trucks, the uncoupling of engines, of guards' vans rattling toward the buffers at the end of side lines.

Now, rereading the newspaper account of the death, he thinks that Keith *must* have planned it. He must have decided to kill himself, or be killed. An image intrudes: that lonely, dejected figure he and Ronnie came across moping about near the woods, who wouldn't talk to them, who must have thought himself as much of an outcast as the lepers they'd been told about in school. Leprosy was a deadly disease. Wherever lepers went they had to ring a bell warning people to keep away. Keith didn't have a bell but the way he hid himself away made him like a leper.

That thought leads to another. Perhaps Keith did, after all, know what had happened to Lorna May. Perhaps some urge drew him down to the woods on Saturday night to see yet again the place where, at the start of summer, her body had been discovered, and that had then pushed him to make his way to the shunting yard and to step into the path of an oncoming truck or engine.

If so, the conclusion must be that Keith killed Lorna May. This is what Mrs Perry thinks. It may be what Mrs Herbert thinks. According to Mrs Bailey, it is what the police think.

And his mother? What does *she* think? For all her friendship with Mrs Bailey, her unwillingness to hear ill of her and therefore of Keith – the lad who "wouldn't harm a fly" – is she in fact beginning to suspect that he hadn't merely found Lorna May's body but that he was in some way involved in her death, had indeed caused it, and that the guilty knowledge of what he had done and which he had been carrying around with him for the past three months finally became too great to bear? And more, does she herself suspect that Mrs Bailey herself knows or at least fears this?

He remembers the words she had used the previous afternoon: "It's his mother we need to protect." And then her suggestion that people think "His mother must have known all along." Does that include the police?

She sits, shoulders hunched, chin in hand, abstracted, her eyes fixed, unseeing, on the mantelpiece clock, as if, it occurs to him, she is trying not to see, not to think about, the contents of the newspaper spread across the table between them.

What does she know? What does she suspect? What does she fear?

23

It is still occupying the space between them when they hear a knock at the front door, hesitant first, then more determined.

After listening for a few moments, as though she hopes the banging may stop, his mother gets reluctantly to her feet. "That's probably Maureen. Let her in will you, love, while I run upstairs and change out of my uniform."

But it is Mrs Herbert, in grey pleated skirt and dark-blue cardigan under which is the familiar buttoned-at-the-neck white blouse, who stands in the porch.

"Is your mother in?"

No 'please', no beating about the bush.

"She'll be down in a minute," he says, standing aside to let her step past him into the hall.

Once there, she appears to lose confidence, hesitates, says, "Should I wait here?"

It strikes him that she is unsure of her welcome.

"We're in the dining room," he says squeezing past her and opening the door.

"Not playing with your friend, then?" she asks, with an awkward approach to affability.

"Ronnie's gone on holiday with his mum and sister."

"Oh, where to?" But she isn't really interested.

"Somewhere up north. To see his dad."

"I expect your own father will be home soon." Her words come out in a short burst. Her attempt at a smile makes plain how ill at ease she is.

His mother comes swiftly in. Her anticipatory smile dims and is replaced by a stare in which surprise gives way to outright hostility. Mrs Herbert's eyes go from her to the newspaper spread across the table. "So you've read what the *News* has to say?"

"I was showing it to Peter." His mother's voice is taut, her hands, he sees, are clenched, as though she is holding herself in check.

Mrs Herbert seems at a loss what to say next. "What do *you* think?" she asks Peter.

Bewildered by the question, he doesn't know how to answer.

"If you mean the innuendo about Keith Bailey *I* think it's disgraceful," his mother bursts out, and at the words Mrs Herbert involuntarily clasps one wrist in the bony fingers of her other hand as she says, her voice now scarcely more than a whisper, "I only hope nothing I said contributed to his … to his accident."

So that is why she has come.

"You mean warning his mother against Keith's 'snooping' around the cemetery?"

The words come out, hard as pebbles, and the other woman, flinching at their impact, doesn't answer.

"Did you know that he was beaten up at work?"

The merest nod.

"And do you know why?"

Mrs Herbert looks up, her eyes full of guilty contrition. "I wish I'd never said anything to her about Keith. Not that it was less than the truth." A pause. Then she says, "Mr Herbert, my husband … "

They wait for her to explain but she bites on her underlip, unable or unwilling to continue. Silently, she looks from mother to son, as if asking, even imploring them to understand a meaning in the words that lies some way below the surface.

His mother hears only smugness. "Told you to do your duty, I suppose. How thoughtful of him. A pity he didn't tell Rachel Perry himself, then. I take it that's who you mean by 'her.' "

Again, a nod. Again, the harassed look. He has never seen Mrs Herbert, usually so certain of herself, so anxious, so fretful.

"She's been nothing but trouble since she arrived. You know about the rumours she's been spreading about us all?"

Mrs Herbert stares at his mother. She looks more anxious than ever.

"Oh, yes, you were included. She may have pretended to find you more sympathetic than the rest of us, but that didn't stop her from having an explanation for those two reporters as to why her daughter had run away from you."

Clearing her throat, as though aware of some sudden obstruction, Mrs Herbert asks, her voice thickened by concern, "What … what did she say?"

His mother gives an impatient shrug, looks away and he wonders whether she thinks she may have gone too far.

But no.

162

"She suggested that your husband's cruelty could have driven Lorna May out of the house and down to the woods where she met her death. So now you know."

His mother's eyes are fixed on Mrs Herbert, and as he watches he sees the other woman wince and half turn her head away as though to avert a sudden blow.

But she says nothing.

In the continuing silence, his mother's words echo in Peter's head. Your husband's cruelty. Yes, he can imagine that cold, unapproachable man could be cruel. A man of cruel words and, even, actions. But cruel enough to make the evacuee run away?

Mrs Herbert's face has stiffened to a grey mask. She opens her mouth to speak but no sound emerges from her thin, pale lips. He watches, fascinated, as the tongue feels its way to the back of her upper teeth, as though cutting off whatever words she may be trying to utter.

When she finally breaks her silence, it is to say, "Do you think it proper for your son – for Peter – to hear all this?"

His mother swats away the attempt to regain moral authority.

"Rather too late for that, isn't it? Given that Rachel Perry made sure her tale was given to reporters and that it's gone around the village as well as into the wider world." A pause, as though she is gathering herself. "And given that she almost certainly hinted to Keith's fellow-workers he was some sort of pervert as well as a killer, hints that, as you can see, are now repeated in the *Morning News* and available for all the world to read."

She takes breath, says, "Now where, I wonder, did she get all *that* from."

The colour is spreading up from Mrs Herbert's neck to her cheeks. "Rachel Perry tried to draw me into … into indiscretions, but I can assure you I said as little as possible." The words are offered as both explanation and justification, and she seems to take some courage from them. "She had shown precious little interest in her daughter until her recent arrival."

And with this revelation, she begins to speak with greater assurance. "I think I deserve some credit for taking Lorna May in. She was almost the last child left at the billeting station, you know." Moral indignation shifts into a note nearer to pitying wonder. "Poor girl. She had precious little with her but the clothes she stood up in."

"Hmm." His mother's anger has, he thinks, softened. She *has* gone too far. "I've no doubt she was grateful to be given a roof over her head," she concedes, if reluctantly and she gestures to a chair. "Please, I should have offered you a seat."

Once Mrs Herbert is sitting, perched on the edge of a chair, it becomes clear she wants to tell her side of the story. Rachel Perry, she announces, has never spoken a word of thanks for all she, Mrs Herbert, had done for Lorna May. "All her talk is about herself. What *she's* suffered, how *her* widowhood has ruined *her* life. Oh, yes, and how she thinks every day of Harold. The name of Lorna May's father, I gather. Lost at sea."

Mrs Herbert lifts her eyes, meets his mother's gaze. "If you can believe anything she says."

Startled, his mother, who is now herself seated, says, "I can't believe she'd make *that* up. That would be a terrible thing to do. Besides," she speaks more briskly now, although her voice is far from assured. "Lorna May would surely have to know the truth about it."

"Lorna May is dead."

"What *are* you saying?" His mother looks aghast.

"Only that Lorna May can't tell us what she knew, can she? But *I* can tell you that we never heard from her mother, that every communication with Lorna May came from a London neighbour of her mother's, a Mrs Hodgins. It was *she* who wrote to tell me of the death of Lorna May's father and that her mother had vanished."

"Her house had been bombed."

The reply is one full of self-righteous affront. "Not then it hadn't."

And again his mother asks her guest, "What *are* you saying?"

"It was hit by a buzz-bomb. Late last year. A lot around there were. That's the part of London called 'buzz-bomb alley,' as you probably know."

"But how do *you* know? About when the house was hit, I mean."

"The neighbour. She's kept in touch, promised to let me have any news of Rachel Perry she might have." She glances at Peter, then says, "I don't know where that woman went, but it doesn't take much to put two and two together, does it, and come up with the reason why."

"And you're saying that in all the time between when you took Lorna May in and when Rachel Perry appeared you'd heard nothing from her?" His mother looks askance. "There must have been *some* communication, surely? Even if she couldn't get out of London to see her daughter, she could have found a way to contact her, to send a message of some kind?"

Mrs Herbert shakes her head emphatically. "Not a word."

And as she speaks Peter remembers Rachel Perry saying "Letters and me don't agree," and the smile on her face as she uttered the sentence.

His mother sits, staring now in disbelief. "I'm sure she mentioned sending cards for the girl's birthday, for Christmas … "

"Christmas, yes. Signed by the neighbour, I could tell from the hand writing. But not for her birthday. I imagine," she says laconically, "Mrs Hodgins didn't know when the girl's birthday was."

"How awful."

"Yes," Mrs Herbert says, "it is."

It seems to be the end of the conversation, but then his mother asks, "You say you never met the neighbour? She wasn't at home, then, that time you and Mr Herbert dashed down to London to look for Lorna May?"

Suddenly uncomfortable, Mrs Herbert shifts in her seat as she says, "We'd hardly begun our search when my husband read about the body being discovered. So, of course, we had to come straight back."

"I see," his mother says. Peter isn't sure she does.

Mrs Herbert is now standing. "I ought to go," she says. Her look has once more become uncertain, troubled.

"Before you do," his mother says, "would you mind telling me why you complained to Maureen Bailey of her son – of his being in the cemetery?"

Mrs Herbert's discomfort increases. "I sometimes go there myself," she says, haltingly. "To say a prayer for the girl. I feel so sorry for her, for her death." Her voice has now sunk to a whisper and she is studying her clasped hands. He thinks she may be close to tears.

"But why should it matter if Keith was there? What on earth did you think he was doing? *Spying* on you?"

Her voice is one of deep scorn, but Mrs Herbert says, "I … I. Yes. It didn't seem right." She looks appealingly at his mother who, still full of scorn, asks, "*Right?* I really don't follow."

And it is then that Mrs Herbert speaks the words that will come to haunt the adult Peter Howard. "Prayers are private," she says.

***

Later that evening, when he comes in from wandering about the field, he finds his mother, in her fireside chair, writing pad on her knees.

"A letter to dad?"

She looks up from the pad, lays her pen aside. "I'm trying to tell him about the events of the past few days. It helps me to clear my own mind."

She screws the cap onto her fountain pen, leans back in her chair, and sighs.

He says, sitting down to face her across the table, "You mean about Keith Bailey."

"Not only that." She hesitates, as though uncertain what next to say. "Do *you* think he might have had anything to do with Lorna May's death," she asks him. "Does Ronnie?"

"Ronnie thinks Keith didn't always know his own strength. And that's what his mum and gran say."

"So the finger of suspicion is being pointed from all round the village. Well, that rather lets Rachel Perry off the hook."

"You mean that she isn't the only one to think … "

Then he stops. He's been going to say that Mrs Perry isn't the only one to think Keith Bailey killed Lorna May. As of course, she isn't. Mrs Herbert probably thinks so, too. Although in that case, why had she come in some sort of apology to speak to his mother – and why not apologise to Mrs Bailey?

As though guessing his thoughts, his mother says, "I made Mrs Herbert promise that in a day or so, when Maureen is better able to cope, she'll apologise to her. Whatever doubts that woman has planted in her mind about Keith she should *never* have said anything to those reporters."

"Besides," Peter says, "Keith didn't make Lorna May run away from the Herberts."

"Going down to the woods isn't running away. You and Ronnie do it all the time, don't you?"

"Yes," he says. "Yes, we do."

"Well, then. For all we know Lorna May could have gone roaming in the woods, as you boys do, climbed on the roof, again as you do, and accidentally fallen to her death, and this whole sorry business of rumour and accusation, the finger being pointed at Keith because he found her body, is … oh, I don't know, built on sand. And once the press get involved … "

He understands. She is trying, hoping, to find an explanation for the two deaths that will soothe Maureen Bailey's mind. Trace the course of events back to their beginning, Lorna May's disappearance, accept that she hadn't intended to run away, and what then?

But something bothers him, something to do with Mrs Herbert, something about how she had spoken to him that Friday afternoon when she asked him if he had seen Lorna May. What was it? Was it the way she'd spoken or the words she'd used?

"Penny for them," his mother says.

But he can't think what it is that nags at him, what he is trying to remember, though years later, when he does, and when he sets them against Mrs Herbert's words, "Prayers are private," everything will become clear.

24

Late August. Summer still, but browner, dustier, and with a heaviness in the air and fields, some of them stripped bare of wheat, others felted with grass that seems as listless as the heavy-leaved trees surrounding them.

The coroner's inquest into Keith Bailey's death has been concluded, the verdict of accidental death recorded, and his body now lies with his father's in the Parish churchyard.

Peter is in the church choir that sings at the funeral. As they begin the last hymn, "Abide with Me," he sees that his mother, sitting beside Mrs Bailey in the front pew, her arm round the older woman, has leant her cheek against the bowed head, her eyes seemingly fixed on his, though he knows that look, and even allowing for the distance between them, knows that she is not seeing him, that she is staring unseeing, ahead.

She seems tired, dispirited, no longer the mother who had earlier in the year shone with delight, whose shimmer of happiness had held from May through to early July. The local deaths, of Lorna May Perry and Keith Bailey, have dimmed her brightness.

Nor has VJ Day, signalling the final end of war, been able to lift her mood. Unlike the earlier day of victory, when in her exuberance she had danced him round their house, this occasion signalled no explosion of relieved joy. Although she has hardly spoken about it, the little she has had to say lies like a chill in his bones. Leaning over the table, studying the front page of her newspaper when he came down for breakfast one morning, she was, he saw, staring at what seemed to be a photograph of an irregular circle of ashy substance, charred and twisted metal girders – or were they the remnants of tree trunks – sticking up into grey air, the whole rather like one of the stamped-out fires left by gypsies. But as he joined her he saw that this circle seemed to stretch indefinitely in every direction.

"What is it?"

She lifted her eyes to his and he saw that they were dark with unhappiness, with some nameless dread.

"This," she said, "is Hiroshima."

"What does that mean? "

" This," she said, "is our future."

Three weeks later, as he sings the words of the hymn, "Fast falls the eventide," her words come back to him. "Earth's vain shadows flee," he sings. *This is our future*, he hears.

***

Of course, she isn't always like that. Her despondency doesn't last long, is usually lifted after a few minutes of what she herself calls her melancholy moping.

"It'll be all right once your dad's back," she says on one occasion when she has been especially inattentive. He is at the table, having his tea, she is sitting in her chair beside the hearth, book open on her lap, though she isn't reading.

The next day, he tells her, he has agreed to help Ronnie clear out the shelter at the bottom of his friend's garden. And when she doesn't respond to his words he asks her, "Don't you want to know why?"

She looks at him, puzzled. "Why what?"

"Why I'm helping Ronnie clear out their shelter."

"What shelter?"

"Oh, Mum. You haven't been listening, have you! The shelter at the bottom of their garden."

She smiles, more an apologetic curve of the lips. "I was thinking."

"What about?"

"Oh, you know." She slips a piece of paper into her book, closes it, and says, "Where we'll be in a year from now."

"That's why I'm helping Ronnie."

And before she can once more ask him why, he says, "Soon as his dad's out of the army they're going to move back up north, to Huddersfield. His dad's been promised work there."

"Huddersfield," she says, feigning interest. "That will be something of an adventure for them all."

"Huddersfield is where Ronnie's dad comes from. But it means I'll be losing my best friend."

"Poor Peter," she says, "you'll miss him, won't you? And he'll miss you." She lapses into silence. Then, "It'll be all right once your dad's back," she says, forcing herself into brightness. "We'll be off ourselves. Back to Manchester, I shouldn't wonder."

"Manchester!" Ronnie is dismissive. "Mi mam reckons that's the wrong side of England, that is. Nowt but rain."

"How does your mother know? Is she from Lancashire?"

"Mansfield," Ronnie says.

They are stacking on the lawn all they have removed from the shelter. Garden tools, including two forks, one with missing tines, plus rusty rake and spade with a broken handle, have been thrown down beside a pair of old Wellington boots, their tops stickily laced with cobwebs. Propped against a packing case into which the two friends lob encrusted paint tins are short rolls of cracked and mildewed linoleum. A tricycle whose front wheel the boys had prised free a year ago, intending to make a go-cart, is half-hidden beneath a strip of rotten sacking they have hauled up the steps leading to the damp darkness into which Peter again ducks.

"What's this?"

Trying to hold his breath against the fetid smells of the shelter, he scrabbles among sacking and strips of carpet and manages to extricate what, under the dim, blue light of the unshaded shelter bulb, seems to be a biscuit tin. He shakes it, hears the rattling, like small pebbles clinking against its sides. "What's this tin?" he shouts to his friend. "Rubbish?"

Ronnie, outside, calls, "Bring it 'ere."

Peter carries the tin up the stairs and then, standing beside Ronnie, eases off the lid and peers in. Then he kneels to shake out the contents. A cracked blue saucer, a pen and holder, a round flat metal disk on a chain that is probably a cheap brooch, and a collar-stud.

He looks enquiringly at Ronnie, who grins uncertainly down at him. "Go on, guess."

Peter looks at the objects. "Give up," he says.

"From Lorna May. She give 'em me. Must 'ave nicked 'em from the 'erberts."

Peter studies the pathetic scatter of objects. "But why?"

Ronnie, above him, shrugs. "Makin' friends, after she shoved me off that branch. I got a tannin' for that rip in them new trousers. Suppose she felt she owed me for that. Wanted to be pals again."

Another memory that in later years will force its way into Peter Howard's consciousness. Some tarnished gold chain glimpsed through a shop window, a cracked saucer in a café, and suddenly he is once again looking up from where he kneels on spiky grass among those tokens of proffered amity, wondering at his friend's embarrassed grin. And then, pushing those memories aside will come another: the bitter twist of Lorna May's mouth and her words. *I thought you were my friend.*

And then he will remember the exercise book.

***

Ronnie hadn't been going to show it him. It isn't with the other objects. But as he crouches to return them one by one to the biscuit tin, Peter becomes aware that his friend is no longer standing beside him but has gone back down the shelter steps.

Straightening up, he calls out, "What do you want me to do with this tin?"

No answer. He follows Ronnie down the slimy steps and in the dim light peers at where Ronnie, his back to him, is on all fours, reaching beneath the camp bed up-tilted against the shelter's rear wall. With a grunt of satisfaction, Ronnie draws out of hiding whatever he has been searching for.

"What's that?"

Startled, Ronnie turns his head.

"Nothin'" he says, scrambling to his feet before brushing past Peter and stumbling up the uneven steps.

Back in the open air, Peter sees that his friend is clutching one of those exercise-books doled out at the beginning of each school term. Buff-coloured card covers, with ruled pages, they are all-purpose possessions: used for sums, for essays, for sketches of the leaves and flower-heads the pupils bring back from nature rambles, for lists of difficult words they are made to copy down.

"That's hers, isn't? The one she gave you."

"Yeh." It is said so softly that Peter hardly hears him, though the next words come more clearly. "Dunno what for, like."

But Ronnie does, Peter is sure. The gift of the book must have been a further plea for friendship.

"What's in it?"

Ronnie shrugs. "Dunno," he says again.

Peter takes a step forward. "You mean you haven't looked inside? Honest?"

"I stuffed it in there" – a nod in the direction of the shelter – "so she'd not get into trouble."

Peter thinks he understands. You couldn't be issued with a new exercise book until you had filled the old one, and the loss of your exercise book had to be explained. Inadequate explanations were deemed punishable. For girls, cleaning chores about the school. For boys, the cane. And the same punishments apply for books that have been defaced or contain "rude" drawings or writing.

"Well," Peter says, "it won't get her into trouble now, will it?"

He reaches to take the book from Ronnie, who at first resists. Then, reluctantly, he lets go. "Look if you want," he says.

Peter flicks through its pages. The usual multiplication tables, some long division, spelling lists, red ticks and crosses in the margins, one or two pressed grasses, a badly drawn sketch of a grasshopper.

Inside the back cover an apparently blank page that had been torn from the book is folded in two.

He unfolds it, sees the pencilled scrawl running down the page.

As Ronnie comes to stand beside him, Peter begins to read what seems to be a letter.

Dear Mum can you come and get me I dont like it heer The peeple I am with make me wurk all the time and I dont get much to eat and I dont like wot they give me just bred and stuff. They say my dad is ded is he I am calling myself Lorna May now because that is his name you sed and I want to remembr him plees come and get me the man is orful to me plees come

And at that point the letter stops.

The two boys stand there, side by side, silent, not wanting to look at each other.

The day seems to have darkened, and under the August sun Peter can feel his friend's body trembling against his own.

Eventually he asks, "When do you think she wrote that letter?"

"Ages ago," Ronnie says. "She give me the book last year, didn't she?" He isn't so much asking his friend as trying to remember. "Before we 'ad that fallin' out, all on us." Then, more swiftly, "Anyway 'er dad got drowned soon after she come 'ere."

"And we always thought she was called Lorna May." And now he remembers Rachel Perry's correcting him that evening his mother took her in. "Lorna, dear. Lorna is – was – her name."

He tells Ronnie, who shrugs dismissively. "Don't care. She's Lorna May as far as I'm concerned. That's what she called hersen. Lorna

May." Then, as the oddness of the name she has insisted on using strikes them both, Ronnie says, as though challenging Peter, "*May*? 'ow can a bloke be called *May*? That's a girl's name."

"Perhaps May was his surname."

Though having suggested that, Peter is still at a loss to understand.

Ronnie seems to be echoing his bafflement. "So 'ow come she's called Lorna May *Perry*. And 'er mum's Mrs Perry."

Then, lifting a hand to smack himself on the side of his forehead, he bursts out, "Come on, it's plain as a pikestaff, like mi gran sez."

He looks at Peter, the flicker of a smile, before his expression becomes serious once more. "Got it? No? It's obvious. Mrs Perry and Lorna's dad, they weren't married. *That's* 'ow 'e come to be called May. It was 'is *surname*. Yeh, it's obvious."

***

Obvious? As with so many of the events of that end-of-war summer, it is only in retrospect that Peter, one afternoon in his final undergraduate year, his friendship with Ronnie long ended but, as so often, rethinking those days at Stonely, makes himself accept how much more perceptive than himself Ronnie had been, how much more the friend of his boyhood had understood about that time. And he acknowledges that Lorna May had also realised this, which was one reason why she pinned her hopes on Ronnie. Those pathetic objects in the biscuit-tin he'd tipped into the grass, they were love tokens of a sort, and also a plea for help.

I thought you were my friend.

I thought, I hoped. But like the letter which Ronnie hadn't opened until that day he and Peter read it, standing side by side in August, nineteen forty-five, the girl's hopes came to nothing. And anyway, Peter thinks, even if Ronnie *had* read her letter, what could he have done about it? Tell his mother? And what could Mrs Slater have done? Who would have believed her? Probably nobody, nobody who counted. Because as he had always sensed from his own mother's scrupulously polite, distanced manner toward her, Ronnie's mum was not "respectable". The Herberts, on the other hand, *were* respectable.

That, of course, was the trouble. As an illegitimate child Lorna May Perry carried within herself the seeds of shame. It comes to him, then, that billeting authorities would have given a copy of the girl's birth certificate to the Herberts or at the very least informed them of her parentage. Lorna Perry, daughter of Harold May and Rachel Perry. A bastard. No wonder they treated her as they did, and why he, Mr Herbert, that upstanding figure in his dark clothes and rigid manner, could dare to – to what? To chastise her, as he might have convinced himself he was licensed to do. *"The man is orful to me."*

Poor Lorna May. She'd been with the Herberts since the early days of the war, and although there was no point in speculating how long Mr Herbert might have been "orful" – cruel, spiteful, prepared to hit her – it had probably been from the start. But on that afternoon in May, nineteen forty-five, he perhaps took it on himself to lash out at the girl in an especially vicious way. Either that, or something in Lorna May herself, some surge of loathing for the man, or even self-disgust, some uncontrollable, primal rage, caused her to run out of the bungalow and away from her tormentor.

Was that what had happened? Yes, Peter decides, it could well have been. It *must* have been. Because, trying to set in order the sequence of events from that summer, the one moment that explains all now comes back to him.

Of course. *Of course!*

Where was he when he first heard that Lorna May wasn't at home? Sitting by the side of the road watching the German POW, Hans, as he drove his steamroller over stones that had to be crushed to make the way smooth for the imminent visit of royalty? Once again, he hears the stones crackling like cellophane under the rollers' heavy weight, the machine's chuntering, clanking, wheezy rumble, he even fancies he can smell the powdery dust rising into the warm air, tingling in his nostrils.

And then Mrs Herbert is calling from the other side of the road, wanting to know whether he's seen Lorna May. Mrs Herbert, who on this occasion is less angry than agitated. Or rather, the two emotions seemed equally mixed in her words, in the expression on her face. There she was, there she *is*, in her pinafore, the woman he'd seen a little earlier in coat and hat marching down the road with her shopping bags. Why had she not come straight back out as soon as she found Lorna May wasn't at home? Tea was overdue, and Mrs Herbert always demanded that meals be on time. Why then wait until she'd changed out of her coat before she came to demand of Peter whether he'd seen the girl? Yes, *why?*

What day was that? Friday, of course, when, he now remembers, the factory was closed for a rare half-day. And that Friday the school, too, had been let out early. Which meant that by the time Lorna May got back to the bungalow, thinking she'd be safe, Mr Herbert was already there, alone. And by the time Mrs Herbert returned from her shopping the girl had disappeared.

Had that stern-faced woman guessed at the extent of her husband's cruelty whenever she was out of the home? Had there been even more to what he did, or tried to do, than she suspected? Suppose he admitted that Lorna May had run away? Had Mrs Herbert then forced herself to drag some sort of confession out of him? And, following that, had she forced herself to pretend to the outside world that all was normal? Was that why she emerged in pinafore to ask him, Peter, if he had seen Lorna May? Yes, all too likely. Indeed, obvious. She was pretending not to know what had happened, not to be aware that the girl had run off.

And then another thought comes. Given Lorna May's origins, the taint of illegitimacy, Mrs Herbert might well have thought of the evacuee as some sort of – of what? Temptress? Of course, he thinks, she'd never have let herself *consciously* use such a word, but someone with her religious scruple probably took for granted that Lorna May had inherited her mother's wickedness. He remembers other children from his junior school in Stonely about whom there had been rumours, children whose company you were – whisper, whisper – supposed to avoid. His mother had been contemptuous of such rumours and angry at any suggestion that the children in question should be shunned at playtime or after school hours. But Mrs Herbert wouldn't have shared his mother's attitude. Quite the opposite. A child born in sin is one who inherits that sin. The flesh is weak. *The man is orful to me.* Mrs Herbert would have done all she could to ensure that her husband and Lorna May were never alone together.

But then, on that one afternoon, her best intentions had been undone. With the factory granted an unexpected half-day off, her husband would already have been at home when the girl, herself let out of school early, arrived back. Whatever then happened, the result was that Lorna May ran away, made some sort of escape. Had Mrs Herbert returned from shopping to find her husband in a panic? Had she forced an at least partial confession out of him? And as the hours went by and Saturday came and still Lorna May didn't return, had that confession become less guarded, more candid, and therefore more frightening?

It was all speculation, of course. But it was at least probable. It would certainly explain why, on the following day, on a Sunday of all days, the day of rest, the Lord's Day, the Herberts had rushed off to London. It was, surely, an act born of desperation, undertaken in the hope that, always supposing Lorna May had made for the city in order to search out her mother, or at least find the neighbour whose name he can't now recall, they might perhaps get to her before she could tell anyone her story. Though goodness only knew what they'd have done if they *had* run her to ground.

But the girl's death had saved them.

No, that was wrong. He thinks, now, of the time – the *only* time – Mrs Herbert came to their house, hoping to make some sort of excuse for the words she had uttered and whose use by a newspaper reporter had led, she must have realised, to Keith Bailey's death. And then there was her telling poor Mrs Bailey to keep Keith away from the cemetery where Lorna May's body lay, the cemetery where she herself went to pray. What were her prayers about, if not a kind of apology for the girl's death, an act of contrition, as were, surely, the retreats or prayer meetings or whatever it was that took the couple away most weekends that summer and for all he knew for the remainder of their lives. Prayers, retreats: they were attempts at atonement for what the man had done and which his wife, by not confronting him, had permitted. That was it. That had to be it. But Lorna May's death hadn't saved them, certainly hadn't saved Mrs Herbert.

And thinking that, he begins to comprehend something of the woman's misery, of her mental and spiritual torture.

***

But in the summer of nineteen forty-five none of this is apparent to Peter Howard. Standing amid the jumble of objects he and Ronnie have between them hauled out of the shelter, he asks his friend as he folds the letter and tucks it inside the exercise book before handing the book back, "What are you going to do with this?"

Ronnie is staring down at the book which he is once again gripping with both hands.

"Well, I ain't gonna give it to the bloody 'erberts, that's for sure."

"How about her mother?"

Ronnie shakes his head. "She's vamoosed."

"She's gone?" Peter hasn't heard, nor, he thinks, can his mother know about Rachel Perry's departure. "When? When did she go?"

"Dunno exactly, but mi mam reckons that with Keith dead she knew she'd better make hersen scarce."

Peter says, "Yes, *my* mother thinks that she was to blame for that."

"What, puttin' them reporters onto it?"

"Yes." Tentatively, he enquires, "That half-crown …? "

Ronnie is contemptuous. "If you're thinkin' that made me tell 'em owt, think again."

"Did you spend it?"

"I give it mi gran. She deserves it, all that lookin' out for me when mi mam's away."

Chastened, Peter says, "And then there's Lorna May."

"What about 'er?"

"We still don't know what happened, do we?"

Ronnie, gazing down at the exercise book, says nothing.

Trying to prompt him into speech, Peter says, "Perhaps her mother was responsible?" And when Ronnie remains silent, he says, remembering Mrs Herbert's outraged words, "She never came to see her, did she, not once, not like other mothers. Perhaps Lorna May couldn't stand it, especially not if the Herberts went on being horrible to her. So she ran off and then somehow she died."

Silence.

Peter tries once more. "That would make her mother, Rachel Perry, responsible, wouldn't it? She'd be the one to blame."

And then, finally, Ronnie speaks.

"'Er an' all the rest," he says.

PART FIVE

25

The wake is coming to an end.

Mourners, most of whom had earlier stood round the open grave in the heat of the August afternoon to join in dropping single roses onto the coffin lid, are now, one by one or in small groups, with increased rapidity leaving the pub's back bar which he's hired for the occasion. Goodbyes are exchanged, together with the customary promises to keep in touch, but he knows few of those who come up to shake his hand, who speak, earnestly he assumes, of the parish's sense of loss, who hope he will soon be back to normal – whatever that means – and that he will find solace in his memories of her.

Only one guest remains.

"Don't go yet," he had asked him a few minutes earlier, "I want to talk."

But now, sitting opposite this last guest, each of them forced into angular postures by the fake-gilt, straight-backed chairs with their padded, plum-coloured seats, each of them with a newly-filled wine glass, he wonders how to break the silence.

It is done for him.

"A sad occasion," the other says, "but I'm glad to be here. I was always fond of your mother." And he raises his glass.

"She was fond of you."

He raises his own glass and together they drink. "She used to say you were 'a caution'." And he smiles at the memory.

"Did she now. And what's that when it's at home?"

As the two of them laugh the chill of uncertainty begins to thaw.

"Do you still use that term or are you indulging me?" And when the other, smiling, chooses not to reply, Peter says, "A caution, let me tell you, is a surprising or amusing person. Droll. Originally American army slang. Mid-nineteenth century."

He speaks the words so as to show that he is quoting.

"And that's the kind of thing writers learn. Or are expected to know."

"I looked it up years past. It's not a word I catch myself using."

"Any more than I say 'What's that when it's at home?'"

"And especially not to your patients."

"Especially not to them."

They lapse once more into silence, each staring into his glass.

"This is something of a miracle, isn't it, this coming together."

"The miracle of radio. I knew it was your voice. Talking about public health issues. Obesity among the young and how to cure it."

"A wartime diet and regular exercise would do them a power of good." He adopts the voice of a crusty old major. "Get rid of the flab, young man. Chasing a cricket ball about Farmer Connolly's field is the very thing to knock you into shape."

"They'd have a hard time trying to do that. The field's been built over long since."

"Hmm." The glass is raised to his lips, lowered. Then, "You're going to have to tell me how you knew the medical man you heard speaking was the Ronald Slater from Stonely. Ronald Slater. Not exactly a rarity among names, is it?"

"It was the way you pronounced 'one', when you said 'one way to help'. O as u, as in 'put'. That didn't give the game away, perhaps, but it made me prick up my ears."

Ronnie, or Ronald, laughs, raises a hand in mock-surrender. "Fair cop. And there was I, thinking I could now go anywhere, dine with royalty – even the Duchess of Kent – and nobody would guess my 'umble origins."

"I couldn't be sure, of course, that the man speaking *was* you, but it seemed worth following up. And my mother had heard from one of the village acquaintances she kept in touch with that you'd done well for yourself, were becoming a big name in the medical world. The BBC wouldn't give me your address, but the woman I spoke to promised to forward a letter, so I took her at her word. What had I to lose?"

"When the letter arrived it knocked me over. To hear from you, Peter Howard, after so many years. More than thirty, by my calculation."

"Long enough for us to have forgotten each other, or so I feared."

"Or for me not to want to be unmasked?" He looks quizzically at his boyhood friend. "I'm more pleased than I can say that you did contact me and that I could get here."

There is genuine regard in his words. For a moment or two they are silent, then Peter's guest says, "That long illness you mentioned in your letter. I assume it was cancer. Lung?"

"No," Peter says. "You're right, she was a heavy smoker, as you obviously remember, but it wasn't smoking that did for her, or not directly. She had a degenerative heart condition."

He stands and reaches for the nearest bottle.

"Not for me," Ronnie says, as Peter gestures to the other's empty glass. "I've a long drive ahead."

His own glass filled, Peter drops back onto his chair. "So tell me," he asks, "if you don't mind talking about yourself, that is. I know damn all about your life after you left Stonely. What happened?"

"You mean how did a working-class oik like me, one of the great unwashed, become a middle-class oik?"

Peter can see nothing in the face of his boyhood friend to suggest that his words contain a hidden, sardonic edge. The smile is, if anything, reassuringly warm. It is also, Peter realises, the smile of a man who knows his own worth.

"Your mother may have thought I was a caution, but she didn't like the way I spoke, did she? She used to repeat my words to make clear her son wasn't to sound like me."

Peter winces at the memory. "I'm afraid she did."

Ronnie laughs. "No need to apologise. It's how things were. When I was a medical student my professor told us that we should get our hair cut and try to speak 'normally'. Ill people, especially working-class patients, didn't like long-haired medics, and they had an almost entire distrust of anyone who couldn't 'speak proper'."

"Is that right? Was what your professor said sound advice?"

"It was what we were told and at the time I chose to believe it. Remember Hutton?"

"The great Len Hutton. How could I forget?"

"One of our heroes, wasn't he. I heard him on the wireless just after he'd been made England's cricket captain, in 1953, over twenty years ago. The first professional to be plucked from the ranks. Oh, how proud the striped-tie brigade were of their daring. But nervous too, you could tell. Would Hutton be able to handle a gin-and-tonic without belching?" This time there is no doubting the contemptuous edge to Ronnie's laugh. "He was being interviewed by some chinless wonder and it was obvious that before allowing him to appear in front of the microphone they'd drilled the poor sod in how to speak. 'Oh, aye think we 'eve a very good chance of beatin' the Orstralians.' I wish he'd told them to get lost. Or lorst. Still, It's how matters stood then." Ronnie grins. "Fortunately I can still speak local like to mi mam and dad when I goes 'ome."

"They're alive?"

"They are indeed. Made a fair bundle from the transport café they ran for years, nicely positioned on the edge of town. Nancy – my sister, remember her? – she and her husband have it now."

"They must be proud of you."

Ronnie shrugs. "I suppose so. But I'm proud of *them*. They've made successes of their lives. I was lucky, that's all, passed the eleven plus, and the rest followed."

Looking across to where his old friend sits at ease, his unostentatiously smart grey suit, jacket unbuttoned to show the dark-blue tie and cream-coloured shirt, the still lean face in which those dark, watchfully-amused eyes scrutinise his own with unfazeable candour, Peter says, "You're a clever man, Ronnie. Far cleverer than me. I think I must always have known that. Hare to my tortoise, and I've learnt to accept that the hare usually wins."

"As I say, luck."

Not wanting to dispute Ronnie's modest disclaimer, Peter says, "I'm afraid my parents' life together wasn't much of a success."

"Your father was a furniture designer, I seem to remember. Or was it textiles?"

"Interior design, he called it. He was good at that. Not so good at marriage."

"I'm sorry. I remember how much your mother wanted the war to end, so she could get her husband back. What happened, if you don't mind my asking?"

Peter drains his glass, wonders about a refill. "No, it's all so long in the past. As soon as my father was in civvies he dashed up to Manchester, but there was nothing much doing there. London was where the work was, so that's where we headed. Bright lights, big city. Perhaps they went to his head. Anyway, not long after we settled in, my mother discovered he was having an affair with his secretary, so she ordered him out. Not an especially happy time for her."

"Or for you, I imagine?"

"Oh, I was OK. I think I spent most of my adolescence dreaming I'd become a writer. A great one, naturally."

Ronnie registers the sardonic note that underlies the self-mockery and doesn't pursue the matter.

Instead, he asks, "Was your father at the funeral?"

Puzzled, Peter shakes his head. Then, remembering that Ronnie had never set eyes on his father, he says, "He lives in France now, with wife number three. I visit them from time to time but my mother cut him out of her life, didn't want ever to see him again. I think she felt that he'd betrayed more than their marriage. The new world she'd hoped for … Well, I don't know, but I'm pretty sure she thought that what he'd done was part of a wider betrayal."

He stops, then says defensively, "That sounds sentimental, doesn't it? But she can't have been the only person who genuinely hoped the world would be different after '45. They built their hopes too high, I suppose."

"Human nature being what it is."

But Ronnie's words, uttered after a moment's silence between the two of them, are, Peter realises, spoken without derisive inflection.

He hauls himself to his feet, and having re-filled his glass, feels suddenly exhausted by the events of the day.

"So, tell me," Ronnie asks, "who were the mourners?"

"Colleagues of hers, mostly." Peter slumps back into his chair. "Fellow teachers from her school in Northolt, some people she knew from her work for good causes, a few of the local Labour party stalwarts, you, me … Not many others."

"She kept up her political interests?" Ronnie seems impressed.

"She did, more out of habit, I reckon, than hope. Rather like her Anglicanism. 'Be Thou my refuge in the day of evil.' She used to murmur that to herself a good deal in later years, like a mantra, though I'm not sure what good it did. Perhaps it brought her comfort. I'd like to think so. She had to put up with a good many disappointments, you know. Husband gone to the bad, the spreading chill of the Cold War, England slipping back into ways she thought had gone forever, and then her son – well, I never quite knew what she hoped for from me, she never complained, and I guess years ago she gave up hoping I'd marry and settle down, produce some grandchildren for her. Instead, she had to console herself with occasional pieces I sent her from my journalistic triumphs. Articles in the weeklies, all of them pored over by mass audiences numbering a hundred or so. She made a habit of pasting them in a scrapbook. And she kept my few novels on show. Just in case anyone asked, which I don't suppose they did. Judging from my royalties I'd guess my mother was my only reader."

"I know about your journalism. I didn't know you wrote novels."

"It's a well-kept secret."

"And are you still writing fiction?"

"Habits die hard," Peter says dismissively. "Habits outlast hope."

"From what I remember of her your mother was certainly full of hope. I can still picture her dancing us round when Labour won the '45 election."

"That, too, was a long time ago."

"Cheer up! They're back in power."

"Wilson isn't Attlee. Still, Heath's being kicked out did something to cheer my mother's last days. But England." He pauses, looks wryly at Ronnie. "England's still the land where the more things change the more they stay the same."

With a smile, Ronnie acknowledges Peter's words without perhaps conceding their justness.

After a few moments, he says, as though to change the subject, or is he continuing it by different means? "What about that nice woman, Maureen Bailey, wasn't she called? She was a friend of your mother's. Did she come to the funeral? Though I don't suppose I'd have recognised her."

"She died a couple of years ago. They kept in touch, and my mother went to *her* funeral. She's buried in the village churchyard, with her husband and son."

"Keith Bailey. The poor lad who killed himself." Ronnie taps a thumb nail against his front teeth. "Since your letter came I've been thinking about those days in Stonely. Awakening some pretty unpleasant memories."

Peter sets his glass down at his feet, intent on drinking no more that day. Too many of his writer friends have disappeared or are disappearing into the alcoholic fog from which they seem never to reappear. "We don't of course know he meant to kill himself," he says. "The coroner's report suggested an accident, don't you remember?" He stopped. "Or had your family already left the village? I can remember a good deal about that summer – I'm still hoping to write something about it – but I'm hazy about various details."

"We were there," Ronnie said. "Though we left soon after. Part of what must have seemed an exodus. Or perhaps diaspora is the better word. People on the move. Emigration. I seem to recall that hardly a week went by without boys I was at school with in Huddersfield disappearing, off with their parents to new lives in – oh, Australia, Canada, South Africa."

"A lot of people left Stonely. Hardly emigration, though the wrench felt severe at the time."

Peter begins to number on his fingers those who'd gone from the village soon after war's end. "Your family, ours – a woman called Sally Parsons … "

"Sally Parsons?" Ronnie raises an eyebrow, remembering. "Wasn't she a friend of your mother's?"

"I'm not sure about 'friend'. I think they rather blew hot and cold."

"My mother – mi mam – couldn't stand her. Parson's nose, she called her. Tilted high to avoid the local stink."

"If you say so."

Peter can't recall much now about Sally Parsons, apart from the fact that she was a widow. "Her husband was a fighter pilot who'd been killed in action early on in the war."

Ronnie nods. "Could be. Although I gather that in the war years, and for a while afterwards, plenty of people invented heroic stories for themselves and their nearest and dearest." He laughs, says, "I have a memory of my mother once telling my gran that Sally Parsons chased more or less anything in trousers. And my gran claimed that she'd even been spotted once or twice in the woods with that German prisoner of war you used to follow about. Or was it Nancy who told us? Not sure who, to be honest."

An image stirs in Peter's mind. Hans running up the road, Hans with a scratch on the side of his face.

But before he can probe the memory any further, Ronnie says, "Drank like a fish, too. Whenever my mother and gran settled down for a glass of something they called it 'Doing a Sally Parsons'." He laughs again, checks himself, says with brisk forgiveness, "Still, those were difficult times."

As though needing silently to measure the weight of that remark, he sits for some moments without speaking, looking at the floor. Then slowly raising his eyes to meet Peter's he says, "Lorna May Perry."

"What about her?"

Ronnie looks at him levelly. "We ought to talk about her, don't you think?"

Peter pretends to consider. "Yes, perhaps." He speaks slowly, as though weighing Ronnie's question, but his heart is pumping. "Yes, you're right," he says, "let's talk."

***

Some two hours later, the two former friends stand together in the pub car park. Soon, the first of the evening's drinkers and diners will be arriving, but for now only a few cars reflect back the light from late afternoon sun as it breaks through the screen of poplars running beside the road that will take Ronnie on the first stage of his journey home.

Taller than Peter, leaner and almost certainly fitter, he stands relaxedly beside his black Mercedes, hand outstretched as he says, "I'll be in touch." Then, on what has to be an impulse, he reaches forward, grasps Peter by the shoulders, pulls his friend to him, hugs him.

"No reason not to stay in contact, is there."

It is less question than statement, one to which Peter, unable to speak, nods.

"No reason at all," he manages to say, as Ronnie turns to go. And, when he can trust his voice, "I'd love to see you again." He raises a hand in farewell salute, "Drive carefully."

As he eases into the driver's seat, Ronnie looks up at Peter. "You haven't mentioned a wife."

"Because there isn't one."

"Should I be sorry?"

"I have a long-term on-off girlfriend. A news reporter. She's in Paris at the moment on an assignment."

He wonders whether to add that, judging from recent occasions when he's let himself into the flat and found Carol quick to put the phone down from calls she claims are from no one in particular, she is probably combining her assignment with an assignation; but he doesn't. Instead, he asks, "How about cricket? Do you keep up an interest?"

"I play occasionally for my local club. Not very well, I'm afraid. How about you?"

"I watch. I'll be at the Oval tomorrow. First day of the last Test and the last chance to see England get a pasting from the Windies. Assuming the weather holds."

"Oh, it will hold," Ronnie says. "Isn't Wilson supposed to be appointing a minister of drought?" He laughs. "That should do the trick. Well, enjoy your cricket."

The window slides up and he starts the engine.

Back inside the pub, Peter finds the landlord, settles the bill, and within twenty minutes the taxi he has ordered is delivering him to the station from where he takes a train to Waterloo.

***

In the jolting, stale-smelling, half-empty carriage, Peter thinks of Ronnie speeding in his discreetly expensive car toward Guildford, where he will no doubt want to tell the wife he had mentioned – Cathy – and the younger of his two daughters, still at home, about his meeting with a friend from his distant childhood, now a writer with absolutely no claim to fame.

Or perhaps he *won't* tell her. How much does Ronnie want his wife to know about her husband's origins? Perhaps success such as his depends on or seems to require a degree of invention about his upbringing. But no, that's unfair. For all that Ronnie has honed his manner of speaking to a kind of southern standard English, there is none of that strangulated attempt at toff-speak which had afflicted, so Ronnie himself pointed out, poor Len Hutton or, for that matter, another working-class hero, Alf Ramsey, Sir H'Alf hisself, as he was cruelly dubbed. Besides, Ronnie has made plain that he isn't ashamed of his background, of his working-class parents and family. "I'm proud of them." And as Peter himself has recently written in a piece about fashion, whereas in the immediate post-war years shop-girls tried to look like duchesses, duchesses now try to look like shop-girls. Not everything stays the same.

At Waterloo Peter shoulders his way onto a tube which takes him the short distance to Kennington. He treads briskly over paving-stones, some cracked, heading to the once splendid, now crumbling mansion divided into flats, of which his is one. Many of the houses along the road, the newer ones, have been built on the sites of those flattened by the Luftwaffe, others, survivors which withstood the effect of incendiary bombs, are, most of them, now rented apartments, from which men and women emerge each morning to various occupations and return at evening to use the same laundrettes, and cafés, and shops, and pubs. Few of them, as he's discovered from casual conversation, lived here during the war. They are in-comers, unaware of that earlier generation which had been bombed or forced to escape during the conflict's terrifying early years, and then, in its last months, become an unwilling part of Buzz-Bomb Alley.

Buzz-Bomb Alley. No, that's wrong. Where had Buzz-Bomb Alley been? Not the part of London where he lives, he thinks, as he feels for his house keys. Buzz-Bomb Alley, the Alley of death, that was surely where Rachel Perry had once lived and where, for all he knows, she may be living once more. He has no interest in trying to trace her, but he tries to imagine what it would have been like, listening out for that drone, knowing you were safe as long as it continued, but aware of trouble heading in your direction as soon as the engine cut out, because that was when the bomb would fall, and if you were in its path, then, as comedians used to say, Goodnight Vienna.

From the top of the stairs leading to the house-porch, feeling momentarily winded by the speed of his ascent and telling himself he needs more exercise, he turns to look at the street below him. How solid it looks, yet how friable it and all the streets around had proved thirty years ago. Yuk. Words, the sounds of which seem to trivialise the brute reality of what had happened, as, for that matter, does the term buzz-bomb. Buzz-bomb. A way of coming to terms – comic terms – with horror. Britain Can Take It. But the horror was real. Thousands of Londoners killed at the very moment they began to hope the end of war was in sight and were daring to imagine how they might pick up their lives as well as repair the city, set about shifting the piles of rubble heaped all around, the vast bomb craters, the streets where the charred, gaunt remains of buildings loomed against the sky, the littered waste grounds that had once been rows of shops and which a student friend of his had, in the nineteen-fifties, prowled in order to research a botanical treatise on the plant life of bombsites. Most of those sites were now built over. But for years they lay unreclaimed from the devastation Hitler's bombs had caused.

And what was true of London was true of so many other European cities. By the time war ended in the summer of nineteen forty-five, Germany, as someone had written, was a wilderness of destruction. Dresden, Cologne, Berlin, Hamburg … Hamburg. Hans …

He unlooses his fingers from the key ring in his trousers pocket. He can't face the thought of making an evening meal for one, not tonight. His local pub does perfectly good bar meals. He can eat there. It also serves beer that doesn't taste like the liquid solder, metallic, chemicalised, that for any of its Fancy Dan names, Tankard, Double Diamond, Red Barrel, is what comes from the taps of far too many 'hostelries', as they are ridiculously called. And if any of the regulars want to join him for a drink, so much the better. He will suggest they lift their glasses to join him in a toast. "To my mother". And then "To friendship".

***

Because, he thinks, as he sits on his own at the rear of the pub's back room, a plate of what had been a serviceable mushroom omelette wiped clean on the table in front of him, half-drunk pint of ale at his elbow, the conversation with Ronnie, now that he allows himself to think about it, has gone far toward making him understand better the events he and his rediscovered friend had lived through during that far-off summer and what followed.

He lifts his glass, and as he does so remembers he has promised himself to drink no more this day. But that was before he and Ronnie had got down to talk, to real talk. And now he's drinking as much in celebration as in solace. No, he tells himself, he's drinking by way of celebration.

"We ought to talk about Lorna May Perry," Ronnie had said, echoing his own silent wish. The death of his mother had once more woken memories of a time, long gone, but though dormant able at any moment to break to the surface, and whenever it did so urging on him the need for some – requital, was that the word he wanted? But no, he decided when he once looked the word up, and found that his dictionary gave as the meaning, "reward, repayment; retaliation, revenge." None of those things. Perhaps acquittal was nearer the mark. Or even quittance. "Release or discharge from a debt of obligation." Yes, that would do. Not that he was clear what the debt of obligation might be, unless it was to the truth. And how to get at that? How else but by asking questions and then seeing what could be uncovered by answers those questions threw up.

He is brooding on this when he becomes aware that the pub's landlord is hovering above him, hoping to clear away his plate. "Everything all right?" the man asks.

It takes a moment for Peter to understand. Then, "Fine," he says, "excellent. Cooked to perfection." And not wanting to seem abrupt or dismissive, "What do you reckon the weather will do? OK for tomorrow?"

The landlord who, as he reaches for the plate gives off a strong smell of stale cigarette smoke, and who plainly understands what lies behind Peter's question, says, "Yeh, no change. Sun and more sun. Rain won't save England. I hear Snow's gonna cry off."

"*Snow?* He's about our only hope."

Straightening up, the landlord snorts. "Not on a featherbed, he isn't. Viv'll cane him, or whoever comes in for him, you see." Then, as he turns to go back to the bar, he asks, "You got a ticket?"

"For tomorrow."

"You'll be all right, then," the barman says. "Wouldn't bet on it lasting till Sunday, though. That's the only day I can go. Just my luck."

Left to himself, Peter takes another mouthful of beer and goes back to thinking about all he and Ronnie talked over earlier, about how, as the two men sat facing each other in the room where the wake had been held and where the crumbed plates and empty glasses now waited to be collected, they had revisited the summer days of some thirty years earlier, trying between them to understand the causes and the consequences of actions that had led to the wrecking of at least two lives. None of it must be allowed to slip from memory. Nothing must be lost.

He pulls out the heavy notebook he keeps always ready in his jacket, puts it on the table in front of him, then reaches in his inside pocket for his pen. Now, he orders himself, write.

***

Wednesday, 11th August, 1976. 7. 30 pm. I am sitting in my local pub, The Admiral Rodney, Kennington, about to set down all I can remember of the lengthy conversation that took place earlier this afternoon between the great friend of my early boyhood, Ronnie Slater, now Dr Ronald Slater, medical consultant, and myself, Peter Howard. Subject: the tragic events of summer, 1945, which, occurring as they did in the Midlands village of Stonely where Ronnie and I lived next door to each other, inevitably made a lasting impression on us both. In what follows I give our talk in the present tense, not only because what passed between us is still vivid in my mind, but because I hope it will show that I aim to provide as accurate a transcript as possible of the talk that occupied us for the best part of two hours. And in order to try to achieve an objectivity I can't, I know, guarantee, I have chosen to write about myself in the third person, as a character in a story, though whether this is how I will present myself in the book I intend to write about that summer I haven't yet decided. Begin here.

"Do you think she *was* killed?" Peter Howard asks his friend, that distinguished medical man, Dr Ronald Slater. And Ronnie says, challenging him, "You mean you don't think she could have fallen to her death accidentally?"

His expression is neutral, gives nothing away.

"A doctor friend of mine said you could die simply by falling over. It all depended how and where you fell. Is that true?"

"It is." Ronnie nods. "But unlikely. Especially if you've young bones. And given that, if she'd fallen from the roof of that hut, the girl would have had a soft landing, I'd say that it's very unlikely her death was an accident. Correction. That she accidentally fell to her death."

"Yes, my friend also said that. But someone could have killed her by accident. Someone who hit her, or pushed her, intending to hurt her, but who certainly didn't mean to be the cause of her death?"

Ronnie considers this.

And while he does so, Peter pretends to think back on a matter which he is endlessly bringing up in his own mind. "If that *is* the case," he says to break the silence, "I suppose the likeliest suspect is Keith Bailey."

"Why?"

"Oh, Christ," Peter says. "I'm not going to be able to recall every detail, not after all these years. But, Ronnie, he found the body, remember. And didn't we think it odd the way he behaved the day before he *said* he found her. Saturday, that was, wasn't it, the day we saw him coming up from the wood, and he warned us we mustn't go down there. He could have killed her then, or even on Friday, come to that."

Pausing to gauge Ronnie's reaction to this, he sees that the other man is staring at him, although the slight smile accompanying his stare suggests scepticism. Or is it professional imperturbability. Don't communicate alarm. Don't frighten the horses. But no, that isn't it. Ronnie is simply waiting to hear all Peter has to say on the subject before offering his diagnosis.

Speaking with an urgency he finds he can't control, Peter says, "I know that some time, I can't remember exactly when, but not long after the event itself, I began to think that Keith Bailey must have killed Lorna May."

And again Ronnie asks, "Why?"

Something in the way Ronnie puts the question irritates Peter. Is the trained doctor implying that layman's thoughts don't merit serious consideration?

He says, "Let's assume, shall we, that he came on her by chance in the woods, that she said something to make him lash out, maybe he even pulled her off the roof, maybe he pushed her, if he was up there with her, and she fell and broke her neck. Could he have strangled her, even? Put his hands round her neck and squeezed. He was strong, after all, and for all his mother made him out to be a softie he had quite a temper on him."

But Ronnie shakes his head. "There's nothing in the coroner's report to suggest she had bruising round her neck."

"But if you're not looking for it … "

And then the implication of Ronnie's words, the confidence with which he speaks, his smile, still Peter's words. When he can speak again, he asks, "You mean to say that you've *read* it? Read the coroner's report?"

"I've read both reports. When you wrote to me, after all these years, to invite me to your mother's funeral, I was, as I'm sure you can imagine, very touched. I'd thought about you a good deal over the years after we'd lost contact, but to be honest I didn't really expect to hear from you again. And then, out of the blue, as the saying is, your letter arrived and with it a whole battalion of memories. We were such close friends, weren't we, so close, and not just because we lived next door to each other. And so, inevitably, I thought about that last summer, the summer of nineteen forty-five, about the death of Lorna May Perry, and about Keith Bailey's death. You don't really forget events like that. Ever."

He pauses, looking for Peter to acknowledge this, then continues. "Two mysterious deaths. So I decided to look up the coroners' reports."

"You can do that?"

"Anyone can. Some reports, a few, are kept under lock and key. Murky secrets of state. But for the most part, yes, Joe Public can get access."

"And there's no mention of bruising round Lorna May's neck," Peter asks. "You're telling me that if Keith killed her he didn't strangle her."

"Oh, Keith didn't kill her," Ronnie says firmly.

"How can you be so sure?" Peter is stunned by the confidence with which Ronnie speaks.

"Like you, I don't say he was incapable of losing his temper, he went for us on a number of occasions, as I remember. But to be brutal," Ronnie looks at his friend,a wry smile tugging at his lips, "Keith lacked the native wit to deceive anyone. He certainly wouldn't have been capable of keeping up a pretence of innocence for twenty-four hours, let alone two whole days. That's why he was destroyed, mentally done for, by the idiots who beat him up. They may have thought or let themselves be persuaded that he'd killed Lorna May. He knew he hadn't."

"So in despair he killed himself."

"Without much doubt. I don't know that he'd have been entirely 'of sound mind' when he walked in front of a train, I'm not even sure what in his case the phrase could mean, but he must have planned to take himself down to the marshalling yard, mustn't he? He got himself out of the house without his mother hearing, and the rest followed."

"You know, I've often half wondered whether he said something to his mother that made her fear he *had* killed the girl."

"What, and she covered up for him?"

Peter says, "It was only speculation." He adds, as by way of apology, " I remember thinking that my mother was afraid Maureen Bailey knew more than she let on."

But Ronnie says decisively, "Not a chance. Keith didn't kill her."

"There's something you may *not* know," Peter says, trying to counter his friend's calm assurance, "an incident, a small mystery, which I only recently found the answer to. It supports what you say – although I don't suppose it would amount to evidence in a court of law."

Ronnie looks expectantly at Peter. "And what's that?"

"Remember that act of vandalism, desecration – whatever – of the wooden cross over Lorna May's grave?"

Ronnie is now all attention. "I remember that someone tried to scratch her name out. We went down to look at it, you and I."

"We did, and so did others, including Keith Bailey. Because Mrs Herbert complained to Keith's mother about him hanging around the cemetery after the act had been done."

"The Herberts. Ah, yes, the Herberts." Ronnie looks keenly at Peter. "The poor girl's guardians, or foster-parents, I suppose they were called." The words are uttered with an ironic inflection, and he looks as though he's going to say a good deal more about the Herberts but then contents himself with a cursory nod, though he adds, "I remember hearing from you about that complaint of Mrs Herbert's. You think she was hinting that Keith was like a dog returning to his own vomit?"

"No," Peter says, "It wasn't that. But listen, what *I* remember, what I remembered, was that the only name on the grave board that had been attacked was her middle name. 'May'. The others had been partly scratched but that was as good as wiped out."

"Go on," Ronnie says, "I'm following though I've no idea where you're taking me."

"It came to me when I was asking my medic friend – my *other* medic friend – about the likelihood of the girl's death having been an accident. I was thinking about her name, and the fact that Rachel Perry said her daughter was called Lorna Perry, not Lorna May. 'May' was her father's name."

Ronnie nods, puts his hands together in silent applause. "Got it," he says. "You're telling me that it was Rachel Perry who tried to obliterate her daughter's middle name."

"Exactly. I don't know when she did it but it must have been sometime just before or after she turned up on our doorstep, because the very next day she and Mrs Herbert went down to the cemetery and came back with the news of what they'd found there."

"That wouldn't have given her much time," Ronnie says.

"She wouldn't have needed it. The cemetery was only fifteen minutes down the road."

"Did she know that?"

"Yes, Peter says, allowing himself a small smile. "She did. I've been trying of late to recall as much as I can about that summer. And it came to me that at some time in the afternoon when she appeared at our house – the Sunday the Herberts were in London – she produced a piece of paper. The police in London had given her the address of the cemetery where her daughter was buried, Old Lane, and I told her how to get to it. I remember that in particular, because something she'd said made me wonder whether she could read and write. But when she showed me the note it was obvious that she could do both."

"Why on earth did you think she was illiterate?" Ronnie looks critically at Peter.

"She said something like 'Letters and me don't agree' and I thought she was hinting at not being able to read."

"She must have loved you," Ronnie says coolly.

"I don't think she liked any of us," Peter says. "I've been thinking about her a good deal of late, trying to write about that time. Trying to make quittance."

But beyond a quizzically raised eyebrow, Ronnie isn't interested in Peter's self-conscious use of the word. "And?" he asks simply.

"And I haven't got very far, I admit. There's too much I can't make sense of. But when it dawned on me that it must have been Rachel Perry who attacked Lorna May's cross I came to two other conclusions. One, that despite some fanciful doubts I'd let myself indulge, she really was who she said she was. The mother of Lorna Perry. The other was that the attempt to get rid of the name 'May' was a sudden impulse. It couldn't have been calculated."

Ronnie looks frankly incredulous. "Why on earth did you think Rachel Perry might be an impostor?"

"Call it boyish fantasy. But she didn't look at all like Lorna May, did she? And that business of her never having been in touch. I let myself wonder whether she might have come across mention of the girl's missing mother and decided to try it on. We took for granted she *was* the mother of Lorna May. But suppose she wasn't. She told my mother she didn't have a ration card – she'd mislaid it, she said – so she couldn't prove her identity. I thought she might have turned up claiming Lorna May as her daughter in the hope she'd make some money out of it. She wanted to see if the Herberts had kept anything of Lorna May's she could take away as a keepsake. I think I let myself imagine she was hoping for a good deal more. Didn't we once fantasise about Lorna May being an heiress? Something like that, anyway."

"If we did," Ronnie says, "I've quite forgotten." He looks at Peter, smiles apologetically but then says, "And I certainly never doubted Rachel Perry's identity. Though I can see why you might have done so. She wasn't much of a mother."

"A nasty piece of work," my mother once called her.

Ronnie purses his lips but doesn't reply to this. Instead, he says, "Tell me why you think that her moment of vandalism, if it amounts to that, was done on impulse."

"Because she didn't know what she was going to find there. I imagine that having gone into the cemetery and located the cross, she saw that her daughter's name had been given as 'Lorna May Perry' and something snapped. The man who fathered her daughter and then left her now claiming her back. Remember when we leafed through that exercise book Lorna May had given you for safe keeping and we found that letter of hers, begging someone to get her away from the Herberts. You realised she had to be illegitimate – a bastard. I should have made the connection between that and what happened to the cross, but I was too stupid. I'm supposing that Rachel Perry saw that name 'May' and went wild with anger. Did her best to erase it, to reclaim the daughter she'd let go, and then made a perfunctory slash at the other names, simply to cover her tracks."

"But why let Keith Bailey become the suspect?"

Peter shrugs. "She may genuinely have thought he'd murdered her daughter. The village idiot who's not fully human, more beast than man. Cliché, I know, but no more of one than thinking a cockney woman may be illiterate. And for all I know the reporter she contacted went along with her theory. He may even have encouraged her. Anything for a good story."

"The history of medicine," Ronnie says, revealing his acceptance of Peter's words, "is full of wrong diagnoses, wrong conclusions drawn from wrong premises."

"That's very depressing."

"That's life."

"Sounds more like death. No, I don't mean that," Peter says. "But like you, partly *because* of you, because of this 'history' between us, which has been on my mind since you wrote to say you'd be here, I've been thinking yet again about Lorna May as well as her mother. As I say, I've been trying to write about the events of that summer. To see if I can't make sense of all that happened. I remembered that Rachel Perry once called Lorna May's father 'my hubby'. Even at the time it sounded false, a kind of fake simpering. I suppose she was trying to throw us off the scent, always supposing we'd been on it, which we weren't. Could have been a one-nighter. We knew only that he died early in the war, went down with his ship and that she'd disappeared soon afterwards. 'My hubby'. Funny the things you remember."

He sits silent for a moment. "I can even remember the exact moment when she used the words."

"Probably because it's linked to some other memory," Ronnie says. "That's how memory can work. Mnemonic memory, it's called."

Peter glances at him. "Really?"

Responding to the ironic inflection, Ronnie assumes an air of cod-professorial gravity. "Memory by association," he says, as though lecturing an audience. "I think, gentlemen, we will find that Coleridge was the first to call it that. His example was Shakespeare's Mistress

Quickly, she whose habit it was to recall one thing by means of another."

A pause, as he pretends to bring to mind some words he clearly knows by heart. "'Thou didst swear to me upon a parcel-gilt goblet, sitting in my Dolphin chamber, at the round table, by a sea-coal fire, upon Wednesday in Wheeson week, when the Prince broke thy head for liking his father to a singing-man of Windsor … '" He stops himself, smiling apologetically. "Henry the Fourth, Part Two. Act two, scene one. Can't remember how it goes on, alas. The vasty deep has closed over my further recollections."

"I'm impressed you remember even that much. Was it a play you did at school?"

"No, it wasn't." Ronnie is now serious. "But I wish it had been. An enlightened tutor at medical school used to quote it and much else beside, as proof, he said, that Shakespeare knew more about the workings of the human mind, including memory, than a roomful of psychologists. I took him at his word. So believe it or not, one summer, as soon as I had been released from houseman's duties, I decided to read my way through the Bard and, yes, I found my tutor was spot on. I was so fired up by it all that I decided to make a study of Shakespeare's use of memory from a medical point of view."

"And did you? Have you?"

"Life got in the way."

"It does," Peter says wryly, deciding to reveal nothing of his own, long-abandoned hopes for a full-time career as novelist.

But as though understanding, Ronnie says "Me Lydgate, you Reardon." Then, as Peter opens his mouth, he says, holding up a hand, "No, don't ask questions about my reading habits. You'd soon find out that I flatter to deceive. Tell me instead about how you remember that Rachel Perry called Lorna May's father 'my hubby'."

"Because," Peter says, "it was the day Geoff Rice was due to play cricket for Stonely. Rachel Perry claimed not to recognise the name – well, perhaps she genuinely didn't know, so I explained he was one of the airmen who'd been on and returned from the Dambusters raid, and in reply she said something about his being lucky that he'd lived to tell the tale. Others hadn't been so lucky, she meant, including her husband, 'my hubby'."

"A fine example of mnemonic memory at work."

Peter inclines his head in mock acceptance of Ronnie's words.

"Except for one error. Geoff Rice didn't return from the raid."

Peter stares at Ronnie. "Yes, he did. You and I saw him. He scored a half century, more or less won the game single-handed. Don't you remember?"

"I mean," Ronnie says, "he didn't *return* because he never *got* to Germany. His plane developed engine trouble, over the Channel, I think it was, and had to turn back to base." He smiles, a wry half-smile. "It came out after the war, in that film about the raid. Sorry, I thought you'd have known."

For Peter is, he becomes aware, staring open-mouthed at his friend.

"Anyway," Ronnie says, his smile now openly sympathetic, "Geoff Rice didn't chicken out, he *could* have been a hero if mechanical failure hadn't let him down."

True enough, but somehow no consolation. For how many other things *could* have been different but for the intervention of chance? His mother's life, his, Keith's, Lorna May's, supposing hers had been a chance death.

He says, when he can speak, "Still, at least Geoff Rice wasn't a fake. Unlike some of those who sat out the war and are now still propping up saloon bars the length and breadth of the nation, recounting their heroic exploits in fighter command."

"Yes," Ronnie says, laconically, "Dambusters apart, Bomber Command never had the same cachet."

"Which reminds me," Peter says. He looks enquiringly at Ronnie. "Hans? Remember him."

"Hans. Our local friendly POW." Ronnie nods. "The fitness fanatic. Yes, I remember. Wasn't he hoping to pick up his footballing career when he got back home?"

Then, registering Peter's perfunctory nod, he says, "But that's not why you've mentioned him."

"It was the scratch on the side of his face."

"Well," Ronnie says, into the silence, "as they say in detective stories, 'go on.'"

Speaking with care, trying to put his thoughts in order, Peter says, "I'd been watching him while he repaired the road in front of our houses. I remember that my mother called me in for tea at the same time as Mrs Herbert came to ask whether I'd seen Lorna May. Then, when I went back out, Hans came running up the road and as he climbed up onto the steamroller I noticed he had a scratch on his face. Quite a long one. Just here." He raises his left hand, sees Ronnie watching the movement of his fingers as he touches a spot immediately below the cheek bone.

"And now you're wondering whether it could have been caused by a girl's nails."

"At the time," Peter says, "when I asked him did he realise he had the scratch, he denied it. But, and this was the odd thing, though it didn't strike me until later, he raised his hand, as I'm doing, and touched the exact spot where the scratch was. He said he wasn't 'blooding'. I think that's what helped to fix the gesture in my memory. 'Blooding'. Anyway, he said he must have got the scratch when he ducked through wires at the bottom of Connolly's field. He'd been running, you see, while he waited for tar to dry sufficiently for him to flatten it with the steamroller."

"Then there's your explanation."

"But there *weren't* any wires at the bottom of the field," Peter said.

Ronnie raises an eyebrow. "You can confidently say that? After all these years?"

"Yes, I can," Peter says. "It came to me the other evening, when I was thinking about who scratched out Lorna May's name from her cross. I'd been thinking that *if* someone killed her it didn't have to be the same person who damaged her name. And then I remembered the scratch Hans pretended not to know about, but which was plain to see."

"And habits of observation start young," Ronnie says, as though repeating a phrase from some medical textbook. Then, as though the words are surrounded by quotation marks, he adds, "You were a boy who used to notice such things."

Peter starts. The words wake a further memory, a vibration that pulses in his inner ear. "You like to watch." Was that it? Who had spoken those words? Hans? But before he can track the long-gone moment to source, Ronnie is speaking again. "Tell me how you can remember something that wasn't."

Concentrating on the question, Peter says, feeling his way, "You and I sometimes took a short cut onto the path that led into the woods, didn't we. Rather than going by way of the stile, we'd dive through a hole we'd made in the hedgerow. I didn't think about that until later, much later, until recently, in fact. I must have assumed Hans had made a mistake and was speaking of a different field he'd been running through."

"So he could have been."

"And the scratch? His denying it, then feeling for it?"

"Easily explained," Ronnie waves a hand in a gesture of confident dismissal. "Have you never been told that you have a fly on your forehead, denied it, and at the same time become suddenly aware of its presence. I could give you a lecture about physiology and consciousness and their strange interconnections. However, I'm not going to." There is no unkindness in his laugh when he adds, "Nor am I about to suggest that what you thought was a scratch could have been a love bite. My sister certainly saw the German together with Sally Parsons in what I think would be called compromising positions, although as an innocent, wet behind the ears, I didn't understand her meaning."

He pauses as, around the two of them, some staff come to clear away plates and glasses.

When they are once more alone, Ronnie says, "Hans didn't kill Lorna May. And I'm damned sure we don't need to point an accusing finger at the old tramp, Whistling Billy wasn't he called, or the gypsies you and I sometimes came across in the spinney."

"Then I'm lost," Peter says. "If it wasn't any of them … "

"You're overlooking something," Ronnie says.

"I am? What?"

Ronnie uncrosses his legs, leans forward, elbows on knees, chin in cupped hands, and smiles across to where Peter sits bolt upright now, watching him. What does Ronnie know?

"The coroner's report said that the girl had been dead for up to forty-eight hours before her body was discovered. Nowadays we could probably be more exact, unless, that is, decomposition had for some reason set in, but in her case it hadn't."

"Oh." There is an edge of exasperation in Peter's voice, compounded by disappointment. "But if you don't want to believe Hans killed her, this is simply leading us back to Keith. And," he is challenging his friend, "you've already ruled him out."

"Because he didn't do it. Nor did he stumble on her body that Saturday afternoon, as you suggested."

Peter is riled by the calm certainty of Ronnie's words. "How can you be so sure? Apart from saying that he wouldn't have been able to keep quiet."

"Because, Peter, the body wasn't there. It couldn't have been."

There is no hint of the triumphalist in the way Ronnie meets Peter's startled gaze.

"How can you *possibly* know that?" Exasperation has given way to disbelief.

"Because if it had been, Keith would have been bound to see it. Which is why, by the way, you can also rule Hans out. If he'd killed Lorna May it would have had to be on the Friday afternoon, wouldn't it? Look," he is now speaking slowly, with careful emphasis. "Keith had gone into the woods, looking for flowers for his mother's birthday. He'd have roamed around, not much, perhaps, but a little. Anyway, we know that the patch of bluebells he found was very near the hut. I'd say it was a thousand to one against the body being there and Keith's not seeing it. And, as I say, if he had seen it he'd have told us."

Baffled, Peter sits in silence. Eventually, he says, "All right, tell me what *you* think happened."

"To the girl's body? I think it was taken down to the woods on Saturday night and left there for someone to discover. And on Sunday someone *did* discover it. Keith stumbled on it. And came running up to tell us. He wasn't hiding anything, nor was his mother. Out of the question."

"And who carried the body down to the woods?"

"Oh, that's easy," Ronnie says. "The person or persons who caused her death."

He sits back now, folding his arms. He is watching Peter, waiting for him to speak.

But for the moment Peter, occupied in wondering who Ronnie can have in mind, can think of nothing to say. Person or persons. What does Ronnie mean.

When Ronnie finally speaks again, he says, to Peter's surprise, "Give it up, Peter." He isn't asking him. He's ordering him. "We don't know," he says with calm emphasis, "we'll never know. And her death could have been, *may* have been, an accident."

"So nobody was responsible."

"I didn't say that." Ronnie leans forward now, his expression one of alert watchfulness. "If you're looking for the likeliest person to have caused the girl's death, the name you need is Arnold Herbert."

A pause. "Or Dora Herbert."

Further pause. "Or both of them."

Yet another pause.

Looking directly into Peter's eyes, he says, "Do you understand?"

Peter drops his gaze. Then, after some moments of silence, "I think I'm beginning to," he says.

"Well?"

Slowly, hesitantly, Peter says, "You're going to tell me that something happened in the bungalow which led to Lorna May's death that Friday afternoon."

"Not *tell* you, nothing so definite, but otherwise correct." Ronnie nods. "To repeat, we'll never know. We can't. But I'd say that left to himself Herbert made some sort of sexual advance, one he may have attempted before but this time went further than any he'd previously dared, that Lorna May resisted, and that somehow or other in the struggle between them she died or, if you prefer, she was killed, though I've no idea how. Not strangled, that's for sure. Though she could have been suffocated, and then her neck broken to suggest she'd met with an accident."

"But not by falling downstairs."

"Not in a bungalow, no. That *would* require some fixing. But one way or another, she ends up dead."

"And then Mrs Herbert returns and is confronted by the dead body and has to ... has to what? Oh, decide what she can do to prevent her husband being had up on a charge of murder, I suppose." Peter tries for a scepticism in which he feels little confidence. He can see the reasonableness that underlies Ronnie's suggestion.

"That's certainly what *I* suppose. The alternative would be to call the police and have them arrest him. But she wasn't going to do that. Not an upright citizen like Mrs Herbert. And what about their faith? Dead set against the sins of the flesh, and all the rest of it."

Ronnie leans back in his chair. I rest my case, his look implies, prove me wrong if you can. But there is no trace of self-satisfaction in his expression. If anything, his look is troubled, or, no, a look of resigned awareness, the expression of a man who is used to the corruptions hidden within the human body, its actions, compulsions, nameless repressions, its hungers, its cancerous needs.

"But why then did Mrs Herbert come to tell me that Lorna May was missing when she should be in for her tea?" Peter asks. "I don't understand that. Surely doing that would risk drawing attention to what had happened?"

Ronnie shakes his head. "No, Peter, it would draw attention *away* from what had happened. Mrs Herbert tells you the girl is missing, you run in to tell your mother, she tells others, they wonder where the girl can have got to, and meanwhile she's there, in the Herberts' bungalow. Dead."

It is possible, Peter has silently to acknowledge. More than possible, plausible. And it helps to explain a matter which, as he set himself to recall the summer of nineteen forty-five, he'd begun to puzzle over. Why had Mrs Herbert looked so agitated when she called out to him, an agitation which, he now realises as he absorbs Ronnie's words, held more than a trace of panic. Of course! She was trying hard not to look distraught, not because she knew why the girl had run off, but because Lorna May had done no such thing. She was there, her body was there, in the bungalow, the victim of a husband who was now revealed as a – as a what? He can't imagine Mrs Herbert using the term child-molester, paedophile. Did it even exist at that time? But even if it didn't what he had done was unthinkably vile. And she was having to cope with the discovery, or, more likely, confirmation of that vileness. No wonder the woman was distraught.

Yet for all that he now grasps the plausibility of Ronnie's explanation, doubts remain. "They told the police that Lorna May was missing. Why do that?"

"They had to. Think about it, Peter. Sooner or later someone would have noticed Lorna May wasn't around. At the very latest, that would have been Monday, wouldn't it? When she should have been in school. But it would look dodgy if her guardians had waited that long before calling in the police. So get in earlier with the story that the girl had gone missing. And it *was* early, you know. When I began to think about all that happened I realised it was odd that they'd not waited longer before contacting the police. After all, Lorna May had run off on previous occasions. She'd stayed out, sometimes for hours at a time, hadn't she? Probably, I now think, when she knew he'd be there on his own. From time to time people had seen her roaming the fields when she should have been at home. I'd come across her myself on more than one such occasion, out and about well after hours. But eventually she always did return to them, no doubt to face a thrashing or whatever. Why, then, alert the police so soon? Why not wait for longer?"

"To put them off the scent, is what you think. Yes, I can see that," Peter says, "but surely there'd have been the risk that once they'd told the police, the boys in blue would come nosing around the bungalow."

"Not much of a risk. Let's say that when they alerted the local copper he went down to the bungalow to take a statement from the pair of them. What reason would he have to doubt whatever they told him? Dear Sergeant – can't remember his name – we're desperately worried. We've looked everywhere for Lorna May in the bungalow, under the beds, inside the wardrobe, but she's simply not here. She's gone off somewhere, and no, there's no note, no reason we can think of why she'd have disappeared, none at all."

"Locker, that was the policeman's name," Peter says. "You used to call him Lock-up. You think that Locker fell for what they told him?"

"Lock-up. So I did. Fancy forgetting that. And yes, my suggestion is that he bought their story. Why wouldn't he?"

Peter can think of no reply. Instead, he says, "So they wait until Saturday night, then take the body down to the woods and leave it where whoever finds it will assume Lorna May fell from the hut's roof?" Meeting Ronnie's gaze, that look of undeflectable certainty, he says, "A long way to carry a dead person." Then, trying to soften the truculence that represents his last attempt to contest Ronnie's assured words, "And surely there was the risk of being seen?"

"Not much of a risk. Not late at night. They'd have been very unlikely to have been spotted going across the field at the midnight hour. And as for the weight, remember that Lorna May was a skinny kid and he was a big man. Someone used to hauling heavy bales of material about a factory floor wouldn't have found that body much of a burden."

"Physically, no."

Ronnie looks at Peter. "You're right," he says, holding his friend's gaze. "I imagine they carried the weight of what they'd done to their graves."

"Which explains the retreats they went on."

"Yes. Trying to atone."

"For the death and for their deceptions. Starting with the flight to London."

"Flight? Yes," Ronnie says, slowly, "I've wondered about that. Did panic make them head for the city in the hope they could hole up there. Become invisible, even." He shakes his head. "There's no knowing, is there?"

Peter says, "We do know they returned. I suppose they felt they had no alternative once the girl's body was discovered. And of course they had a story about going to look for her. It was almost a perfect alibi."

"True."

And it is then Peter remembers Mrs Herbert telling his mother that prayers are private. When had she said that? Ah, yes, of course, when she was explaining that she feared Keith Bailey had been snooping on her. She must have gone to the cemetery to pray for forgiveness. In all likelihood, he now thinks, she was praying aloud, praying not only for herself but for her husband, begging forgiveness for a man in far greater need of it than she herself was. He imagines her on her knees in an agony of contrition, then hearing a sudden noise, and turning to see Keith gawping at her. *Prayers are private.* They are not for sharing with others, especially not if they will incriminate her and, in particular, her husband.

He tells all this to Ronnie in a rush, a tumble of words that, as he speaks them, he knows must provide as full an explanation as they will manage to piece together of what had happened thirty years ago.

When he finishes, Ronnie says simply, "Yes, you're right."

The conversation seems to have run its course.

But then Ronnie speaks again. "I should have helped her."

He sits, face now averted, staring at nothing in particular.

Then, more determinedly, he repeats, "I *should* have helped her."

Helped who, Peter is about to ask, but he knows. Instead, "How?" he asks. "How were you to know what was going on? None of us did."

Suddenly Ronnie is staring at Peter. "*Of course* I knew," he says. "That damned letter."

He drops his gaze now, as though he can't bear to meet his friend's eyes, brooding. When, after some moments of withdrawn silence, he raises his head it is to stare unflinching at Peter. "I know I told you I hadn't looked inside that exercise-book she gave me, but I lied. I had, *of course* I'd looked. I'd read what she'd written, *of course I had.*"

Pause.

Then, speaking more reasonably, as though he's managed to tamp down whatever emotion – anger, resentment, bitter self-accusation? – had momentarily surfaced, he says, "To be honest, I thought you must have realised."

He waits for Peter to say something, and when his abashed friend stays silent, says, "I ought to have shown the letter to my mother but I was still sulking because of the whacking I'd had from her after I'd torn my shorts. All Lorna May's fault, I thought, so let her stew in her own juice."

"Poor girl," Peter says.

"Yes," Ronnie says, "poor girl. Poor, poor girl." His look is troubled.

Again, they sit in silence, musing.

"You know." Peter's memory is again at work. "It comes back to me now that when, after we'd looked through the book she'd given you, and I suggested Mrs Perry was responsible for what happened to Lorna May and to Keith Bailey, you said 'and the rest'. Who did you mean? Apart from yourself, that is. That we were all responsible? How could we have been?"

Ronnie shrugs, weary it seems of the discussion. Then, "We all failed her," he says, as though forcing the words out. "All of us. No one to love her, to show her any affection. She was as good as chucked out of her own home, so she must have felt, with a father she probably never knew, a mother she probably thought couldn't wait to get rid of her, who never *once* came to see her – and then to find herself not much more than a prisoner of the Herberts, the man free to do whatever he wanted to her. And us – me, in particular, too damned selfish or blind or indifferent to care." He shakes his head, sombre now as he meets Peter's own troubled look.

"Well," Peter says, "if all that you say is true, and I accept it's the best explanation of what happened, some responsibility surely rests with the billeting officer. They were meant to make regular checks on evacuees. Why didn't *they* realise what was going on at the Herberts?"

Ronnie flaps the question away. "Oh, come on. I don't suppose there'd have been more than one visit. Who's going to doubt the ways of the God-fearing Herberts. Anyway, I don't imagine Lorna May would have dared to breathe a word against them. She'd have feared what would happen. No, it was *me* she turned to. And I let her down."

Why take all the blame, Peter is going to ask. But doesn't. He knows why his friend is full now of remorse, of self-blame, denies himself the merest hint of exculpation. *I thought you were my friend.* She had looked to Ronnie for help. It was Ronnie she trusted. Ronnie had meant far more to her than had he, Peter. No wonder that their running from her that long ago afternoon, trivial though it seemed to them – to Peter, anyway – had for Lorna May been an act of betrayal. She trusted Ronnie, and Ronnie had let her down.

And as if to confirm this, Ronnie now says, "All these years it's been on my conscience and now, meeting today … " His voice trails away, his eyes are hooded, his head once more averted.

"'Be thou my refuge in the day of evil,'" Peter says, speaking, he thinks, to himself.

But Ronnie has heard. He jerks his head up, stares at Peter. "What?"

"I've just remembered that those were the words our vicar at Stonely, Chard, took for his sermon the Sunday after the war in Europe came to an end, the weekend Lorna May went missing."

"Well, neither Lorna May nor Keith found their refuge, did they?" Ronnie says savagely. Then, with a brief, caustic laugh, "Accept the burden of the past. Just what the doctor ordered."

"Meaning?"

"Oh, face the past, confront your demons, acknowledge your guilt, and feel free." He pauses, the glare replaced by a look of weary, sad resignation. "It doesn't work like that, does it?"

Peter looks across at Dr Ronald Slater, friend of his boyhood years, highly esteemed man of medicine, as he sits, grave-faced, his look turned inward, unflinching.

A memory of Rachel Perry comes to Peter then, a sudden recall of her uncanny, flickering eyes, their unwillingness ever to rest on any one face or object. Letting his eyes slide away from Ronnie's face he begins to wonder about that seemingly endless shifting of focus, of attention. What, if anything, did it mean? What had she been wanting? What had she been fearing? Did that restless movement, the skittering from eye contact, imply evasion, the fear of being recognised. The bad mother, the true evacuee, running away from her responsibilities. Or was it reassurance she was after? I did my best, I'm not to be blamed for what's happened.

The home psychologist explains.

On the other hand, it might simply have been a case of strabismus.

He ought to ask Ronnie whether he has an explanation for any of this. But Ronnie is speaking again.

"Not that I regret this talk," his friend says, as he gets to his feet. "I wanted to do it, to have it resolved between us, and now it's done."

A brief, wan smile. "All as the doctor ordered," he says.

End here.

Finishing the pint left unattended while he has been absorbed in the act of writing, Peter pushes his pen back inside his jacket and closes the notebook. All as the doctor ordered, he thinks. Well, yes. Following doctor's orders has brought him to acknowledge the comfortless explanations for the two deaths which, between them, scarred the summer of nineteen forty-five, the summer of peace, the harbinger of a new age. Sweet dreams. He has noticed that of late people have begun to speak of the need to achieve closure from some tragedy or grief, or loss, or pain, any discomfort, any pea under the mattress which has thrust itself into lives meant to extend smoothly until the final moment when screens will be wheeled into place round the plumped-up, antiseptic deathbed.

Allow us to forget, take memory away from us. Unburden us. We meant no harm, therefore we did none. Idiots. Facile, gritless, gutless, bland. You can never be free of the past, nor should you want to be. Understanding is impossible without memory, and understanding is its own cure, not because it frees you but because it brings you to acknowledge the ties that bind you to others. Just what the doctor ordered.

Standing at the bar to pay for his food and drink, he waits while the landlord switches on the bar radio in time for the ten o'clock news. As the chimes of Big Ben begin to sound out, Peter is lost in memories of his mother as she sat in her hearthside chair listening to the six o'clock news, eager with anticipation of her husband restored to her and his son, of a new tomorrow, of a refreshed world.

But now the chimes fade and it is nineteen seventy-six, and almost immediately a government minister, speaking with grave emphasis, explains how the threat of yet another strike, this time by car workers, will endanger the country's economic well-being, and with stern vehemence a union official explains that the strike, which he regrets, has, because of the government's refusal to discuss the union's proposals, become unavoidable.

Peter looks about him, and realises that nobody in the pub apart from the landlord and himself is paying the radio any attention.

As he takes Peter's money, the landlord says, "They want shooting, all of them." For a moment the remark echoes in Peter's mind and he tries to recall where, once before, he heard such words, or ones very like them. He can't, but anyway it doesn't matter. The landlord doesn't mean what he says. It's talk. No more than talk.